LONG RUN
SOUTH

Alan Williams

SAPERE
BOOKS

LONG RUN SOUTH

Published by Sapere Books.

20 Windermere Drive, Leeds, England, LS17 7UZ,
United Kingdom

saperebooks.com

ISBN: 978-1-80055-149-7

To Peter Jenkins

PART 1: The Sack

CHAPTER 1

One October morning just after sunrise a small boy was rooting about on a disused building site outside the city. He had a shaved scalp and bare brown feet, and he came out here to hunt for scrap-metal and rubbish to sell in the market.

He rarely found anything better than cans and bottles and old tyres. Few people came near the place any more. The building crews and digging machines, which had been withdrawn months before because of the inflation, had left behind them miles of scarred earth. Along the horizon the slender skyscrapers rose sugar-white above the sweep of the Atlantic, but further inland on the edges of the city the newer buildings, which had begun to shoot up during the brief boom, were now huge husks of girders and cement. At night the wind came off the plain behind the city and moaned among the dead blocks, and even lovers and stray dogs kept away.

On this particular morning the boy had wandered from his usual hunting grounds and had come to a cleft which ran along for several yards like a trench. It had probably been started for a sewage pipe or gas main. At the end of it something lay covered under weeds and lumps of earth. It was a sack. There was a very bad smell about, as when a rat has been picked up by a buzzard then dropped to rot in the open. The boy crept forward, knowing with the cunning of a wild animal that something was wrong.

He reached it and pulled the weeds away, and there was a fierce buzzing through the stillness. One end of the sack glistened with flies. He leant down and poked at the sack, and tugged it and felt a weight inside. He pulled harder and the sacking moved, and something came out of the other end — the end away from where the flies were. He stepped round and saw a pair of feet.

He looked at them carefully, his big eyes solemn with curiosity He looked down at his own feet, then at the feet in the sack, and saw the ones in the sack were almost twice as large as his own and were white. Then he ran away.

He went nearly a mile before he found anybody. The sun was coming up, and on the dirt track leading into Casablanca two Arab labourers were ambling along pushing bicycles. The boy ran up to them, shouting in a sing-song voice of what he had seen, waving back in the direction of the trench, but the men shook their heads and pointed towards the city.

One of them then hoisted him over a crossbar of his bicycle, and they began wobbling along the track into Casablanca. The men were scared of what the boy had said; and the further they rode the less they wanted to have to do with it. He kept asking them to take him to the police. If he wasn't lying, and the feet in the sack were really white, it could mean a lot of trouble for anyone involved. Even since the French had left the country the poorer Arabs still guarded an obstinate deference for Europeans, especially where the police were concerned. A European found in a sack would make the police work hard. The two Arabs already saw themselves enmeshed in the sophisticated machinery of the law; they began muttering to each other and shaking their heads, and just inside the outskirts they suddenly stopped and told the boy to go away. He started whining at them, and one of them rushed at him and cuffed him round the ears. He whimpered a little, then walked off, and the two got back on to their bicycles and pedalled on into the city.

The boy said nothing more about what he'd seen until that evening, when he mentioned it to one of his friends while they were kicking a football about in the street. His friend repeated it to some of the other children, who went off howling with excitement to tell their families; and soon everyone in the street was talking about the pair of white feet in the sack outside the city.

That night a police officer in a uniform the colour of dried mud, with shining belt and holster, knocked on the door of the boy's house and asked to be shown where the sack lay. There was a jeep outside the house, with a few Arabs huddled round it, chattering and whispering.

Three other policemen sat in the jeep, and as the boy was passed up among them his eyes were wide with terror. They drove off down the dark streets with the police siren sending its panting scream into the night, like the wheezing of an asthmatic. The boy was crying. The officer took him under the chin, turned his face up and said gently in Arabic: 'Tell us where you saw it.'

They came to the building site and stopped. Two of the men took down a portable searchlight and switched it on. The boy went on crying and said he couldn't remember. They walked round and round for nearly an hour. It was the smell that first attracted their attention. Then the boy sobbed and put out his hand. 'There!'

The officer led the way down, while the boy hung back at the top of the slope. He watched the four of them moving along the trench, the shadows swinging with the searchlight. They stopped and bent down. There was a hush. He heard a slither and the scrape of boots, then they all began shouting and one of them came running out with his hands over his mouth making a gurgling noise.

The officer ordered the boy to be taken back into the city. Two of his men were to stay on guard while a special police van was called.

The four policemen in the jeep were all staunch Moslems; they had looked upon what they found not so much with revulsion as fright. Each had the Moslem's terror of putrefaction, and when the officer had pulled away the sack they had run back, believing it would defile them. What they all dreaded most was having to touch the corpse.

They were spared. It was collected by a special squad from the morgue and driven in a van to police headquarters. A tarpaulin was thrown over it, and the driver, a very young, round-faced Moroccan, gripped the wheel all the way back, murmuring little prayers under his breath.

At headquarters there was chaos. By an unhappy misunderstanding the body had been rushed out of the van by two orderlies, hurried up a flight of backstairs and laid out, still under the tarpaulin, in a room that was being used temporarily by one of the duty-sergeants while his own office was being repainted. The policeman who had found the sack had been delayed downstairs filling in forms for the night detective. Upstairs the duty sergeant returned, saw the shape on the table, pulled back the tarpaulin, and ran out screaming into the corridors. It caused near panic. Mature officers with red and gold shoulder-flashes thrust their way into the night captain's office and ordered that the abomination be removed at once. Most of the men at headquarters refused to approach the body. The staff at the city morgue claimed that they had no facilities to deal with the case; it would have to be held in a deep-freeze. There were angry words in the corridors and several men threatened to resign their posts.

In the duty room they were busy putting through a number of urgent telephone calls. The stench had already infected the entire building, and a detective was delegated to find a swift means of disposing of the corpse. He eventually arranged to have it stowed in one of the deep-freezes used by the fishing companies down by the port. The manager accepted a polite bribe, called up his labour to have the fish moved elsewhere, and most of the men at headquarters enjoyed a round of good French cognac.

Meanwhile for the second time that night, the police van moved off with its terrible load, driving along the modern boulevards, down towards the clammy salt smells and the lapping of the great Atlantic.

In a whitewashed room under a naked light the police doctor began his autopsy. It was the body of a girl aged between about eighteen and twenty-three who had been dead some twelve days. She was naked, wrists and ankles lashed together with wire; the throat had been cut, the face mutilated with heavy blows, and decomposition of the head and torso was advanced. She had been European, with possible Arab blood, and had not been a virgin; but there was no sign of sexual assault; no distinguishing marks, nor the least trace of identification.

It was dawn before it was finished. The doctor washed his hands and went out on to the promenade over the harbour where he lit a cigarette and stood for some time watching the fishing boats putting out, their fine nets suspended behind them like insect wings.

He wondered what the detectives would make of the case. In his view it had probably been a crime of passion. It was impossible, of course, to tell whether the girl had been pretty or not.

PART 2: The Bus Ride

CHAPTER 1

The Australian, Patrick Bates, squinted over his glass and groaned: 'Oh God, here comes the Jesus Man!' He hoisted his sandalled feet off the table and tossed a fifty-franc piece to an Arab in sackcloth who had just shambled on to the hotel roof carrying a drum and a wooden box.

Then he turned to his companion, a young Englishman called Rupert Quinn. 'The poor bugger used to be the star-turn in Marrakech before they banned him. Hitchcock even had him in a film.'

He swallowed his drink, his face turned out of the afternoon sun — a big, wild-looking man with a blond beard and canvas trousers rusted about the crutch. He was working in Morocco as a guide with a travel agency and had met Quinn in a bar the night before. He began explaining about the Jesus Man. 'Belongs to a religious sect out here — followers of the Eighth Prophet, Christ. The Nationalists decided they were reactionaries, so they've been banned from performing in public.'

The Arab had opened the box and hauled out what looked like a length of black rubber tubing. He dropped it on the hot concrete where it squirmed for a moment, then lay still. They watched him take out a flute from under his rags and blow a quavering note. Nothing happened. He picked up the drum and waved it, and slowly the snake — a cobra, with its hooded neck puffing out like a shining black seashell — reared up and began swaying to the motion of the drum.

'Snakes are all deaf,' said Bates. 'The music's just a gimmick. They only dance when they see things move.' He turned back to the table. 'What happens if you don't get the job tonight?'

Quinn peered into his glass of foggy green Pastis — his fifth since lunch — and scooped out a dead fly. He grinned. 'Something'll turn up. It usually does. There must be a few private armies in Africa looking for paramilitary advisers.'

'You mad English bastard!' said Bates happily. 'I didn't think they made them anymore.'

The snake-charmer had stunned the cobra with a blow from his drum, and was now coaxing a fat yellow serpent which was refusing to perform. He looked towards the table and showed them a mouthful of gold teeth. Quinn watched him absent-mindedly. 'I could always spend my last francs getting a lift with a petrol-truck down into Black Africa.'

'They only sell one-way tickets down there,' said Bates. The Arab was approaching with the yellow snake round his shoulders like a stole. 'He's not going to put that thing on us, is he?' Quinn cried. The man came closer, bowing. Bates shouted, '*Allez, va-t'en!*' and threw him another fifty francs. A waiter arrived and slapped the Arab with a napkin and bundled him swiftly through the roof door. Bates clapped for more Pastis.

'Not to worry, sport! You'll get the job. We can do with a few more lunatics like you.'

'Let's hope you can,' said Quinn. He sat looking on to the huge market of Djema el Fna spread out below. A figure covered in bells, like a medieval clown, was scurrying lopsidedly between the stalls and tents with a contraption on his back the shape of bagpipes. Bates explained that he was the local fresh-water carrier.

The Pastis arrived, without ice or sugar, scented and sharp as medicine. 'What made you choose Morocco?' said Bates.

'Oh, it seemed a good idea at the time. Anything seems a good idea after two years in the north of England. Two years of spitting black.' Quinn listened to the hum of the market. The air was hot and bitter-sweet, full of the age-old smells of the Casbah: of sandalwood and pepper and urine and orange blossom.

He had been in North Africa now for ten days, was almost broke, had no job, and with the Pastis burning in his belly he was beginning to feel reckless. The night before Bates had told him he might be able to hire him as another guide with his agency. They ran a trip each month over the Atlas Mountains into the Sahara. There was one leaving next morning, and the man who ran the agency — a Moroccan tycoon called Sebastien Izard — was staying in Marrakech and had promised to meet Quinn that evening in the Mamounia Hotel.

'Make out you're a little mad,' Bates said. 'Izard likes adventurers. But whatever you do, don't mention you've been a journalist, and keep right off politics.'

'What sort of man is he?'

The Australian grinned slyly. 'A bit of a pirate.' The grin stayed and he lifted his glass: 'To a long run south, sport!'

'In what way a pirate?'

'Well, Izard is what we call here an entrepreneur. That doesn't mean he buys and sells on the Stock Exchange. Just let's say there aren't many honest ways left in Morocco of making the money he's got.'

Then as though to change the subject he took out a dog-eared Michelin map of north-west Africa, and showed Quinn the route the bus would take in the morning. The line crossed the blotched contours of the Haut Atlas, down into the yellow spaces of desert where even the ubiquitous postes et télégraphe stations give out, and there is only the fierce sand sheltering a civilisation that has not spoilt for more than two thousand years.

Down in the square a veiled woman rode past on the pillion of a motorcycle, a pair of crimson lips painted clearly on to her yashmak.

Bates was explaining that some of these trips were hard, and people fell ill, and it was always useful to have an extra hand around. Izard liked to employ Europeans — independent young men who could speak French and were willing to pick up a few thousand francs by going out for two weeks into the wilderness. 'How is your French, by the way?'

'It used to be pretty fluent. I studied a year in Grenoble.'

'That'll be a help. Now this part here' — he pointed to the desert that runs north of Mauretania — 'used to be called under the French the "Zone d'Insécurité." We still need special papers and escorts to go through it.'

'Is there any danger?'

He shrugged. 'Nothing's happened so far, and I've been doing the trips all winter. The tribesmen down there are pretty docile and introverted — unless you get drunk in front of them or smile at their women.'

'Only smile?'

'That's all it needs, sport. Just try it, and you're likely to be good for nothing but singing treble in the church choir.'

'I'll remember that.'

'The woman situation here,' Bates went on, 'is a little precarious. I find on the whole that boys are more satisfactory. They're cleaner, safer, more co-operative, and generally prettier than the girls. But it's a matter of opinion, of course.'

Quinn asked about the work.

'Just keep the idiots happy. See they get fed and put to bed and don't get the screaming hab-dabs. Otherwise, it's nice to give 'em a lot of local facts that you can make up as you go along. Almost anything's believable in this country. Did you know that in the eighteenth century the University of Safi ran a course for piracy?' They had a couple more drinks and the sun began to go down, and Bates' eyes grew heavy. He talked a lot, but very little about himself. From odd things he said Quinn gathered that he had read law at an Australian university and had practised for a short time in some obscure town in the back-country; had thrown it up to work as a deckhand on a Norwegian coaster; had once sold his blood to a hospital in Rio when threatened with gaol for not being able to pay a nightclub bill; and he now lived in a flat in the modern quarter of Casablanca and ran a car.

He told Quinn a lot about Morocco — how the old feudal life in Marrakech had been dwindling since the French left. The Nationalist government, aping the Europeans, had swept away the embarrassing spectacle of dancing boys and storytellers and public letter writers; had rounded up the 5,000 whores and sold them to the army, and banned the medicine men whose potions of powdered snake skull and lion's blood had been known to cure female ailments, where aureomycin had failed.

On the great Djema el Fna, the Place of the Dead, where a generation ago the Sultan had exhibited the pickled heads of his enemies, half the cobbles had now been torn up and replaced with a tarmac car park for ramshackle American cars run as taxis. The rest of the market was lined with tents and stalls where they sold razor blades, instant coffee and Egyptian paperbacks — love stories and political propaganda indiscriminately. And the palace of the notorious old Pasha of Marrakech had now been turned into a student hostel full of ping-pong tables. Bates claimed that once, after a bomb had been thrown in the mosque, the screams of tortured prisoners in the palace had kept the tourists awake in a nearby hotel.

'You've got to go south of the Atlas now if you want excitement. The sods have cleaned this place up as though it had been conquered by the Salvation Army.'

'There's the Casino,' said Quinn.

'There is that, but you have to wear proper shoes.'

They watched a posse of jungle-green soldiers slouching across the square swinging machine pistols. These were the modern substitutes for the dancing boys and the medicine men — members of the Armée de Libération, a mutinous hangover from the struggles against the French. They would come down from the hills and maraud through placid towns, jeering at the regular militia and spitting at pictures of the king, then disappear again. The Nationalists had once promised to reward them with gold and French girls on Independence Day, which they never did, and now these privateers controlled great areas of the country — although no one seemed to know who controlled them. Bates claimed, quite seriously, that they were equipped with arms from the Belgians and the Czechs as an experiment in peaceful co-existence.

He always looked Quinn straight in the eyes when he spoke, and his own eyes were blue and beguiling, but there were moments when they rolled up and showed the whites, and an odd craziness crept into the face that was not altogether pleasant.

They had a last drink, as the sun slid behind the minaret of the Katoubia and prayers began to wail like sirens into the green evening. Bates paid the bill out of a wallet fat with money, and they agreed that if Quinn got the job they would meet at the café downstairs next morning.

CHAPTER 2

Quinn still had two hours to wait. He went back to his hotel which was cheap and dark, in the heart of the Arab Medina. In the alley outside, four blind beggars sat calling for alms. They had been there for two days now, crouched under the wall, their eyes misted over like burnt-out flashbulbs.

In his room the shutters were closed and the fan on the wall had broken. There was a chipped enamel bowl on the floor half-full of tepid water which he splashed over his face and neck; then he lay naked on the bed and began taking stock of his position. He had five pounds in travellers' cheques, six thousand Moroccan francs and a return ticket, deck-class, from Tangier to Algeciras; a knapsack with shaving-tackle, changes of underwear, a mohair sweater, some hard shoes and one clean shirt. That was all.

For the last two years he had worked for a provincial newspaper in the north of England: two years in the reporters' room sitting back-to-back with a white-faced Christian who wrote sensible articles about church affairs and the preservation of rural England — of which there was precious little within many miles.

For Quinn, a relentless hammering at a typewriter between mugs of tea and interviews with tiny-minded borough councillors and civic dignitaries. Two years of it — like living on a plate of cold porridge.

He lay listening to the beggars outside. After a while their melancholy bleating became confused with the hundred other sounds, of mules and children and bicycle bells and radios blaring Arab music.

Then there had been the evening not long ago when he'd disgraced himself at one of the editor's parties (cocoa and brown sherry) by arriving drunk, retiring to a room upstairs where he'd taken off his trousers, got into a bed and passed out, returning to the party a couple of hours later, only to find himself standing in the middle of the room with everyone gaping at him. He had forgotten to put his trousers back on. The incident had not gone down well.

He grinned in the twilight, swung off the bed, shaved and pulled on the clean shirt, put on a tie and combed his hair, and in the slice of broken mirror saw that his face was darkening with the sun and his hair bleached, almost blond. He was twenty-seven, had good eyesight and good health, his teeth were all his own, his feet weren't flat, and he was single. His principal vices were a tendency to be lazy and impetuous; and his idea of Hell was to be confined for eternity in a fish-and-chip shop with a cinema-organ playing non-stop. Otherwise, he was a normal Englishman.

On his way to the Mamounia Hotel, he passed one of the last nightspots in the Arab Medina, 'Le Bar des Amis', which before the new régime had been the haunt of the Pasha's private police and had won a notorious reputation. He glanced inside and now saw a row of Arabs huddled under the hoods of their jellabahs, getting quietly, deeply drunk to the strains of an Egyptian 'pop' song from the jukebox. There was an advertisement on the wall for 'Dentifrice Colgate', with a blonde girl who was all teeth and legs. The Arabs did not look at her. They were drinking bad local brandy.

Through the submarine lighting of the Mamounia bar M. Sebastien Izard's head appeared to be made of plasticine. He was a small man in a dinner jacket, stooping slightly out of his armchair, eyes like black stones and a mouth that was a curved slot just wide enough to take a fifty-franc piece. He reminded Quinn of some deep-sea fish.

He had not talked much, except to ask a number of personal questions about Quinn's background, his previous jobs, why he had come to Morocco, what he wanted to do there. Quinn had taken Bates' tip and did not mention that he was a journalist. To each reply Izard simply nodded, never once taking his eyes off him.

There was a second man with him, a Moroccan of about thirty with a complexion like cork. He was introduced as M. Beloued, the chief guide with the travel agency. He did not speak a word throughout the interview, and, like Izard, never moved his eyes from Quinn; but once or twice, for apparently no reason, he smiled and showed a pair of nickel-capped teeth.

Neither of them smoked, and they drank only orange juice, while Quinn ordered himself a discreet aperitif. Under their scrutiny he felt that he was being sized up exactly and that very little escaped either of them. Even the small deceit of omitting to say he was a journalist began to make him mildly uneasy. Izard struck him as a clever, ruthless old man — the sort of person whom it would be unwise to cross.

The bar was almost empty. Out of the corner of his eye he kept catching a glimpse of a little man with spectacles at a table across the room, watching the three of them closely.

Izard told Quinn that he would pay him three thousand francs a day, all found, and that the trip would last twelve days. 'Your duties will not be severe. You will meet Monsieur Beloued and Monsieur Bates at the Hotel de France tomorrow morning at ten o'clock. There is a third guide, a Mademoiselle Soissons, whom you will meet later.' He paused; then, as though to make the interview seem less formal, he concluded with some random remarks about England, which he had visited a couple of times. He talked of Ascot and Newmarket, and mentioned a T. S. Eliot play he had much enjoyed seeing in London, calling it, by some slip of the tongue, *The Confidential Agent*. He made conversation with ease, but dispassionately, as though all the time thinking of something else.

There was only a moment, towards the end, when he became enthusiastic. He was speaking of the isles on the west of Scotland and of the wild flowers he had found on the mountains. 'It is, of course,' he said, in his stilted, accurate English, 'due to the volcanic rock. Some of the most magnificent flora I have seen was on the Virunga volcanoes in the Congo. You are not interested in flowers, Monsieur Quinn?'

'I'm afraid I don't know much about them.'

Izard suddenly broke off and thrust himself up with a black cane. He took Quinn's hand. 'Monsieur, it has been a pleasure. I hope that you enjoy the journey. Good evening.' He did not smile. Behind him, M. Beloued showed a glint of nickel-teeth, like fangs.

Quinn watched them both move away across the lounge, then took out his wallet and counted out enough to pay his hotel bill. He was left with the five-pound travellers' cheque and about five pounds in Moroccan money. He ordered a large excellent brandy. A three-man band came in and struck up some tunes from *Pal Joey*. Nobody got up to dance.

The little man with the spectacles across the bar was still sitting alone watching him. Quinn felt happy and at ease. He had a job under his belt for a couple of weeks and a long run south into the desert; and at the end of it would have just enough for a one-way fare down to Black Africa. He wondered

24

why Izard should be wary of politically-minded journalists. He sipped the brandy and smiled at the idea of being placed so high, remembering the usual stuff he'd had to turn out: '…Councillor Pendlebury then moved that the showing of "X" films on a Sunday would lead to a serious decline of morals among the youth of Stokington.'

The little man was still watching him. In a moment he would come over and try to start conversation. Quinn finished his drink and left.

In the reception lobby there were posters for the Haut Atlas advertising winter sports, fishing, riding and tennis. Outside he passed a group of chalk-faced girls piling out of a horse-drawn caliche, carrying Air France overnight bags. *Probably Paris models*, he thought, *flown in by Caravelle jet, their narrow haunches squeezed into skirts like two legs in one trouser leg.*

It was still early. He climbed on to the caliche and told the driver to take him to the Casino. They rattled out of the city gates, down a wide floodlit avenue of cypress and eucalyptus trees. There were fountains playing at the foot of the Casino steps and two red-fezzed Moroccans stood at the doors like sentries. He gave up his passport, bought a ticket and cashed his travellers' cheque. In the salle de jeu about a dozen Europeans were gathered round the one roulette table; the other two, and the baccarat table, were under shrouds. It looked like a cocktail party that was beginning to break up.

He bought twenty 500-franc chips and placed one on red; then glanced round the table, hoping for a pretty girl who looked bored and in need of champagne. Most of the faces were grey and middle-aged.

The ivory ball spun and clicked and came to rest against red. He left the chips on, and won again. This time he collected the

2,000 francs and bought himself a champagne cocktail; went back to the table, put 1,000 francs on red again, and lost.

He was standing directly behind the croupier, whose rake was deftly sweeping in the unlucky chips. Quinn saw his own pile being whisked off the baize, and as he watched, the handle of the rake jabbed back and hit him neatly in the testicles.

He gave a gasp and sank almost to his knees. A woman next to him touched his arm and said, 'Are you ill?' The croupier's face appeared, unruffled, and said *'Je m'excuse, monsieur.'* Play had stopped for a moment. One or two faces eyed him dubiously. In a casino the least disturbance, outside the fluctuations of play, is regarded with suspicion.

He straightened with a twinge of nausea and limped over to the bar, where he had another champagne cocktail, his skin prickling with sweat.

'No luck?' enquired the barman, without interest. The champagne was making Quinn feel sick; he told the barman what had happened. *'Ah, faut faire attention!'* said the man. Quinn walked away and cashed in the few chips he had left.

Outside, the night smelt of jasmine and eucalyptus. Somewhere across the darkness, behind the walls and minarets, lay the Atlas Mountains. And behind the mountains lay the Sahara and the whole continent of Africa.

There was no caliche or taxi, so he walked back to the hotel.

CHAPTER 3

Bates and the Moroccan, M. Beloued, were sitting at a pavement table in front of the Hotel de France when he arrived at ten o'clock the next morning. The Australian's breakfast appeared to have consisted principally of a bottle of Algerian wine, which he had almost emptied, his head slouched back under a floppy bush hat. M. Beloued sat behind him sipping a thimble of muddy coffee; he looked like a well-scraped knife.

Bates stood up with a crash. 'Join the party, sport! Drink some of this filthy wine.' He grabbed up another chair, almost upsetting M. Beloued's tiny cup. 'And what did you think of the old man?'

Quinn looked sideways at M. Beloued, who sat with his face just within the shade of the roof. Bates said, 'Don't worry about him, he doesn't have any English.'

'Well, he asked a lot of questions. Is this job really all that important — to Izard, I mean?'

'Just routine. Izard likes to be sure of who he's hiring.' He ordered Quinn some mint tea and a plate of kebab.

'By the way, he mentioned there was a girl coming,' said Quinn.

'Oh, Leila! Yes, I forgot to tell you. She's joining us tomorrow morning at Tarourat up in the Atlas.'

'What's she like?'

Bates grinned, his teeth black with wine. 'A lovely angel! She's got a figure like…' He flapped his big hand out — 'like as though her legs started up at her shoulders!'

Quinn laughed. 'A swagman's vision!'

'Honest to God no! You wait till you see her. She's riding up from the south with the Blue Men.'

'And who are the Blue Men?'

'Tribesmen from Mauretania. Negroid, nearly seven feet high, faces like eagles, bodies stained ultramarine. They say the dye sinks in so deep that even some of their kids are born blue.'

'And this girl travels with them alone?'

'Why not? She's a lot safer with them than she would be at night in one of your dormitory suburbs.'

M. Beloued had finished his coffee and said in French: 'Good day. I will meet you at the bus.' Bates nodded absently and went on: 'She's a marvellous girl. Half Algerian — refugee from the war.'

'But what's she doing alone in the desert?'

Bates didn't answer. He tilted his chair back at a perilous angle against the railings, pulled the bush hat over his eyes and said: 'Riding all tonight with her sweet little rump jogging up and down on a donkey's back, over the mountains through the dawn.' He belched noisily. 'You know,' he said, pushing the hat up and glaring at Quinn, 'I should have married that girl. I had a wife once. A proper bitch she was!' He laughed and rolled his eyes up, his face suddenly sad, the colour of old newspaper. 'I'd marry Leila only she won't look at me. She'll come up with her hips swaying and fingers splayed out like starfish and say: *"Salut, Paddy, ça va!"* and that's as far as Poor-Bleeding-Paddy gets. Oh Hell!' he said, and called for the bill. 'People used to come out here to get away from girls. Now they've hauled the Foreign Legion off to Algeria and I get Leila Soissons waving it all right under my nose. Come on, let's go!'

Quinn asked again: 'But what's she doing alone in the desert?'

'With the job.'

'But what job? As a guide?'

Bates turned. 'You ask a lot o' questions, sport.' He pushed past the table. 'Too many bloody questions!'

Quinn said nothing. They started to walk towards the bus terminal. The sun was climbing high over the square, where pariah dogs panted for shade and figures lay rolled up asleep in their jellabahs under the walls. Bates gave him an advance of ten thousand francs on his wages and he stopped at a shop and bought a straw hat and a brass-studded belt with a concealed pouch to carry his money.

At the terminal a deluxe coach stood in a departure bay marked: Haut Atlas: Sahara. M. Beloued was waiting at the door with a typed list of the passengers. Quinn was surprised to see that there were only six names: an American couple, a Frenchman, a Swiss and two Moroccans. Bates said something about it being the off season. He told him to look after the two Americans and not to worry about the others. It seemed a lot to pay him thirty thousand francs for, but he didn't argue.

The passengers arrived just before eleven o'clock in two caliches. They struck Quinn at once as an odd assortment. The American couple, a Mr. and Mrs. Whittaker, were normal enough: husband criss-crossed with cameras and binoculars, and a dumpy wife with a mauve rinse and clothes that had probably cost more than an Arab labourer makes in a year.

But the one who interested Quinn most was the Frenchman, an anthropologist called M. Bloch. He was the man who had been watching them in the Mamounia bar the night before. He was small and hairy, his suit flecked with ash and his pebble-glasses so thick that they made his eyes look like oysters.

The Swiss and the two Moroccans were the last to arrive. The Swiss was a middle-aged man, compact as furniture in a bank, with a pitch-black suit that looked far too hot for the climate. The two Moroccans were identical with fleshy blue faces sheltering behind dark glasses. They might have been business men or bank clerks or civil servants or waterfront gangsters. M. Beloued wrung them both by the hand. They sat up at the back of the coach, which was three-quarters empty.

When they were aboard, Bates took out a bunch of keys; one of them looked something like a corkscrew which he began to turn into the lock of the luggage bay. Quinn hung around waiting to help him stow the baggage aboard, but Bates ordered him on to the bus. Inside, M. Beloued was making a short speech about stopping that evening in the mountain city of Tarourat just below the snow line.

They drove out of Marrakech through one of the arched gates, round the crenellated mud battlements, past wells where exquisite children squatted down scrubbing heaps of washing on stones and waving excitedly as the bus went by. Ahead, the horizon seemed at first as flat and empty as the sea; then slowly the mountains emerged, a dim azure ridge far above them, like storm clouds hanging between the glare of the sky and the haze off the sand. A few miles on they could see the peaks tipped with white and looking clean and very distant.

The wooden aqueducts along the roadside were flowing swiftly back into Marrakech, and soon the bus left the plain and began swinging round hairpin bends, with M. Beloued at the wheel sweating through his drip-dry shirt and the tyres screeching on the tarmac. They drove into gullies of rock veined with savage greens and purples, where the road sliced the hills into precipices hundreds of feet high, cutting out the sun.

Bates slept, his long body collapsed over the folding seats. The Whittakers followed the landscape clicking their

Rolleiflexes, and at the back of the bus the two Moroccans and the Swiss snoozed under the blue windows, no more interested in what was going on than if they'd been on some urban bus ride.

Quinn was sitting up near the front. Shortly after they'd started, the French anthropologist, M. Bloch, had appeared at his elbow with a packet of cigarettes out, smiling eagerly, his eyes swimming behind their bifocals.

Quinn soon discovered that the man was a skilled bore. He chatted incessantly, punctuated with small inconsequential questions, until Quinn realised that in the space of a few minutes he had told him more about himself that he had told Bates in an afternoon.

The man had a small bunched face with tufts of hair springing from his ears and nostrils, and smelt strongly of tobacco. He seemed always the one to open a fresh track of conversation, and although persistently inquisitive, he carefully evaded any questions that Quinn put to him. He seemed especially interested to know how he had got the job and had met Izard; but when Quinn asked him if he knew Izard too, he tacked away on another subject.

After they had been going about an hour they ran into a roadblock, with two jeeps of royal Moroccan soldiers. An officer came on board and asked to see all passports. Bates and M. Beloued were very alert, springing down on to the road and quick to show the passenger list and the permits for the Zone d'Insécurité. The officer asked to see the luggage. Bates made great play with his bluff charm, pleading that these delays made a bad impression on tourists and that they were already behind schedule. The officer finally relented and waved them on.

Quinn had tucked his passport into the sleeve of the seat in front, in case they were halted again. He had noted that while the Whittakers had been obviously excited by the delay, snapping up the soldiers in a whole reel of film, the two Moroccans, and even the Swiss, had seemed quite agitated by the incident.

Bates got back in and explained casually that it was a routine check that was made on everyone going into the Atlas.

A few miles on they stopped at a mountain restaurant, famous for its French cuisine. The meal, although excellent with plenty of good wine, went off awkwardly. M. Beloued and his two compatriots refused to drink; the Swiss talked only to the Moroccans — Quinn noticing that he spoke fluent Arabic — and Bates consumed a large quantity of wine and became tight and noisy, breaking into lewd Bush ballads that made Mrs. Whittaker giggle nervously, while her husband stared hard at the table.

Back in the coach Quinn made elaborate efforts to escape M. Bloch and his endless questions; but the little man fastened on to him again, thrusting his packet of cigarettes at him as though it were a pistol compelling instant friendship. Quinn tried yawning, even feigned sleep, but the Frenchman seemed immune to hints. Hardly a minute was allowed to slip by without his making some trite but probing remark which demanded a response.

Quinn was lying back with his eyes closed, trying not to listen to M. Bloch. He had thought of seeking refuge with Bates, but he saw that he was fast asleep again, and there was nothing for it but to bear with the Frenchman as patiently as he could. The man was now talking to him about journalism. 'That must indeed be an interesting job? I expect you get a lot of opportunity to travel?' No, Quinn had never been beyond

Blackpool on a story. So he wasn't in Morocco on a job? No, he was on holiday. 'Do you get many opportunities to take such holidays from your work?'

'No, very little…' Then Quinn realised something that gave him quite a start. He came wide awake and looked closely at M. Bloch, who avoided his eyes, and in the same moment became suddenly quiet. Perhaps he too had detected his mistake. For Quinn remembered that at no time since they had met had he ever told the man that he was a journalist. The only person on the coach who knew was Bates, and Quinn thought it unlikely that he would have told M. Bloch. It was Bates, after all, who had been anxious that the fact was not spread about.

There was just one explanation. For some reason M. Bloch had gone back to the coach during the lunch and had examined Quinn's passport, which he would have seen him put in the seat sleeve in front of him.

Perhaps the little man was insatiably curious. Quinn was puzzled. After a few minutes the Frenchman excused himself, saying the front of the coach made him sick, and went back to sit with the two Moroccans and the Swiss.

CHAPTER 4

They came in to Tarourat just after sunset. It was a harsh medieval city with walls and blind towers hanging down the mountain face, bone-white under the African moon.

The hotel was very modern, standing on a rock above the city — layers of plate glass staring down over the mountains to the great plain below. A monument to an alien culture. The dining room was like a gymnasium, and outside, a fountain dribbled in a cement patio the size of a small barrack square.

Quinn and Bates shared a room with a balcony that faced the Casbah, with curtains handwoven by the Berber tribesmen, which drew on large brass hoops. There were spiders in the bath, and in a drawer they found a lump of bread as hard as a stone.

Bates' luggage consisted of a leather holdall that he kept locked, and a wooden medicine chest filled with extensive prophylactic and anti-venereal kits, which he now began checking carefully through in case of damage by the heat. Quinn was about to tell him about the incident with M. Bloch, then thought better of it.

After dinner Bates announced an excursion into the town to see some Berber dancing. Besides Quinn, the only ones interested were the Whittakers. The two Moroccans went into the lounge to play backgammon and M. Beloued and the Swiss disappeared to their rooms. As Quinn left the hotel he saw M. Bloch sitting alone in a corner of the lounge with an old French magazine, chain-smoking, occasionally glancing up at the two Moroccans at their game. He looked as though he were waiting for someone.

Bates led the way down through the Casbah into the covered souks, which were closed up and black, with a hush that seemed to hold in suspense a myriad of tiny ticking sounds, like a room full of clocks. In one of the alleys the ground was white with wood-shavings from the shops where they carved sandals and Moorish slippers; and further on was the flinty smell of foundries where they made lanterns and forged daggers and beat out silver goblets and plates and tea sets. Bates pointed out the openings to the Jewish quarter, with the shutters bolted over cells full of families, skull-capped and gabardined, asleep in suffocating communion by night, sitting by day behind trays glinting with gold rings and bracelets.

The dancing was given in a room above a Berber café. They had to climb a stepladder through the café ceiling, and Mrs. Whittaker cried: 'Oh, isn't this crazy! — it's so original!' The hooded Arabs in the café watched them with dark impassive faces, their eyes following them up the steps, communicating nothing.

A very handsome young Berber, in a jellabah stitched with gold thread, bowed them in and invited them to sit on leather pouffes, bringing them mint tea in cups of silver and dishes piled with pastries. An old man with a beard like a cobweb sat cross-legged against the far wall and played a flute, and four boys in turbans of brilliant yellow, with white robes and daggers, swept in holding drums above their heads, stamping their naked heels on the matting, rapping the drums in a steady, monotonous rhythm.

Bates watched them, leaning forward with hands clenched, breathing quickly. The Whittakers looked on enraptured, applauding after each dance, at which the boys would stand to attention and Mrs. Whittaker would cry: 'Formidable! Oh, aren't they just divine!'

The young Moroccan came smiling and bowing and refilling their cups, until after about twenty minutes the boys vanished and the young man brought the bill. It was unexpectedly steep, but Mr. Whittaker insisted on paying it all himself.

As they rose to leave the Moroccan murmured some words to Bates, who turned to Quinn and said: 'Look, sport, I'm staying on here. You wouldn't mind taking these two back to the hotel?'

'Anything to oblige, cobber.'

All the way up through the Casbah Mrs. Whittaker enthused about 'those gorgeous little boys!' and her husband agreed that it was very exotic. It was only ten o'clock when they returned, but the guests had already retired and the hotel was like an office block after hours.

Quinn said goodnight to the Whittakers and went to fetch his key from the desk. It wasn't there. Bates must have left it in their room. He went upstairs and found it in the door; and as he stepped through he heard a ring of metal. The curtains were swaying on their hoops. He ran out on to the balcony and heard a sound below. The moon was on the other side and he could see nothing. There was perhaps a ten-foot drop to the courtyard and no visible way of getting up. He decided that it must have been a cat burglar from the Casbah.

He turned back into the room. Both Bates' holdall and medicine chest had been opened. They had simple snap-locks which could have been easily picked with a hairpin. Nothing appeared to have been touched. The holdall contained a couple of bottles of French brandy, a pair of boots, bundle of clothes, compass and maps, a flask of expensive eau de Cologne and an open razor.

At the back of the bag was a zipped compartment. Quinn opened it. Inside lay the bunch of keys which Bates had used to unlock the luggage bay of the coach, and a chequebook on an American bank in Tangier, with a statement that showed that his current account stood at $1,839. A lot of money to save as a part-time travel guide.

There was also a holster with a well-oiled revolver, French Army issue, and several unopened cartons of ammunition. The weapon was loaded.

Quinn went out to the balcony and paced about and felt restless and excited. He wondered if he ought to warn M. Beloued about the thief. He lit a cigarette and let it burn down till it nearly scorched his fingers; threw it away and made up his mind that whatever happened on this trip he would remain an interested observer. If there was something odd going on — and he was pretty certain there was — then so much the better. He was not feeling in a cautious mood.

He went downstairs. Through the stillness the fountain in the patio was making a noise like a tap that had been left running. He went outside and began walking down again into the Casbah.

A voice called: *'M'sieur, tu Français?'* He stopped. An Arab slid out of the shadows. *'Tu cherches jolie fille?'* He was a scrawny man with a woollen cap and a European jacket that might once have been part of a blue suit. He smelt like a goat.

Quinn began to follow him. 'How far is it?' The Arab cocked his head and smiled: *'Tu viens — bel amour!'* and made a familiar gesture with his fingers.

Quinn wondered where the man could have picked up the phrase *'bel amour'* — out of some French novelette perhaps, or an ancient number of *Marie Chantal*.

They started down towards the walls of the city. The alleys grew steeper, descending in steps that twisted under arches where he could see nothing and kept tripping over the Arab's heels. Figures crouched and lay in corners and doorways, and rolled their eyes up and watched them like cats.

'How far is it?' he said again. The Arab gave him an encouraging leer and beckoned towards an arch shaped like the ace of spades. '*Tu viens!*' he called coaxingly.

For the first time since his arrival in Morocco Quinn sensed the tenuous link with law and order being stretched to snapping. There were no police, no good men from Cook's to restore the illusion that this was just another country in the twentieth century opening its frontiers to tourists.

The Arab stood waiting for him under the arch. Quinn began to walk forward, suddenly feeling very alone. The Arab took his hand and led him into what seemed like a tunnel burrowing below the city. He drew a deep breath, remembering how it had been back in England — drab and easy, with the evenings hanging around coffee bars and the local dance hall; creeping past his landlady's door; the girl standing buttoned up against the Lancashire cold, while he put a shilling in the gas meter — enough for one hour.

They came out under the city walls. A raw wind blew off the mountains and whined among the blind towers, stinging his eyes and nostrils. The Arab had stopped and was banging on a door in the wall. It was opened by an old woman in a yashmak, and they followed in, stooping down a passage with tiny wooden doors on either side. She led them into a room with no windows and a ceiling of finely carved cedar wood, lit with oil lamps.

A woman came in and smiled at them. She was barefoot, wrapped in a towelling-gown. She sat down and let the gown fall open. Quinn caught a glimpse of the dark belly and drooping teats. Her face had a gash of lipstick like blood, and the corners of her eyes were crinkled-grey and heavily made up. She was probably no more than twenty.

She gestured to them to sit on the cushions round the walls and clapped her hands. Through the door came a younger woman in an embroidered robe carrying a tray of mint tea. Quinn watched her as she set it down, and the Arab tapped him on the knee and said: '*Deux mille francs pour madame.*'

The woman in the towelling-gown smiled again and showed teeth the colour of impure wax. The younger woman began to pour out the tea; her black hair was wound in plaits and she had the same face as the dancing boys: wide and pencil-grey in the half-light, with almond eyes spaced far apart above the flat Berber nose.

Quinn nodded at her. The Arab simpered and arched his hands as though in prayer, then said something in Arabic to the older girl, who just shrugged. The younger one finished pouring out the tea and stood waiting; she gave no sign of understanding what was being said.

The Arab turned back to Quinn and began to speak in fluent French. He told him that the younger woman was a virgin called Tamalda and that she was promised to a man in Tarourat; but if Quinn gave a cadeau he could take her away and live with her. 'How much?' Quinn asked. The Arab talked more with the older girl, then said, '*Cent mille.*' Quinn laughed; he asked how much it would cost to be with her. The Arab said twenty-thousand. Quinn said he would give five. Twenty-thousand, said the Arab, because she was a virgin and very beautiful. The young woman had not moved.

Quinn said he would pay six. The Arab and the older woman sipped their teacups empty, and Quinn went up to seven. The Arab put his head on one side and spoke to the girl, Tamalda. He turned to Quinn, '*Elle dit qu'ti es beau!*' he grinned.

'Seven thousand,' repeated Quinn. They agreed on seven thousand five hundred.

All three of them watched as he peeled off the notes from the roll inside his belt pouch. This would be cutting severely into his savings, but he wasn't thinking about that now. The older girl took the money, and the Arab put his arm out and whispered '*Pour men p'ti pourboire.*' Quinn gave him five hundred francs, but he did not look pleased. Tamalda tugged at his elbow and led him out into the passage, disappearing with him into a room like a cell. There was a lamp in a red vase and a couch draped with Berber rugs. She closed the door and stood against him, taking his hand in hers, which was cool and tiny, and ran her lips along his knuckles, then pressed her mouth against his and began sliding the soft lips over his cheeks and neck.

He tried to take her round the waist, and she broke away, and with one swift movement pulled the robe over her head and threw it into a corner. Underneath she wore only a pair of wine-red trousers held fast at the ankles and the dip under her belly. She put her hands above her head and began to dance, her feet together, her stomach rolling and swelling as though there were some live creature inside it. The dancing became faster, frantic, shivering up her whole body, although her breasts were so shallow that they hardly quivered. Then her hands flashed down and unfastened the trousers, and she gracefully slipped out of them and went on dancing, her flanks and bottom as slender as a boy's.

He pulled her down on the couch, but she lay quite still, panting slightly, dry and closed up and rubbing her mouth over his face and neck. He tried speaking to her in French, and she murmured a few guttural Arab words and rubbed her lips harder against him. He tried again to make love to her, but each time she tightened up and began to shake like a bird. Once he thought she was crying. He looked down into her face and stroked her cheeks, but there were no tears, the eyes staring at the ceiling.

He wondered what she was thinking about: what her life could be like, promised to a man she had probably never seen, living with a whore in this odd little house among the towers and heat and desolation.

He stayed next to her and the oil lamp guttered and went out. He was lying in pitch dark and heard her stir up beside him. For a moment he didn't move; then he felt her fingers between his thighs beginning to caress him, and his senses quickened, when he suddenly got violent cramp in his foot.

He tried flexing the toes to hold the pain off, but it came jarring into him, and he sat up wincing and stretching out to massage the foot, and heard a rustle quite close to him. He leant out and touched the girl's leg. It darted away and he grabbed her arm. She was holding his belt and a little fistful of notes. He tried to pull the belt from her and she began to scream — a high, shameless, animal scream. 'Shut up,' he said quietly. 'Shut up! Tamalda!' At the mention of her name the scream stopped.

He started groping for his clothes. He had his trousers and shirt on, and was looking for his sandals, when she began screaming again. He tried to put his hand over her mouth, now thoroughly scared, and she snapped at him with needle-sharp teeth. '*Tamalda, tais-toi!*' He had leant down to fasten the strap of his sandal, when the door burst open and he was kicked in the head with a wooden shoe.

He pushed his way stunned into the passage, one sandal on his foot, the other in his hand, hopping against the door, head reeling The door swung open and he fell into the alley.

Somewhere behind him an old woman was screeching abuse at him in Arabic. He got his other sandal on, and heard footsteps coming towards him down the passage. He got up and ran. The footsteps came padding after him, and he turned into another alley, very dark and narrow, leading upwards. The footsteps passed at the bottom. He ran on; up into a square; past a pump. He felt for his belt. It was round his waist, but the pouch was empty.

He had no idea where he was, and went on up crooked alleys and stairways, thinking of the posters in the Mamounia Hotel with their promises of tennis and winter sport. He was following any turning that led upwards, and all round the figures lay in corners watching him. He began to shout, 'Anyone for tennis!' — when he saw the hotel silhouetted on the rock above.

Bates had still not returned. Quinn went into the bathroom and saw a blue duck's egg swelling up under his hairline. He dabbed water on it, then went and stretched out fully dressed on the bed. He was half asleep when Bates came in. 'Jesus! What happened to you?'

Quinn groaned. 'Give me some aspirins or brandy or something. I got kicked in a whore-house. Kicked and fleeced. I've no money left.'

Bates had gone over to his medicine chest, then swung round. 'Hey, sport, have you opened my things?' He started back towards the bed and Quinn remembered about the thief. He explained what had happened. Bates stood very still. 'You didn't see who it was, then?'

'It was too dark. He got out through the balcony just as I came in.' Bates was going quickly through his holdall: opened the compartment at the back, zipped it up again and said, 'So the bastard got clean away? Did he get in by the balcony too?'

'I think he came through the door. The key was in the lock.'

'I left the key at the desk when we went out.' He paused, fingering his jaw. 'Do you remember who was downstairs when we left?'

'The two Moroccans. And the little Frenchman.'

'Monsieur Bloch? What was he doing?'

'Nothing. Just reading. You don't think it was him, do you?'

When Bates didn't reply Quinn began to tell him about the incident with the passport.

'You're sure of this?'

'Well, unless the man's telepathic.'

Bates stood staring in front of him. 'He could have been waiting last night when the others went upstairs,' he murmured, half to himself.

'We don't have any proof.'

'No. Not yet.' He handed Quinn some codeine tablets and a couple of inches of brandy in a tooth-glass. Quinn swallowed them and said, 'But why would he have done it?'

'I don't know,' said Bates slowly. He stood for some time in the middle of the room, flipping his lower lip. At last, just as Quinn was dropping off to sleep, he said, 'By the way, if you notice anything else funny about this fellow Bloch, let me know, will you?'

Quinn woke with the sun in his eyes and one side of his face feeling like a football. The rest of the party, including Bates, were already breakfasting in the patio when he arrived downstairs. A girl was sitting at a table with Bates and M. Bloch; she watched Quinn come across the patio with long sliding eyes over the rim of her coffee cup. He saw, with a catch of excitement, that she was extremely pretty.

Bates introduced them: 'Leila Soissons — Rupert Quinn.' She gave him her hand and smiled. She had a wide mouth, and her hand was slender and deeply tanned. Bates grinned at him and said in French, 'Well, what do you think of her?'

She wore a khaki shirt and jeans, and a legionnaire's képi with a white linen shield down to her shoulders.

He said, slightly confused: 'You look like something out of *Beau Geste*.' (*Not the sort of girl*, he thought, *you find in the Midland Hotel, Manchester.*)

She looked puzzled. 'Comment, beau geste?' Her French had only a trace of accent. She was very dark, with a straight nose and delicate tilted features that looked more Latin than Arab, her skin the colour of brown eggshell.

Bates said, in his correct, nasal French: 'It was an English novel about the Foreign Legion.'

She frowned, and said sharply: 'The Foreign Legion? I have nothing to do with it!'

'I didn't mean you were in it,' said Quinn; but Bates broke in in English: 'Don't talk to her about the Legion, sport. She's Algerian — doesn't care for them.'

Quinn nodded rather foolishly at her. There was an awkward pause; then she suddenly leant over and touched his bruised head with the tip of her finger. 'What happened to you?'

'I walked into a tree.' He looked past her, straight-faced at the fountain.

Bates said: 'He had a fight last night in a whore-house.'

'You won, I hope?'

'No. I never saw who it was.'

Bates patted him on the shoulder and said smiling: 'And they took all his money, too.'

She threw back her head and let out a spray of laughter. 'What you men do in pursuit of pleasure!' M. Bloch hunched his shoulders and smiled obsequiously. None of them had taken the least notice of him. Bates said to Quinn: 'By the way, what was the girl like? You didn't tell me.'

Quinn stirred his coffee and said: 'Very pretty but too young.'

'No girl's too young in this country,' said Bates.

'Well, this one was. She was a virgin. They wanted me to buy her.'

'Then why didn't you?' said Leila. 'Virgins are very rare in Morocco.' Bates gave an enigmatic grunt. 'Wasn't she nice to you?' she went on. She was watching Quinn closely. He said, 'Well, I told you, she was too young. Then she stole my money and someone kicked me in the head.'

'Poor boy! But didn't you seduce her first?' She showed him her small white teeth.

'It didn't work,' he said.

'Shame on you, monsieur!'

M. Bloch suddenly stood up, bowed to each of them and left.

Leila said: 'Who is that dreadful little man? He's been hanging around me ever since I arrived.'

'I'll tell you about him later,' said Bates. 'We may have a problem there.'

'Oh?' She raised her eyebrows, and Bates made a short gesture. Quinn felt that whatever had to be said to Leila about M. Bloch was not for his ears.

She then began telling about the trip with the Blue Men: how they had brought an ostrich with them, a huge creature that ran with the caravan and which they exhibited in the towns, standing it in a bed of its own eggshells and bones of its ancestors, plucking the feathers from under the wings and tail and selling them as love potions. She leant over to

Quinn and said: 'They say that if a woman dips the feathers in mint tea and drinks it she goes mad with love!'

He looked at her, narrowing his eyes, and said: 'You ought to try it sometime.'

She put her fingers to her lips and gave him a mischievous smile that was somehow not all mischief.

Bates stared into his cup and said sourly: 'You're flirting, Leila.'

'I am not!' She looked back at Quinn, and the smile returned. 'No,' she said, 'I have to be in love with someone first.'

'Bravo!' said Bates. She was still looking at Quinn. 'What do you think of him, Leila?'

'I think he has very beautiful eyebrows.'

Quinn felt that he was going to enjoy this trip.

CHAPTER 5

They left the city after lunch and drove till dusk down through the mountains to the brown plain to the south. On the lower slopes they passed valleys full of olives and fig trees, and tall hill-towns immured behind Moorish battlements.

Bates had lent Quinn another 10,000 francs on his wages. At first Quinn had wanted to go back to the brothel and threaten them with the militia if they didn't return his money; but Leila had dissuaded him. She had laughed and said he had got what he deserved. He didn't like being influenced by girls, but this time he had given in. She had a certain authority and ease about her which fascinated and rather disturbed him.

On that second day of the trip complications set in. The Whittakers, in their passionate pursuit of the exotic, were swiftly defeated by the lavatories. These became smaller and fouler and rarer, while Mrs. Whittaker complained of bites and headaches and pains in her stomach.

That night they stayed in a town with a hump-backed mosque and a market that seemed to have nothing but poles hung with pale bleeding meat. The hotel consisted of a courtyard and mud rooms with rugs and straw palliasses. The proprietor lay in the yard rolled up in a blanket, brushing flies from his face. There was a well in the yard and a lavatory inside a wicker screen — a hole in the sand which Mrs. Whittaker refused to use. She also refused to eat the meal of skewered white meat, and complained of bedbugs; and after they had all gone to their rooms they could hear her ranting at her husband saying that Ischia would have been much nicer.

For the next couple of nights Leila did not sleep in the hotels, but stayed outside slipped into a sleeping bag, and was always up with the dawn looking crisp as celery. The sight of her threw Mrs. Whittaker into even deeper depression. Leila did the best she could for the woman, tending her corns and dabbing calamine lotion on her raw face; and finally tried to persuade her, using Quinn as a stricken interpreter, that these lavatories were just as healthy as Mrs. Whittaker's own china throne. After a particularly miserable scene, with Mrs. Whittaker in tears and her husband looking like a whipped dog, Leila threw up her hands and cried: 'Oh, you poor Americans! Can you do nothing without your beautiful bathrooms?' And Bates laughed at her and said: 'You can tell she's an Arab! If you took her to the Ritz she'd still squat on top of the seat!'

It was this kind of jibe that seemed to constitute Bates' only defence against Leila. He was clearly in love with her, in an obscure, hopeless way, and in his eagerness to project the image of the easygoing romancer he became pathetically awkward and self-conscious. He had only to sit at the same table with her to sweep some glass or cup to the floor, and if he had to open a door for her he usually managed to trip up or fall over her. He was also a little frightened of her and obeyed her like a well-disciplined schoolboy. Quinn at first found it hard to calculate what she thought of either of them. During the first few days she seemed to treat them both with a bold camaraderie, like one of those tomboy heroines out of children's adventure books.

She was very resourceful and could build fires that survived desert winds, and pitch tents, and brew mint tea as well as any Berber woman; and whenever they stopped at a market she would buy maize and slivers of meat and fruit, and mash it and chop it and mix it with Bates' cognac, then roast it over a bucket of flaming newspaper, and finally serve up a meal that would have fetched a fair price in any expense-account restaurant.

The more south they went the more they came to rely upon her, particularly for the task of placating Mrs. Whittaker. On the third day the unhappy woman was close to giving up and demanding her money back. It was only the prospect of having to linger days in one of these burnt-brown Casbahs swatting flies and waiting for a return bus that deterred her. Her bowels were still playing havoc with her, but she was now possessed by a new dread — that of snakes. She remembered hearing somewhere that they came up one of these hole-in-the-ground lavatories, and it was in vain that they explained to her that snakes were rare in this part of Africa. Her husband grumbled that it was a disgrace the French had not taught the Arabs more hygiene; and Quinn suggested to him that the United Nations set up a commission to teach the Arabs how to go to the lavatory. The American took this idea quite seriously.

Meanwhile, the heat had become terrific. The sky was a ceiling of white lead, an aching ultraviolet glare that stabbed at the eyes and made clothes cling like bandages. Quinn even found the strap of his wristwatch growing tight as a handcuff.

The ground lay cracked open like a loose jigsaw puzzle; palms hung shrivelled in the static air and crops of vegetation were parched the colour of old straw. The only signs of life were the mud villages and the occasional Biblical figure in brilliant white, strolling behind a herd of goats.

Besides the Whittakers, who were crushed to exhaustion, the other passengers seemed to be taking the trip in their stride, as though they had done it before and knew what to expect. The two Moroccans and the Swiss had changed out of their dark suits into lightweight tropical outfits that looked oddly like uniforms; and M. Bloch, after insinuating himself into everyone's company, being shrugged off by each of them in turn, and bluntly insulted by Bates, had become mute and thoughtful, smoking incessantly. As for the apparent reason for the whole trip, that seemed to have been forgotten. With the Whittakers in revolt, and the wrappings of Western civilisation growing increasingly thin, the last pretensions at a sightseeing tour were abandoned.

All through the third day they had been driving between mustard coloured cliffs, down a valley that was like the bed of a broad river; and along the foot of the cliffs they passed burial grounds where the tombs whitened among the bones of camels and wild dogs. By evening they had come out of the valley, and reached a fortified town on the edge of the desert which looked from the distance like a sandcastle crumbling on an empty beach.

After supper — a communal bowl of cous-cous and rice in the hotel yard — Quinn wandered down by the walls and watched the molten disc of the sun sink into the sand. Behind the town he came to a slope dotted with black tents. There was a figure standing on a ridge in front of him. As he came closer he recognised Leila.

'You're out here all alone?'

She nodded. 'There's nothing to do at the hotel. Paddy's getting drunk, I think.' They stood looking down at the black tents. 'Who lives there?' he asked.

'They're Touaregs. They come up to buy girls and take them down with the caravans into the desert.'

'As slaves?'

She shrugged. 'The girls don't mind. It's a great honour to ride down with the nomads. They call it in Arabic, going down to drink tea in the Sahara. All the girls either want that, or to go to the big cities in the north. It's strange,' she said, 'how everybody seems to have somewhere they want to escape to.'

'And you?'

'Sometimes I do. I'd like to go to England.' Her face had a grave beauty.

'You wouldn't like England,' he said. 'It's too cold and it rains.'

The tip of the sun had slipped under the horizon, and they began to walk back towards the walls. The dusk fell swiftly, making the landscape look like an old photograph. He asked her about the Blue Men and what she had done on the trip over the Atlas. She said something vague about arranging hotels for the tourist run. It didn't sound very convincing. He asked her what she talked about with the Blue Men.

'Not very much,' she said. 'They're very polite, but they're not very interesting. They talk about the moon and the seasons, and what they're going to sell in the Atlas.'

'They sound like farmers in England. Don't you ever get lonely out here?'

'Yes, I do.' She looked up at him, 'And you? Why did you come to Africa?'

'To see what it was like. To get away.'

'Were you very unhappy in England?'

'No. I was just bored.' He used that bleak phrase, '*le cafard.*'

She nodded. 'Didn't you have a girl?'

He smiled. 'Nobody that mattered. And you? — don't you have anybody?'

'Not like that,' she said. 'I don't belong here really. I live up in Casablanca at the moment, but my real home was in Algeria. I had to leave because of the war.'

She stopped and stared into the darkening horizon of desert. 'My father was French. He was a schoolmaster in Algeria. And my mother was a Moslem. They put her in prison. She was very beautiful.'

She began to tell him haphazardly about her life — how she'd been brought up in Oran as an only child, and that her father had been a Communist who'd gone to fight with the Resistance, and that her mother had heard from him just once again, soon after the Liberation. He had been planning to bring them both back to France, when he'd been killed in a riot in Marseille. Life had become very bad for them after that. The authorities had discovered that the father had been a Communist, and his war record, which would still have meant something in those days in Metropolitan France, had been eclipsed in Algeria by the growing European dread of the Left. 'The colons all wanted Hitler and Rommel to win, anyway,' she said.

Her mother had been drawn into political life, and at school she herself had caught the sweet smell of nationalism which she'd at once found seductive and exhilarating — and then, before she could quite realise what had happened, it had exploded round her in a cruel war.

'Did you fight with them?' he asked.

She had her face turned from him, and said, without answering directly: 'I was only sixteen at the time. We got caught up with it. It was very bad in Oran. They arrested my mother and put her in prison. I didn't hear from her much. They only let me see her once every month, then one month she was ill and I couldn't see her, then her letters stopped coming and I didn't hear from her again because I left Algeria. Then I heard from the Red Cross that she died.'

'I'm sorry,' he said. She was silent for a moment. Later he tried to ask her how she'd got the job with Izard, and more about her trip up with the Blue Men, but she shied off the subjects, and scooped her hair up in her fingers and cried: *'Ça ne me gêne pas!* I'm not worried. I'm young — I've plenty of time.'

They had come to one of the gates where a group of children sat in the sand around an older boy who was writing with chalk on a slate. He talked as he wrote, and the children, with their shaven scalps and huge eyes, watched him enthralled. The writing looked like shorthand seen back-to-front in slow motion.

None of them took the least notice of Quinn and Leila. She gripped his arm and said: 'He's teaching them to read. Aren't they beautiful!' He felt her close to him, and the touch of her made his heart beat hard. 'What's he writing?' he asked. She walked round behind the boy, who bowed to her, and read the words on the slate. 'He's telling them a story.' The boy held out his hand, let it circle the group and gave a hoarse cry, and the children bowed their heads, terrified. She laughed. 'He's just said, "And the king commands that the beautiful princess's head be cut off!"' She looked at them lovingly, as they kept their eyes fixed on the little scholar's lips.

On the way back she said: 'One day I shall have lots of children like that!' He said nothing. She began to ask him about himself, and he gave a sporadic account of his life and how he'd thrown up everything to see the world. She interrupted in mid-sentence, turned to face him and put her fingers against his cheeks: *'Tu es bien sympathique!*' She asked him if he'd ever been in love, and he said, 'once or twice,' but that it hadn't really been love; and he asked her the same, and she smiled secretly and said: 'Perhaps. I don't know.'

It was suddenly dark, almost as though lights had been turned down in an auditorium. She pulled his sleeve and cried: 'You tell me about your love affairs — everything! How many girls have you slept with?' then instantly put her hand over his mouth: 'No, don't! — it might make me jealous.'

'It would,' he said, feeling excited and puzzled by her.

They stopped at a café just inside the walls, with kerosene lamps swinging in the wind. Somewhere a radio played: a woman singing a sad, interminable lament that was half peace, half pain, cawing and twanging through the night.

There was a row of tables in a courtyard off the street. They sat and drank glasses of tea, and all the tomboy camaraderie had gone now. Sitting there alone with her, watching the robed figures pass like moths in the dark, he knew that if he put out his hand she would take it and hold it, and that touch would be as meaningful as any kiss. But he made no move, afraid to give anything away — to betray himself a fraction too soon, in this cautionary manoeuvring of emotions.

A hooded man had stopped in the street; he came over to the table and stood murmuring at them. She tried to wave him away, without looking at him, but he came closer. His face was eaten away like a stump of dead tree, without nose or lips. After a moment he sat down at the next table, still talking at them, and Quinn said nervously: 'What's he saying?'

'I think he's telling us about some god. I can't understand properly. He's not a beggar.' The man's face was mad and terrible, nothing to do with the human race at all. Quinn looked at her and next to this obscene intruder she looked very frail and he felt frightened for her. The man stayed with them till they left the café and followed them all the way back to the hotel. Once Quinn confronted him; but he went on murmuring, shaking his arms as though he had something vital to communicate. 'Perhaps he wants to convert us,' she said; 'he says he's seen a vision.'

He did not try to come into the hotel, but stood for a few moments contemplating the gates, then turned and ambled silently away.

Leila had spread her sleeping bag in the hotel courtyard. Later that night Quinn crept out beside her and touched her shoulder. She started up, crying out in Arabic. 'It's all right!' he whispered. 'It's only me.'

She sat up, wearing a cotton shift like a kimono. 'Are you all right alone out here?' he asked.

'I'm all right,' she said sleepily, lying down again.

'Why do you sleep out here?' he said after a pause.

'I like looking at the stars.' She yawned. 'It goes on forever up there. There's no end to it. Have you ever thought of that? — millions and millions of miles, going on forever.'

'I don't like leaving you out here alone,' he said obstinately.

'I'll be safe. If I scream you can come running to save me.' She giggled, and he lost his head and said: 'Can I sleep here with you?'

'No.' Somewhere outside the town a camel started to bray with a metallic rasp like an old-fashioned claxon.

'Not yet,' she whispered. She curled up and her head and shoulders vanished into the bag. He leant over and said: 'Goodnight,' and her head came up again and called: 'Sleep well! Dream about me.'

He lay awake thinking about her — of how he would save her up and enjoy her properly and completely. He would wait till they were back in the north and he had collected his salary, then he would take her to Mogador or up to Fez. Instead of the one-way ticket down to Black Africa, there would be an hotel room with fresh linen sheets and a telephone to ring down for iced wine; and this lovely dark lithe girl between the sheets, loved by him all through the Moroccan night.

He woke early. The morning was still cool as a northern spring. He went into the yard and found the sleeping bag rolled up empty.

He went out of the gates and shouted her name. There was no answer. A camel stared contemptuously down at him. He came to a slope that led under some palms. There was a stream at the bottom, clear as a mirror. He found her at the edge of the water, sitting on her heels, naked except for a triangle of blue pants. She hadn't seen him. Her back was speckled with darting shadows from the mesh of palms; and he stood counting the bumps of vertebrae as she leant down and splashed water over her face and neck. The hair seemed to glisten blue-black on her shoulders. He felt his throat drying up as he watched her.

She got up and wrapped a towel round her neck, and stood with her legs astride, calmly looking at him. She was quite expressionless and made no attempt to cover herself. Then she turned her back to him and began rubbing herself down, and slipped on her jeans and khaki shirt, and he came up behind her and touched his lips to the nape of her neck. She slithered round and kissed him quickly on the mouth. He tried to hold her, and said: 'You are very beautiful.' He kissed her again, on the lips and throat and under the ears, and she said: 'Am I more beautiful than the others?' She pulled his face down level with hers: 'What about that little Moroccan girl the other night? Am I prettier than her?' She bared her teeth in mock rage. 'Fighting for your woman — like an animal!'

He said solemnly: 'There's only you, *Il n'y a que toi.*' He felt more at ease with the French language; one could say things that would sound ridiculous in English — and besides, French didn't seem to implicate him so much. Later on there might be other things to say which would be harder; but for the moment he could enjoy fooling about with these flirting little phrases of less than three syllables.

She drew away and said: 'We must go.' He kissed her again, and she shivered and said: 'Please!'

'What's the matter?' he said, teasing.

'No, no, please! You don't understand. If I start I can't stop.' She frowned and started casting about for her sandals. He said roughly: 'I want you!'

'I know,' she said. 'Now please, let's go.'

Back at the hotel Mrs. Whittaker was just stumbling into the open, like a cow with straw in her hair. She said she hadn't slept a wink, and her husband grumbled about the smell and the snoring Arabs, and she snapped at him that it was all his idea to come out here in the first place.

After breakfast Bates came up to Quinn. He had drunk a lot of brandy the night before and looked rheumy-eyed. 'So you're getting on pretty well with Leila, eh?' He kicked at a stone which bounced across the yard.

Quinn said defensively: 'She's a very nice girl.'

'Don't worry, sport, I'm not in the running! Let the best man win, and all that crap. Did you get your end away last night?'

'No. I'm very fond of her.'

He laughed gloomily. 'Good luck to you! It should be fun in a sleeping bag.' And he slouched off to help M. Beloued check the coach.

CHAPTER 6

Quinn went to call on the local militia post to have their papers stamped and collect an armed escort across the next stretch of desert. Their destination for that evening was a town two hundred and seventy kilometres away called Asouf Mrimina. They were now on the edge of the real Sahara, and the militia at either end had to be informed of their exact timetable. If they had not arrived by midnight a search party would be sent out.

In the militia post three men with rifles sat drinking tea under a fan. The one who was to come as an escort rung Quinn's hand and fetched some cognac from a drawer. He had a stout face like leather, with black pork-chop moustaches. They touched glasses, and he told Quinn how much he admired the British Constitution and wanted to go to London and watch the Red Coats parading on horseback. '*Ça, c'est le militaire!*' he said, slapping the table. His face streamed with sweat. They had another brandy and he explained that he always escorted Izard's parties when they passed each month. He said sadly: 'This is a terrible place for a soldier. I've been here a year now, and I'm a Moroccan and I've only seen Casa once — for two days.'

He collected a spare clip of ammunition and they walked back to the coach. Fuel was taken at a pump outside the gates — the last before Asouf Mrimina — with a hundred litres in reserve cans. Just beyond the town the scrub of the valleys died out and the sand became fine as beach sand blown into smooth dunes; and through the shaded blue of the windows the dunes became the waves of a sea, transfixed under a glass dome of blinding whiteness that played strange tricks on the eyes and could kill a man in a few hours.

Bates told him about four Danes in a Land Rover who'd recently set out to cross this desert without telling the militia. They had been found eight days later by an air patrol, sixty miles off course, with a faulty compass and a seized engine — all four of them picked almost dry by birds and insects.

Leila sat beside him trying to concentrate on a paperback volume called *L'Histoire de Mouvement Socialiste en Allemagne, 1914-1933* — probably the sort of book her father would have encouraged her to read if he'd lived. The bus moved slowly, its tyres dragging through the soft tracks. In the late afternoon the sky darkened and a hot wind came up, whipping the sand into long drifts. Quinn fell asleep on her shoulder and woke with a sore throat and his limbs aching as though he had flu.

Along the horizon he could just see the smudged line of Asouf Mrimina under a sky veined like bad marble. The hotel was on the edge of the town and had once been the palace of the local ruler: full of rotten wood painted in delicate peeling patterns of blue and orange, with rooms as spare as cells in a monastery, standing round a gallery over a patio. Quinn and Bates had one each, and Leila was so enchanted by the building that she decided not to sleep outside, and had a room a few doors along.

Quinn opened the fragile shutters. There was a little yard to the left of the window with the coach parked under some palms. He wished it would only rain.

He went out and walked round the gallery and stopped at Leila's room, and found her asleep on the bed, her head in her arm. He went on, downstairs. His throat was very sore. There was no sound in the hotel. The Whittakers had gone to bed with aspirins and headaches. Outside, there was a hard grey light and the town seemed quite empty. He walked to the end of the street, which led to another that was identical, and the walls had no windows and the doors were locked, without handles.

He went back to the hotel and up to his room. The silence from the town seemed unnatural. He stood at the window again and watched the palms trembling in the wind. Somewhere far away a dog began to bark. When it stopped the silence became total and frightening.

Bates came in. 'What a bloody hole!' He sat down on the bed and yawned. 'It's the wind. It drives some people mad if they're out here long enough.' He took off his sandals and began picking between his toes. 'By the way, there's a place here where we can eat hashish. Do you want to have a go? Leila's coming.'

Quinn thought he saw something move under the palms near the coach. He said: 'I'll try anything once. I think I've got flu, or something.'

'Probably the heat,' said Bates. He came and stood beside him, looking out of the window. It was getting dark. Quinn said: 'I thought I saw something down there.' They peered between palms. 'There's nothing,' said Bates.

'What does this hashish do exactly?'

'Makes you feel good. It's not as wicked as it sounds. The Arabs take it instead of alcohol. You can smoke it and eat it as much as you like down here, but one glass of wine, and you're a social outcast. It's also an aphrodisiac.'

'On girls too?'

'Certainly. More than on us.' He laughed. 'Otherwise there wouldn't be much point, would there?'

Down in the yard they now distinctly saw someone move behind the coach. Bates gave a shout and ran out of the room.

Quinn caught him up at the hotel entrance. They sprinted round the wall into the yard and almost collided with someone coming from the side of the coach. Bates grabbed him by the shirt, and a pair of spectacles dropped on to the sand. It was M. Bloch.

'What are you doing here?' Bates yelled, hauling him up on to his toes. 'Come on, answer! *Qu'est-ce que tu fous ici?*' The little man jerked his head about, his eyes screwed up and half-blind. 'Please monsieur, this is outrageous!'

Bates let him slowly down, searched the man's pockets and drew out the bunch of keys that came from the holdall. 'Second time not so lucky, eh!' he sneered. 'Couldn't you manage the locks on the coach too?'

M. Bloch shook himself like a dog. 'There is some mistake,' he said. 'I wanted to find you earlier to ask you to open the compartment. I thought I had left something in it.' He began groping for his spectacles.

Bates laughed nastily: 'Did you find what you wanted?'

The little man did not answer. He hooked on his spectacles, and said, with an attempt at dignity: 'I admit my fault. But I assure you my intentions were honest.'

Bates smiled. 'Please go back to the hotel, Monsieur Bloch.' The Frenchman said nothing, but walked away round the wall.

'So it was him,' said Quinn.

'The little bastard!' Bates was looking worried. 'You go on back too,' he said, and walked round to the back of the coach.

Quinn went and lay on his bed and tried to sleep. What could M. Bloch have been after? An Arab might have wanted to steal the spare petrol cans or emergency provisions, but not a humble-looking French anthropologist.

At supper he could eat almost nothing. His sore throat was growing worse. He sat with Bates and Leila, and at one point she tried to spoon-feed him some damp rice. He said: 'I'm sorry, I think I've got a fever coming on.'

Bates, who seemed preoccupied throughout the meal, said: 'You'll feel better after you've tasted some hashish.'

'No, I'm not in the mood.'

Leila said pleadingly: 'No, no! You'll feel all right.'

Bates kept looking at his watch. The soldier who had escorted them on the coach now came in and sat down at a table with the three Moroccans and the Swiss. M. Bloch did not appear.

Both Bates and Leila seemed to hurry through the last part of the meal. Neither of them mentioned M. Bloch. Quinn said: 'I think I'll go up to bed.'

Bates seized his arm: 'Come on, sport. We'll cure you.' The soldier came over from the next table; he had the rifle over his shoulder. Bates nodded to him, and he and Leila got up to go. The soldier clapped Quinn on the back: '*Ça va, mon Britannique!*'

As they walked across the patio towards the street Quinn noticed that all the doors of the rooms round the balcony looked the same. They had no numbers, and he remembered wondering how they would find their own rooms when they got back.

They went into the town, with the wind stinging their eyes with dust, and came to a bamboo pagoda strung with oil lamps. Arabs squatted on the mats drinking from enamel mugs. There was a backroom that smelt of burnt sandalwood, with a wind-up phonograph crackling out European dance music. The soldier came in last, still carrying his rifle.

The room was very dark. A figure in a turban glided up to them and Leila began talking quietly to him in Arabic; he disappeared, bringing back a pot of mint tea and a plate of cakes. Quinn tried one of them and it melted in his mouth, soothing his throat; and while the Arab was pouring out the tea he ate two more of them, before Bates stopped him. 'Jesus!' he cried, 'you're going to be high! Each of those things has a dose of hashish in it.'

Leila burst out laughing. 'You'll lose your soul on the ceiling!' she said. The phonograph began screeching the shreds of a foxtrot. She said to Quinn: 'Dance with me!'

'I can't dance,' he said. She pulled him on to the floor. *Victor Silvester in the Sahara*, he thought. *Mint tea in the Palm Court.* 'How long does this stuff take to work?'

'About half an hour. You'll go completely mad!'

They began to shuffle to the music. 'Look, we can't dance to this!'

'Shhh!' she whispered, and laid her cheek against his. 'Just hold me.'

He caught the musky scent of her skin. They made no attempt to dance. Once he thought he saw Bates watching them, and he felt foolish, swaying alone with her to this preposterous music. His watch said just after ten o'clock. The half hour passed quickly; he felt no particular effects, except that his sore throat had eased. They drank a lot of tea, and a couple of times Bates got up to dance with her to the Arab's apparently inexhaustible supply of ballroom loot. Quinn found himself peering keenly to see how Bates was progressing with her, but the two of them seemed to be doing no more than going for a long walk together round the floor.

Quinn danced more with her, and felt her body alive against him and her breasts hard through the khaki. He said: 'Did you hear what happened with M. Bloch this evening?' She didn't answer. Her eyes were closed as they balanced against each other. He kissed her, and her wide mouth opened gently; he moved his hands down her spine and she trembled. The music stopped. It was now well past the half hour. He said, as though stating a fact: 'Isn't hashish an aphrodisiac?'

'I don't need it,' she murmured.

The music blared out again, suddenly very loud in the little room; and they went on swaying together, and he said: 'I can't go on like this much longer.'

She didn't reply. He pulled her head back: 'Come back to the hotel and sleep with me!'

She nodded.

He kissed her and closed his eyes, and something very strange happened. He tried to open his eyes, and the lids were battened down, heavy as lead. Then his legs folded up beneath him like a card table.

He was lying on the floor, his body light and agile. He sprang up, took Leila round the waist and twirled her round. The room was large and pleasant, full of Bates and this sweet, beautiful girl whom he was going to spread out on a bed and love to exhaustion. He was laughing, and the Moroccan soldier was laughing, talking to him, and he couldn't quite make out what was being said.

He was lying against Leila, and something was happening to the walls: they were moving inwards, closing in, very hot, driving down on him, and he closed his eyes and again the lead-weight fell on the lids pulling his head down on to the table.

He tried to keep his balance, holding his head perpendicular, but he was still going down — slipping, falling into darkness. He struggled and choked for breath. He tried to get his head up, but the muscles of his neck had jammed. The table gave way and he was hanging over the wall of a dam more than a mile high.

There was a rushing in his ears, and far away he could hear Leila and Bates talking, like voices caught on the edge of sleep. Below him the brickwork of the dam sheered away, black and slimy, and he tried to cry out, but his tongue stuck to the roof of his mouth like a strip of leather.

He was on the other side of the dam now — the side with the water lapping against the top of the wall — and the sun shone on to a vast lake, transparent as glass. He could see down through the water five, ten miles. He dropped over the side and began swimming. Far beneath him he could see the wreck of the *Titanic* — a great hunk of ironmongery full of fish and bones and smashed crockery. He began to scream with terror, and a voice a long way off said: 'Give him some sugar.'

He was yelling in French and English, and he felt Leila's fingers in his mouth, emptying a packet of sugar on to his tongue.

His mind cleared. He was talking to them, and they were all round him, like a crowd at a party, laughing and wagging their heads. He thought of Leila and felt worried. He was taking her back to the hotel, lying with her on the springy bed, going through the act in every detail. He must contact her: get her back to the hotel. His limbs were numb: he struggled but nothing would move.

He couldn't find her. Something lifted him; he was standing, with the Moroccan soldier holding him under the arm, saying: '*Doucement, ami! Doucement!*'

It took just over eight minutes to reach the street. He timed it with his watch, one part of his brain still lucid, his speech measured and normal. He tried to ask the soldier about Leila; he said: 'I must go back and find her. I'll lose her. She's with Bates. I must find her.'

The soldier said: '*Doucement — allons!*' It was very black all round, freezing cold. His watch said one o'clock. Soon it would be too late. The night was slipping away, he was losing his chance.

He was back in the hotel, climbing the stairs on the soldier's arm, heaving himself like a man moving up a mountain face. He was lying on his bed and Bates was not there, and suddenly he was terrified of being left alone.

He began to whimper and felt a rush of panic. Where was Bates? He must find him — find Leila, find her room, climb in with her under the blankets.

He was out in the corridor, staggering beside the rows of doors — opening one of them and finding her on the bed naked in the darkness, waiting for him. His legs wobbled, his groin like jelly; he was shaking and whispering, 'Leila, where are you?'

He put his hands out and groped about, going down on his knees. His fingers touched newspaper. It was all over the bed — sheets of it — and there was someone lying on top of it. He said: 'Leila! Leila!' softly, touching her.

There was a man on the bed, stretched out on his back fully dressed. A pair of spectacles had fallen across his throat and the front of him was wet and sticky.

Quinn thought: *She's still out there with Bates!* He cursed and went back to the door. He got out into the corridor and there was one thought in his head: Leila had said she would sleep with him, and now he had missed her and it was too late.

He found his room; got under the blanket and fell into a heavy sleep, full of dreams that he could not remember in the morning.

PART 3: The Set-Up

CHAPTER 1

It was past midday when he woke. His sore throat was now savage and his mouth tasted like a boiled-out kettle.

He stood up carefully. His body was full of pain as though he'd been bruised all over. He couldn't concentrate on anything. All he wanted was a glass of water. He dressed and went downstairs. There was no one about. He walked into the room where they'd eaten the night before and found some remnants of breakfast. There were flies everywhere. On one of the tables stood a nearly empty bottle of Vichy. He drank it and leant against a pillar.

A very dirty Arab came in and stared at him. Quinn asked him where he could find something to drink, and the man grinned: '*Pas comprends Français.*'

He sat down and tried to steady himself. His throat felt as though he were swallowing on a nail. He rested his head on the table, and it was only then that he saw that the inside of his fingers were brown with dried blood.

Something in his mind clicked at once; he ran upstairs, trying several doors round the patio. They were all locked except his own and Bates'. He went down and called to the Arab, pointing up at the doors, crying: '*Ouvrez!*' — but the man only smiled again apologetically.

He shouted the Whittakers' name, but there was no answer. He went back to his room and sat for some minutes on the bed, trying to recall exactly what had happened the night before.

He remembered Leila saying that she would come to bed with him — then the confusion, wanting her and losing her and being helped back to the hotel by the Moroccan soldier.

But there was now something else — something that came back to him like an episode from a film seen a long time ago. There was a man lying in a small room on a bed covered in newspaper.

He looked to see if there were any cuts on his body — if his nose had perhaps bled in the night. There was nothing: only some blood on the sheets near the pillow and a smear on his shirt.

He tried to think out rationally what he ought to do. Before he could take any direct action, he would have to be quite sure that it had not all been a dream. But if he really had stumbled on a dead body who would believe him? The militia would laugh at him and say it was the hashish. The Whittakers probably wouldn't believe him either — and in any case, they would be useless.

Then there were the people who had done the murder. This brought him to the nastiest thought of all: Bates and Leila. He remembered how they had both coaxed him out to take the hashish, and how he had eaten a double dose before they had warned him. Had they both tricked him and the Moroccan soldier out of the hotel, while someone else — M. Beloued, one of the Moroccan tourists, the Swiss? — was killing M. Bloch? Had Leila really wanted to go back to the hotel and sleep with him? Or were she and Bates in league — she only playing for time, delaying him, keeping him away, doped and silly, while M. Bloch's spectacles were knocked off his nose and he was stabbed and laid out on the newspaper?

He decided the only course would be to try and find M. Bloch. If the Frenchman had disappeared, he would go to the militia and tell them everything. He wondered what sort of excuse the murderers would think up for the man's absence. They'd no doubt say he'd just gone away, hired a car, taken a bus or camel, vanished into the desert. Quinn remembered the four Danes. It would not be difficult out here. Nobody would look very far for M. Bloch — and even if they did send out planes and search parties, he would be just one of those they never found.

Downstairs the hotel was still and deserted. He supposed that everyone must have gone on a sightseeing tour. He went outside and walked round the wall of the hotel to the yard where the coach stood. He had no idea what he was looking for, but the sight of the coach reminded him of the incident the night before with M. Bloch. It might have been this that had given him the nightmare about the body; it also now gave him a reckless idea.

He went back, quietly and quickly, up to Bates' room. The holdall and the medicine chest lay on the floor by the bed. It looked as though Bates had gone out in a hurry; the shutters were still closed, and he saw with surprise that the holdall was not locked.

He opened it and unzipped the rear compartment. The revolver had gone, but the bunch of keys was still there. He took them and slipped out, downstairs and round to the coach. His hands were trembling as he selected the spiral key for the luggage bay; it screwed in about three inches. There were two clicks and the sound of a heavy spring being released. He pulled and the gull-wing door opened upwards.

On the floor in front of him, wrapped in a blanket, lay M. Bloch. The face was covered, but he recognised at once the pudgy clay hands, curled stiffly outside the blanket. Behind the body were some steel-bound crates and jerrycans of petrol and fresh water.

There was a slight sound behind him. He swung round and saw M. Beloued and the Moroccan soldier standing less than a yard away. M. Beloued's face was yellow as parchment, and the soldier was grinning behind his jolly pork-chop moustaches. M. Beloued made a movement with his hand, and Quinn jumped sideways and ran round the wall. As he got to the front door he collided with Bates. The Australian said something and tried to grab his arm as he passed; he stood blocking the entrance to the street, and Quinn ducked into the door and ran upstairs, shouting for the Whittakers. Once he called out Leila's name, but it was like shouting in a church.

He flung himself into his room, noticing his knapsack hanging over the back of the chair. He remembered that it contained his passport and about nine thousand francs. Outside, he could hear sandals smacking along the balcony. Bates came in and closed the door; he stood with his back to it, looking at Quinn with a funny hang-dog expression. The revolver was in his hand, pointing at the floor.

'You damned fool.' He shook his head sadly. 'You're in trouble, sport.'

Quinn said nothing. Bates picked up the knapsack and tossed it into his lap. 'Go on, get out o' here! — you've got about thirty seconds.'

'I don't understand,' he murmured. 'It doesn't make sense. Monsieur Bloch…'

'Get moving! I like you, boy, and I'm giving you just the ghost of a chance. Now get out — through the window and run!'

'But why? What about you?'

Bates stepped over and opened the window. 'I'm just the hired help,' he said wearily. 'Jump — it's not far.'

'And Leila?'

'Get out, boy — quick!' He brought the revolver up, and Quinn grabbed the knapsack and was through the window, landing in some sand about ten feet below. There was a wall separating him from the yard with the coach; he saw M. Beloued and the soldier had gone. He scrambled over the wall on the other side, chafing his hands and knees, and dropped into an alley that zigzagged along for about three hundred yards, turning under an archway into a square with a mosque. A row of children sat under the wall watching him, their eyes gummed up with flies. Near the gate of the mosque stood a mule and an ancient low-slung Citroën, its windows blistered yellow, tyres half flat. It was probably used to take rich families to worship. An old Arab lay rolled up asleep on the back seat. Quinn opened the door and tugged at him, shouting, 'Taxi!'

The Arab climbed slowly out, rubbing his face: *'Tu Français? Tu vas hotel?'*

Quinn thrust a one-thousand franc note at him. 'Police!' he said. 'Commissariat!'

The old man took the note and crinkled it in his fingers and said at last: *'Ça va!* Police.'

Quinn got into the car, which was stifling hot with lumpy seats and a smell of scorched leather and goats. He glanced fearfully at the archway into the square, but it was as black as a tomb.

The car started after the fifth snort of the ignition; crawled out across the square, down an alley, honking every ten yards. The Arab said: *'Tu Français, toi?'*

'Oui — plus vite!' The heat was appalling. Quinn tried to wind down one of the windows but they were all jammed.

The militia post was on the edge of the town near one of the gates — a shabby house with a corrugated-iron roof and a painting of King Mohammed V over the porch. The old Arab stopped the car and said, '*Ta-voila, police!*'

Quinn climbed out and stood for a moment blinking into the sun. A man had appeared on the porch and was looking down at him. Through the glare Quinn recognised the pork-chop moustaches against the leathery skin. He must have come round here very quickly. Quinn noticed that for once he was not carrying his rifle.

The man said pleasantly: '*Salut, Britannique!*' and took a step forward.

Quinn looked at him, then at the Arab standing by the taxi, and saw that the key was still in the ignition. The soldier took another step, and Quinn pushed the Arab aside and jumped into the car. He slammed the door, pressed the handle, and there were shouts and fists beating against the windows.

The engine started the first time. The car bucked forward and swerved round the bend, through an arched gate; and he had a glimpse of figures running in the street behind; then he was driving along the city walls, trying to work out what he was going to do.

He drove for perhaps half a mile, and all he saw were the walls and the wilderness of sand, dry as a bone. He came to another gate where there was a signpost in Arabic pointing into the desert.

He swung the car round and headed out across the faint tracks in the sand. There were now two images in his mind. One was of the crippled Land Rover and its crew of Danes going mad in the heat and dying. The other was of M. Bloch.

He thought of Leila — of her long legs and kisses and promises; of Bates, with his floppy hat and stained teeth, taking Quinn up as a friend. Trying to save him from being killed like an animal.

He had his foot full down on the throttle, but the car was doing a bare twenty kilometres an hour, spluttering like a 1914 reconnaissance plane. His shirt and trousers were drenched with sweat. He struggled again to get the windows open, but they wouldn't budge, and the air seemed to grow thicker, hotter, choking him. He kept looking in the mirror for a glimpse of something coming up in pursuit. There was nothing but the dazzle of sand. Perhaps they wouldn't even bother to chase him out here.

After about twenty minutes he saw that the petrol gauge showed empty. At any minute he was going to faint. His knapsack still lay on the back seat. He tried to remember what it had in it — if there was anything to drink. The inside of his mouth was sticking together like the sides of a squeezed-out toothpaste tube.

He stopped the car, opened the bonnet and tried soaking the end of his shirt in the boiling water from the radiator. He sucked at it and the taste of water only drove him to a frenzy. He searched through the sack, and all he found was a bundle of old clothes, including his clean shirt which he tied round his head and shoulders. Outside the heat was even worse than in, and he clambered back, pushed the starter, and there was only a whirring sound. He pushed it again and again, but the engine was dead.

He hunted for a cranking handle, but couldn't find one; and then he began to pray. He was going to die out here. He didn't deserve it — it had just been bad luck, and perhaps a bit of bad judgment. He felt, with a curious disinterest, that it would have been better to have stayed: to have argued, made a bargain with them. Every man had his price. They could have bought him — he wouldn't have quibbled. All he wanted was a drink, a bit of shade, to slide out of his clinging clothes and be cool and rest.

He pushed once more at the starter, and the engine broke into a sudden roar; and he moved forward again, watching the dunes coming up at him through the yellowed windows.

At the same time he knew that the further he went the more hopeless were his chances. Perhaps Bates had told him to get out simply to spare them the trouble. And if he had stayed, who would have done the job? M. Beloued — professionally, with a knife and no fuss? Or the soldier — shooting him down in cold blood? Or Bates, with a word of apology and one fell blow? He wondered whether Leila would have pleaded for him, or hidden and pretended she didn't know.

The dashboard meter showed that he had covered more than 50 kilometres. If only he had some sedatives or a strong drink. He could get high and pass out and die with a little comfort. How did one die in the sun? Were there the dreams of a drowning man? The sweat dripped off his nose, ran into his eyes, stinging and blinding him. He felt the track tilt downwards. The car was going faster. He wiped his eyes and peered forward; threw the wheel to the left, and the car bumped against the rocky edge of a ravine.

The sand sheered away in a clean rift; the front wheels had missed the drop by perhaps six inches. There was a slight gradient, and he found he could coast in neutral, saving petrol but needing all his wits to hold the steering.

He went about a mile along the margin of the precipice. Below the sand glowed like beaten gold. Now that he was higher he lost the immediate sense of being trapped; his head cleared a little, and he screwed up his eyes and stared out over the horizon for some sign of life.

The gradient was levelling out, the car slowing down. He dreaded trying to start the engine again: as long as he was moving he could still enjoy some instinct of hope. He was down to a crawl, and with a mutter of prayer and his fingers crossed, he put the car into second, carefully let out the clutch and jogged forward.

Then below him he saw what looked like a village — a blotch of huts against the haze.

About a mile further on, the cliff shelved down, carrying the road with it. He put the car into neutral again and bumped over bits of rock. He could now see the village quite clearly. There was the finger of a minaret and palm trees, spider-black against the sun. The road levelled and the car carried him just another half mile. He passed a signpost in Arabic rotted like driftwood, and the village was only a few hundred yards away. He could see two Arabs walking with a donkey.

There would be a well here, and a roof and shade and peace. If it was on a main track through the desert there might even be petrol, and he would be able to move on after dark.

The engine coughed, jolted and died. He tried for several minutes to restart it: waited for it to cool, pumped at the clutch, but it was no good. At least he'd had more than his share of luck. He was not at all religious, but he offered up a quick thanksgiving by way of an investment in future providence.

With his clean shirt flowing over his head and shoulders, and the tails of his other shirt hanging wet out of his trousers, he staggered into the village. A few Arabs came out and stared at him; a dog as thin as a stick began limping at his heels.

Children and veiled women came out, and soon there was a crowd watching him and looking back at the marooned car.

A man called to him and asked if he was French, then began leading him down the street to a door with a bead curtain, into a room where a woman sat on the floor without a veil, heavily tattooed. Quinn lurched in and collapsed on the matting and shouted for something to drink. The woman didn't move. The dog sniffed at his feet and whined.

The Arab then came over to him and began chattering to him in pidgin French that suddenly made him furious; he yelled at the man, almost crying, and put his head in his hands. The woman came timidly over with a bottle of synthetic fruit juice; he grabbed it and gurgled it down; it was too sweet, but he drank three bottles of it, then lay still, panting.

The Arab laid a piece of damp cloth over his forehead. The doorway was filled with faces. He lay for perhaps ten minutes and no one moved; then he sat up and began trying to ask for petrol.

The Arab smiled and shook his head. '*Essence, benzine!*' said Quinn. A face in the door said something in Arabic, and the man said to him: '*Ça va!*' beckoning him outside and down the street with the crowd following.

They reached a house with steel hoops hung over the entrance. The Arab went inside and came back with a rusted Esso can. It was empty.

Quinn said again: '*Essence, benzine — auto!*' and the fury swelled up in him, a blind, nervous frustration, and he began swinging has arms about, and some of the crowd backed away terrified. The Arab disappeared again, then came back with the can about a quarter full. There was certainly petrol in it, but Quinn tried to explain that he needed thirty, forty litres.

He said it over and over again, holding up his fingers, repeating the words as though trying to explain to a child, and the Arab listened patiently, then tapped the can and said with a smile: '*Essence!*'

Quinn thought, *in a moment I'm going off my head. They must have more petrol than this.* He began again, trying to keep calm, to explain clearly what he needed.

The crowd watched as though it were all some show put on for their benefit. No more cans were brought. There was no more petrol. Perhaps if he fetched the car he would have more success. He began leading the way back to the Citroën. The Arab insisted on carrying the petrol can, and the crowd followed dutifully.

As they approached the car it began to look like a skeleton in the sand. All four wheels had gone; the headlamps had been ripped off, the leather of the front seats stripped and the springs wrenched out. The crowd stared without interest. Quinn was not even angry. A flat despair came over him. He looked at the wreck of iron, then at the crowd of faces behind him, and thought it could be any of them. An abandoned car on their doorstep; a lunatic white man stumbling into their village. It didn't mean anything in their daily routine. The car had been put there to be ransacked. To Quinn it would have meant perhaps forty or fifty more miles; a postponement of death.

He turned and walked back into the village, and they all followed and no one asked him for money. In the room behind the bead curtain he was given a pot of tea, then curled up on the matting and slept. In his sleep there was a regular ridge of pain slicing through his subconscious every time he swallowed. He woke feeling tired, shivering.

Outside it was getting dark. He had slept more than four hours. He stirred and felt a strange heaviness in his body. He automatically checked that everything was as he had left them in his belt and knapsack. Nothing had been moved. The knapsack was hard and awkward under his head.

The Arab came out of the darkness of the wall: he touched Quinn's forehead and smiled: '*Ça va, ami!*'

Quinn could not see his face properly; he stood up and tried to reach the door.

CHAPTER 2

He found himself lying on the matting, with the Arab and the old woman bending over him. The man was wiping vomit from his chin and shirt, and the woman was trying to get him to swallow some tea. There was a singing in his ears and the tea dribbled from his mouth, very hot. He found he could hardly swallow.

There were two men in the doorway dressed in shabby European clothes, bare-headed. Quinn saw them come towards him and he was lifted up, with hands under his feet and head, and carried to the door like a sack, but not roughly, hanging down between them, swinging across the street.

He knew he was very ill, and realised suddenly that his knapsack had gone. He tried to speak but no sound came.

The Arab followed beside him, rummaging in his clothing; he felt him prising back the belt and the pressure on his stomach made him howl. The Arab extracted a five-thousand-franc note which he gave to the two men. He had seen that Quinn was ill and knew it would be better to get him out of the town. It would not be good to have a European die in his house. He had kept none of Quinn's money for himself; and when they reached the truck, which travelled across the desert with olive oil and paraffin, he tied the strap of the knapsack tightly round Quinn's wrist and made sure the belt was properly clasped.

Quinn was unconscious when they put him aboard. The back of the truck was empty except for two olive oil jars, and they laid him in the middle of the floor with his head on the knapsack. The two men had been told he had dysentery, which is not infectious. They were content with the five thousand francs.

He came to after a few hours and felt the steady jogging of the floor, the rattle of steel supports under the canvas. The noise was somehow comforting. Every few minutes there was a violent spasm in his bowels, and he would hunch up, gripping his stomach, feeling a pocket of hot air rising in his gut, bursting with a pain under the heart.

This went on for perhaps an hour. His watch had stopped at just before nine o'clock. Once the truck came to a halt, and one of the men pulled back the canvas for a moment and looked at him, then went away.

He slept for short stretches, and had always the same dream: he was running across the desert, trying to get back to Marrakech, and every few hundred yards there was a high wall that he had to climb over, and the effort was a wrenching pain in his throat.

When he was awake the act of swallowing was like the motions of a slow machine: he could feel the muscles grinding into action, the rubbing of skin like wood rubbing on wood, the pain, then the machinery falling back and the sweat breaking out on his face.

Towards the early hours he slept more soundly. His body was still stiff, but inside he was all hot and melting. He woke suddenly and found that he had soiled himself. At first he felt disgusted and futile, trying to remember what one did when this sort of thing happened. The last time had been when he was five.

Then it didn't seem to matter. He wondered where they were going. If the truck was empty they would perhaps be going north where he could send a telegram to the British Consul, Marrakech. He thought of his passport and the inscription on the inner flap, demanding that the Bearer be allowed to pass without Let or Hindrance. He saw the pompous assembly of Privy Councillors, pink and pinstriped, representing Her Majesty in her Annigoni loveliness, all marshalled to the aid of their loyal subject, one Rupert Quinn, lying lost in a truck in the Sahara, escaping from murderers and mucky as a baby.

Sometime before dawn the truck stopped, the flaps were stripped back, and he was carried out and laid at the edge of a street. The two men left his knapsack, threw a piece of sacking over him, and he heard the truck roar away, and there was silence.

A mangy dog came and sniffed at his face and trousers; he tried to kick at it, but was too weak, and the dog took its time, then ambled off.

He fell asleep, and was woken by the sun coming up over the houses. A crowd of Arabs were gazing down at him. The sight of a European in this condition excited no sympathy in them; a few looked scared, thinking he carried some pestilence.

One of them pulled the sacking up over his face, and they left him there all day as though he were something unclean. He had tied the strap of his knapsack round his wrist, and kept his fingers secured to his belt. No one touched them, but in the afternoon some children came and stole his sandals.

Dogs visited him periodically, and he was tormented by flies; they crawled under the sacking and settled down, big and lazy, without fear. Several times he tried to wipe them from round his mouth and eyes, and could even feel their wings vibrating under his touch as though they belonged there.

After dusk he was hauled up and put across the back of a mule; it was led a few hundred yards, then tethered to a post, and he was left bound to it, with the sacking still over him like a winding sheet secured with a rope across his back and under the beast's belly. He had eaten nothing for two days, since the evening before taking the hashish; no one tried to feed him, and he was not hungry; and in the moments of consciousness he had no sense of time or of fear or even of curiosity: only a sickness and pain and a great tiredness. Once during the day a man had come and poured boiled water down his throat from a skin-bottle. But most of the Arabs had cringed away from him. There had been rumours in the town that he was a mad Frenchman with leprosy.

After he had been on the mule's back about three hours he was given some more to drink by a man holding his head upright and another forcing the spout of a kettle between his teeth. The liquid tasted spiced and bitter: then they wiped the flies off him again and began to lead him away on the mule. They came out of the town, on to the smooth swelling desert with the dunes clear as silver and the dips black under the moon. There were mules and camels, and Arabs shrouded in jellabahs. They threw a blanket over him and the mule began to move with them across the desert. The night was so cold that his teeth chattered even in his sleep. He dreamt that he was an ostrich going down with the Blue Men, and that they were crossing into the heart of Africa, keeping him in tow as some pet that they were going to exhibit in the jungle villages.

The mule moved under him with a slow, deliberate rhythm. He imagined the line down into the desert like the course of a ship through the ocean, to where the jungle began. He woke in terror and thought he felt the undergrowth scraping past, trailing green slime over his hair and face and body. But the desert went on endlessly, and just before sunrise they stopped and put up tents. He was laid in one on a soft woollen rug. It was cool and dark and he slept all day. Later an Arab came in and fed him rice and nuts and scalding tea; then after dusk he was strapped again over the mule, and they set out for the second night.

Some time before dawn they passed under the gates of a town, and he was taken down and carried into a room that smelt of straw and dung. He did not know how long he was left there. When he woke it was daylight outside. He was half delirious, watching a crowd of hooded faces peering at him. He tried to say something: to tell them his name, that he was ill and dying. He felt fingers separating his hands from the strap of the knapsack and unclasping his belt. He could do nothing to stop them; his body was like a pool of water spilling out across the floor. Later he was picked up again and carried out; he could see only black and red patterns spinning and breaking in front of his eyes. They were going up some steps; he was laid down on a bed; flies pinged against a wire mesh over the door. A young Moroccan in a white jellabah began undressing him. He lay there feeling helpless and decayed; the young man and a companion carried him out naked and washed him under a pump in the yard. Then they gave him soup and tea; but it still hurt badly to swallow, and he found the only real peace in deep sleep. Once he woke with a spasm in his bowels and began yelling with pain, and the young Moroccan came and helped him outside to a cubbyhole in the wall, splashed and stinking, where he stayed crouched for a long time. The pain made him gasp and weep. When he came out he was sweating, still very weak, but a little better.

He slept through most of the next few days, knowing little of what was happening. His mind was at its most active in his dreams which were wild and terrifying. The first signs of his recovery came when his throat began to hurt less, and he was able to swallow a little meat and pastries.

The young Moroccan spoke not a word of French. Several times other people came into the room and looked at him. As he began to regain consciousness he tried to talk to them, but they shook their heads and went away.

He had a growth of beard by now from which he guessed that he must have been lying there at least ten days. He began to sit up and take notice of things. His clothes had gone, along with his belt and knapsack, and he could not make the Moroccan boy understand anything he said. One day he was visited by an old man who seemed to be some sort of dignitary in the town. He commanded perhaps a dozen words of French, and kept talking to him about a bus that would come from the north, from Marrakech, speaking as though it were somewhere in another continent.

Quinn asked when it would come, and the old man bowed and said soothingly, 'Soon — very soon!' Quinn tried to get him to tell him about his clothes and money and passport, and after a long time he made him understand enough to translate to the Moroccan boy, who went away, and after some time brought them all back and placed them by the bed. The clothes had been washed and folded, and there was a pair of pointed Moorish slippers to replace his sandals. The knapsack was untouched, but all the money had gone from the belt.

Quinn tried to ask the old man what had happened to the money — whether they had taken it as payment — but the Arab only smiled uncomprehending, shaking his head like the others, and went away; and Quinn began to feel trapped.

Later he was able to get up and sit on the verandah; and he practised waddling crab-footed in the slippers, which were of supple white leather and kept falling off his heels.

He could not work out what sort of place he was in. Out in the yard there were only mud walls; and he never saw anyone about except the young Moroccan who looked after him.

In a few days he began to venture into the town. There was a square so wide that a voice calling from one end barely carried to the other. On one side was a row of palms as tall as the masts of a schooner which in the full heat of the day threw only a few feet of shadow; and across the square the line of buildings shimmered like shapes seen through water.

In the afternoon caravans of camels lurched into town with tribesmen from below the Tropic of Capricorn — nomads dressed in fierce colours, speaking tongues strange to the Moroccans, bartering with their hands over endless glasses of tea. And when the day's trading was over they would stride away to seek out the whores, who in this town were famous throughout the Sahara — proud women with arms tattooed to the shoulders, heavy with gold bangles.

In the twilight Quinn would wander round the perimeter of the square, through the souks to the fortified walls, where the desert rolled away with the curve of the earth. Along one horizon lay a rim of hills; he calculated from the position of the sun that they were somewhere to the east. He thought of the bus from Marrakech; and each day he tried to ask the Moroccan boy when it would come, but he didn't understand. Once he saw the old man again, and asked him, and he repeated 'Soon, soon!'

Now that the sickness had left him, and he could move and think clearly, the solitude began to frighten him. The people in the town paid him far less attention than they had done in the north, where Europeans are common. He could find no one who spoke any language he could understand; yet each day he was fed by the young Moroccan, and in the evening there was the door with the wire mesh and the little room behind, with the blankets smoothed out for him on the bed; and each morning the Moroccan woke him with mint tea. Yet the bus still did not come.

There seemed to be no police or militia in the town, no telegraph office or petrol pump; and the only wheels he ever saw were the pulleys and spinning wheels in the souks. The women were all veiled, with foreheads tattooed against the Evil Eye. They moved gracefully, balancing pitchers and bowls on their heads, their eyes large and black and tempting. Quinn could only tell if they were old or young by their hands — some like claws, others plump and pale brown, peeping out of the wide sleeves.

It was eight days now since he had been told about the bus. One afternoon he was lying asleep in his room when he was woken by voices outside. The Moroccan boy was standing on the verandah beckoning to someone. Quinn saw a figure move up behind the wire mesh of the door, and the Moroccan called out excitedly to him. The door swung open and Bates came in.

CHAPTER 3

He came in grinning, polite enough to remove his bush hat, and sat down on the edge of the bed. 'Well, sport, how are you?'

Quinn dropped back on the pillow and closed his eyes.

'I hear you were banging on Death's door. Are you all right now? You look like a resurrection.'

'Have you come to finish me off?' Quinn said, not opening his eyes.

'That depends.'

There was a pause. Bates got up and walked round the little room. 'Not a bad place this, all considered. I hear it's some sort of Moslem sanctuary. It's a lot better than the hole we're all staying in.'

'How did you find me?'

'It wasn't hard. We were coming here anyway with the coach — it's the end of the line. About the only place you can come after Asouf. We heard about you as soon as we got in. They're probably talking about you down in Timbuktu by now. I heard you were lucky to survive.' He had taken out a packet of cigarettes and flicked one at Quinn, who ignored it. 'It's good to see you again, sport. Leila's been missing you.'

'I bet she has! And what are you going to do with me now?'

Bates took his time answering; lit a cigarette, blew the smoke up to the ceiling and said: 'We've both missed you — God's truth we have! They're never much of a crowd on these trips.'

Quinn felt tired and confused. The relief of having someone at last to talk to had dispelled some of his fear; he lay back and waited.

Bates said slowly: 'I've come to make a deal with you. I managed to persuade the powers-that-be to give you a reprieve and try you out.'

'That was nice of them.'

'First, I'm going to give you the facts — and when I'm through, you'd bloody well better do the sensible thing!'

Quinn said nothing. Bates leant back against the wall and began: 'This place, as I said, is as far as the coach tour goes — and about the last big town before Black Africa. About twenty miles to the east of here are some hills. Behind them is Algeria. Once a month this little outfit of Izard's comes down here with tourists. Only the real cargo's not tourists at all. We carry a crate of light machine-guns and ammunition which we take in for the Algerian rebels. The tourists are just a front. The Moroccan authorities are very keen to encourage them, and they don't normally search coach parties. Besides, it doesn't arouse suspicion with the French secret service boys in Morocco.'

'And Monsieur Bloch was an exception?'

Bates sucked his little finger. 'I don't know how he got on to us. He was working for an agency in Casablanca that supplies information to the Deuxième Bureau. Poor little sod! — died a natural death.' He grinned. 'Typhoid, I think they said it was. Nasty. You probably caught it from him.' He shook his head sadly. 'We fixed him up with a proper death certificate — all quite regular — and our friend the soldier, who came as our escort to Asouf Mrimina, very kindly had the little man laid to rest in a proper cemetery. I don't suppose anyone'll check very far.'

The Moroccan boy came in with tea. Quinn said: 'And which of you did the blighter in?'

Bates spread out his hands. 'Look, sport, there's a war on, and in war that sort of question is not asked by one officer-and-gentleman to another. Let us now enjoy our tea.'

'Back at the hotel,' said Quinn, 'were you told to kill me?'

'Please, you're embarrassing me! In all truth, boy, you were an awful damned problem. Izard hired you on my recommendation because I thought you might come in useful. Then you started nosing around — I hoped you had more sense. It put me in such a difficult position!' He sounded genuinely aggrieved. 'No, you'd have been dangerous to dispose of just like that. We reckoned that if you got out there in the desert alone you wouldn't last long. I must say, I give you credit for endurance. We hadn't counted on you being ill as well.

'Anyway, now that you're still alive, perhaps we'd better think again. On the last trip, it was awkward. Those two Moroccans on the bus were in fact members of the FLN — the Algerian National Liberation Front — and the Swiss was one of their agents in Geneva who handles the arms purchases from behind the Iron Curtain. We were taking them in across the border on that trip — and I'm afraid they were a little tough about you.'

'I see,' said Quinn. 'So they wanted me out of the way like Monsieur Bloch — and you were the Good Samaritan who gave me a break. You should get a medal. And how long's this neat little business been going on for?'

'Since the autumn. The stuff used to be run through Tunisia from Cairo, then the French built about a thousand miles of electric wire, and put down bombs and God knows what else, so it all had to be started from this side. As you say, it's very neat — and you wouldn't like to go and spoil it all, now would you?'

Quinn ignored this. 'And where does Leila come in?'

'Ah well, sweet Leila is a Believer. She's not in it for the money, but for the great cause of Independent Algeria. She's a member of the FLN — been working for it since she came over from Algeria nearly three years ago. She's a kind of liaison officer and knows most of the rebel commanders in this area, and has recruited a lot of useful contacts inside Morocco. God help her if the French ever got their hands on her.

'And she's marvellous for publicity!' he added. 'The international Press goes for her like a film star. She's been all over *Life* magazine, and about half a dozen Arab papers, and for her sins she once got herself described in *Izvestia* as a "Daughter of the Arab Revolution".'

'Hooray,' said Quinn. 'What was she doing down with the Blue Men?'

'She'd been down contacting the FLN agents inside the border. She puts on a jellabah for the crossing if it's far inside. It doesn't attract attention. The police here, and the French Army, don't trouble about the Blue Men. It's the safest way to travel in this country — better than a bus. Just join up with one of the nomad caravans.'

'I'll remember that next time,' said Quinn. 'And where do I come in?'

Bates paused. 'I don't like to see a good man go to waste. And in your case, sport, it would mean the end of you. We can't afford to take risks.'

'You're sure I haven't already given the show away?'

He shook his head. 'Not from down here, you couldn't. Not even up north, until you could put the evidence before the French authorities. The Moroccan government's sympathetic to the Algerian Nationalists and they prefer not to take any action against them unless the pressure comes straight from the French. That's why Monsieur Bloch had to go.'

'Then I don't seem to have much choice. What am I supposed to do?'

'You work as an ordinary travel guide. When we get down here we transfer the guns to a truck we keep hidden here with an FLN agent. The plan is that if the worst happens, and we get picked up taking the stuff over by a French patrol, we try to bluff it out — pretend we're just a couple of hen-brained explorers with a pretty French girl who've got lost making some trek from the Med. down to Cape Town.'

'What about Monsieur Beloued?'

'He stays with the tourists. He's Izard's personal assistant and neither of them have anything directly to do with the FLN. They're just in it for the pickings — which are big.'

'And you?'

'I'm in it for the pickings too. I'm no patriotic idealist I can tell you! — Queen and Commonwealth or anything else.'

'And what can I hope to get out of it all?'

'Cash. Lots of it. At the end of six months you'll have made more than a thousand pounds, untaxed and banked in Tangier. And if you rub him up the right way, Izard'll throw in a flat, too, in Casablanca.'

'Considerate of him. And what's the risk?'

'Very small. The French patrols don't get down here much, and the nearest garrison post is more than a hundred miles to the north. There's no risk unless one's damned unlucky, or damned careless. And on the Moroccan side the worst that can happen is a deportation order.'

'You make it sound too simple.'

'It is simple. That's why it works. It's been working for more than five years all round Algeria. How do you think this war's been able to go on for so long?'

Quinn was silent for a moment. *Every man has his price,* he thought again. 'So you think I'm worth paying more than two thousand a year to keep quiet?'

'It's not my money,' said Bates. 'We'll have to get Izard to agree. But I don't think he'll make trouble — after all, it's not easy to kill you, and we need another hand on the trips. Besides, Leila likes you. She wouldn't want to leave you rotting in some sandpit.'

'All right, I accept. I want it all in writing — and the first instalment in advance as soon as I get back.'

Bates slapped his shoulder. 'I knew you were no fool! And I should have hated it if you'd refused.'

Quinn got up and dressed. 'Where is Leila? Does she know I'm here?'

'Yes. She's with the tourists — the most ghastly gang: three Hun maidens in search of the Mysterious East. She's taking them round the souks — preferred not to be here, just in case you said no.'

'How sensitive of her!'

'We're taking the guns over tonight,' he went on. 'You'd better come and get an idea of the set-up. It's a tough drive, and it'll be a relief to have someone to take turns at the wheel. Leila does the navigating, and seems to be able to do everything else in this man's world, except drive.'

They went out across the yard, into the town. The sun was going down, but it was still unpleasantly hot. They followed the alleys into the square. The hotel where the coach party were staying was the usual arrangement of poky mud rooms round a courtyard. The one refinement was a makeshift café with rugs spread on the ground under a corrugated-iron roof. There were only two people inside: an old Arab woman crouched beside a tea urn, and Leila, who was sitting against the wall reading Saint Exupéry.

She stood up and greeted Quinn with a solemn stare. He watched the belt move on her hips as she unfolded her legs off the rug, and found himself swallowing hard.

She took his hand and said. 'Are you well now? I heard you were terribly ill.' Her hair was piled up from the neck, tumbling over her ears and forehead. 'You are very, very pale.'

He grinned sarcastically: 'I ought to thank your charming Algerian friends!' Bates broke in quickly, speaking to her in French: 'And how were the Walpurgis witches?'

'They wouldn't buy anything,' she said, 'they said the souks were too dirty.'

He turned to Quinn: 'Well, at least we haven't got that Whittaker woman with us this time. These three German Fräuleins have all got bowels like battleship boilers.'

He disappeared to fetch some wine from his room. Quinn sat down on one of the rugs, and Leila sat down very close to him. 'Please understand,' she began, 'we are all fighting a very hard war here.'

'I've nothing to do with your war,' he said. They looked at each other without speaking. The old woman with the urn mumbled something behind her yashmak. Leila ignored her. 'Tell me what happened to you,' she said at last. Bates came back with a jar of wine and three Bakelite mugs; the wine tasted like vinegar. Quinn had begun an account of as much of his adventures as he could remember; when he had finished she looked at him with her enormous eyes, sloping and sad, and said: 'It is horrible what you suffered!'

When he said nothing, she went on hurriedly: 'I am very sorry about what happened. But it is not easy for me. We don't know whom we can trust as friends, and we are fighting for our freedom, and there are many people who are against us and betray us.' She spoke with a gloomy passion, her face set hard, straining to make him understand. When he still said nothing — only drank some more of the sour wine — she said: 'We have a proverb: "Tell me who are your friends and I will tell you who you are".'

He nodded, digesting this piece of gratuitous wisdom, and said: 'Yes, I have a proverb too: "Tell me your address and I will tell you where you live".'

She paused a moment, then flared into anger. 'You are laughing at me! I am trying to explain to you!' She put her hand to her mouth, fist clenched, and scrambled to her feet. 'You are stupid — you don't understand!' Her eyes glazed with tears. 'I did not want to see you die!' she cried.

'Now come on, children!' said Bates. 'Nobody wanted to see anybody die. We're all one happy family!' He swung up the jar of wine and refilled their mugs. The old woman grumbled again from the corner, and Bates whispered to him in English: 'Don't mess it up, sport. I explained what happened.'

'You damned well did! But I don't see why I have to be polite about it. She was in on it too, wasn't she? You may have tried to let me escape, but she's one of them. I just like to know who my friends are, that's all.'

'We are all your friends,' said Bates, reverting to French. Leila sat down again and clasped her knees to her chin, frowning at the ground. 'Are you coming to Algeria with us tonight?' she asked Quinn.

'It seems I do what I'm told,' he said. She sat for a moment in silence, then said: 'We must be sure that you sympathise with us. Hundreds of brave people depend for their lives on what we are doing tonight.'

He said nothing. She swivelled the mug of wine in her fingers, and asked, without looking at him: 'What are your politics, Rupert?'

'Nostalgic nineteenth-century liberal.'

Bates whispered: 'This is important, for Christ's sake!'

'I'm being quite honest with you,' he went on. 'My entire political activity has been restricted to two general elections in both of which, I am proud to say, the candidates I voted for lost lamentably.'

She looked puzzled; then said at last: 'Are you in sympathy with the Algerian National Liberation Front?'

He leant over and took her by the shoulders, smiling as charmingly as he knew how — which was quite a lot — and said, 'Listen, my beautiful freedom-fighter, I will do many things for money, and almost anything if my life is threatened. As for Algeria, I don't give a damn. I don't give a damn about Algeria, Cuba, Communist China, Fascist Portugal or whether Wales is given self-government.'

'Wales?'

'It's a beautiful place,' he said, helping himself to more wine; 'I'll take you there some time.'

'You are not being serious?'

'Leila, I am being perfectly serious. In this matter I have no alternative. I am a soldier of fortune, a freebooter, an old-fashioned mercenary. As for world affairs, I think the world would be a lot happier if everybody drank more and slept more in the afternoon and had more sex.'

Bates laughed. She said: 'You are an anarchist.' Then slowly she smiled. 'All right — but please be loyal.' It was a slight, girlish appeal as though she were asking him to keep some private secret; it had nothing to do with war, demanding from him an oath of loyalty in a business that meant fighting and famine and torture. He said quietly: 'Of course I'll be loyal.'

They stayed there till late in the afternoon, playing liar-dice on the rug and drinking the wine till it fell low in the jar, and she finished by winning from both of them — altogether seven thousand francs. 'I'll pay you outside the bank in Tangier,' said Quinn. And as the day drew on he felt her growing closer to him again, watching over him with an almost ponderous affection, worrying if he were really well enough to come on the trip, asking him not to drink too much wine and get too tired. And he sat basking in the glow of her attentions, steadily losing money to her, thinking of her as wife, mother, mistress, slave — smiling under her legionnaire's képi from the gloss of *Life* magazine, along with the ads for next year's Pontiac convertible.

The twilight began to fall like grey silk. They left the hotel in time to avoid the tourists, who had gone to look at some tombs with M. Beloued.

The three of them walked down some alleys to a house built like a Chinese box, walls within walls, with the doors unbolted for them by a little veiled woman. They were met inside by the FLN agent, a shrivelled Arab with a turban wound round his head like a bandage. In a back room there was a powerful two-way radio set. They squatted down on mats, and the woman brought them a bowl of steaming cous-cous which they ate with their fingers. Leila sat next to the transmitter, her head caged in earphones, tuning in the wavelengths — first making sure that there were no French radio signals in the area, then contacting the rebel unit over the border, finding out the position for the arms transaction that night, which she marked on a large-scale contour map. The whole operation took more than half an hour.

Behind the house the coach was parked in a yard next to a small olive-green truck. The four crates of guns had already been removed from the luggage bay and screwed down under a steel floor at the back of the truck, which was also stacked with explorers' equipment: tinned food, tents, compasses, maps of the whole of Africa. Bates had also lugged aboard his medicine chest — a prop he calculated would not be viewed unkindly by most professional French soldiers if the worst happened.

Inside the truck the four-wheel-drive engine set up a vibration like an electric current. The journey was fifty kilometres to the border and fifteen inside Algeria; but they were carrying enough petrol to take them in an emergency nearly five hundred kilometres.

Leila sat squeezed up between them both, with Bates taking first shift at the wheel. There was a half-moon, like a copper-coloured bowl suspended above the desert. It was very dark, with the headlamps throwing a flat arc over the sand. There was no road and they drove due east from the town, bumping along at about twenty miles an hour. Leila pored over the contour map under the dashboard light, and twice they had to stop while she took bearings with the compass.

After about an hour the ground began to climb between rocks which grew into high peaks and fell away into treacherous ravines. Quinn was baffled at how she could know where they were going. They crossed the hills, on to a plateau where they were able to drive fast over wastes of sand, then followed for some miles under a precipice, up a winding track as sharp as the Haute Corniche, coming out on to a ridge above a huge valley.

They saw not a village nor hut nor living creature. The noise of the truck thundered through the night, and a ground patrol could have heard them twenty or thirty miles away.

After they had been driving about three hours Leila suddenly cried, 'We are in Algeria!' Bates dipped the headlamps to a range of less than ten yards; five kilometres further on he turned them off altogether and they drove on a fog-lamp, crawling at less than ten miles an hour. He explained that it was not the noise which was likely to give them away: the danger was of being spotted by an air patrol.

They had been moving like this for some time, when a light flickered towards them. Two men slid out of the darkness gripping Sten guns, one of them with a hurricane lamp strapped to his waist. They were Algerians in camouflaged battledress, their faces sallow under the fog-lamp, absurdly young, like schoolboys. Bates switched off the engine. In the stillness they crept up to the truck, peered inside, then saluted shyly. They said something to Leila, and through the window Quinn could smell them, rancid as butter.

They waited squatting outside, their guns at the ready. The truck now became bitterly cold; the night as quiet as a vacuum. Quinn tried nodding off to sleep, his head slipping on to Leila's shoulder, but each time he was jerked awake by the cold. They found some blankets in the back and wrapped themselves up; sipped some brandy, smoked and whiled away the time. They started telling each other jokes, which for Leila's sake had to be rendered in to French. Bates began with the one about the Englishman and Frenchman on their wedding nights, and Quinn followed up with one of Max Miller's better known pieces which didn't translate well. Leila laughed at them all, except the one about the three Catholic girls in the confessional, which she didn't understand; and Bates told a story about the time he had been a barrister in Australia and had successfully defended a Tasmanian accused of interfering with a duck, arguing that a charge of bestiality cannot apply in law to a fowl — at which Leila laughed so much that she banged her head against the dashboard.

Quinn thought of the two of them coming out here month after month, sitting alone in the truck at night while he'd been knocking away at his typewriter, plodding through the rain after road accidents and drowned dogs in the Union Ship Canal.

Once they heard the distant drone of a plane like a mosquito in a dark room, throbbing nearer, further, dying away altogether. 'Airliner,' said Bates casually; 'you can hear them fifty miles away.'

Suddenly the two Algerians sprang up and one of them began signalling with the hurricane lamp. A few minutes later a group of soldiers appeared leading two mules. They were all in the camouflaged uniform, strapped across with Sten guns and belts of grenades. They saluted, and without a word two of them climbed into the back of the truck and began unscrewing the false floor, hauling out the four steel-bound crates and tying them swiftly on to the mules. They worked in silence; when it was finished they handed Leila a receipt in Arabic, saluted again and moved off into the night.

'Well, that's that,' said Bates. 'It's the same every time — simple as going shopping.'

Quinn took over the wheel for the return journey, with Leila giving him directions every few hundred yards. 'Don't the French suspect anything down here?' he asked.

'They suspect the whole frontier,' said Bates, 'but they haven't got enough men or planes to cover it all. Five years ago the generals said they had the rebels beaten, and today the

FLN's got more men and weapons than ever. Trying to fight a war in a country like this is like conquering Russia. As it is, it's sucking France dry.'

'Then France should stop the war,' said Leila.

Bates laughed. 'Try telling that to most of the French! Or to the colons!

'You know,' he said, putting his hand on Quinn's shoulder, 'Algeria is part of France. No, really! The Algerian Moslems are French — like the Indians and Cypriots and the Gyppos were all really loyal British subjects. *Algérie Française!* He thumped out two short and two long blasts on the truck horn, and Leila cried, 'Are you mad!'

'That's right,' he said, '*Algérie Française!* You go on saying that long enough and they'll even forget they lost the Battle of Waterloo.'

'Now they've found petrol in the Sahara,' Leila said glumly, 'they'll never stop until we drive them into the sea.'

Quinn asked her: 'What do you think of De Gaulle?'

'De Gaulle is a fool. But the French in Algeria are bigger fools.'

'Maniacs,' said Bates. 'If those boys could get their way, they'd be fighting the second Hundred Years' War.'

'Only the Communists want the war to stop,' said Leila.

Bates snorted. 'The Communists want this war to go on as long as it gives the West a dirty name. They're about as against a peace here as the big landowners round Algiers.'

'In France,' she said firmly, 'the Communists are against the war.'

'Ah yes, the French Communists!' he said. 'Let me just roll those sweet words round in my mouth. The great French Communists, shouting their mouths off against the Americans and the fascists and making bloody sure they keep the Moslem labour out of the factories too!

'Leila,' he said, 'I find it amazing how an intelligent girl like you comes to be so fooled by those decrepit old bigots at the top of the French Communist Party, most of whom have either gone mad or been sacked or are bedridden in Russian hospitals.'

'You are ignorant,' she said, 'you know nothing!'

'Yes, I'm ignorant. And I look forward in ignorance to the glorious day when the Russians tramp in to run your free Algeria. The new white colons from Metropolitan Russia. I suppose you could call Russians white?'

'Oh, shut up!' She gave Quinn a beseeching look, but he just grinned and said, 'You can't argue with the Ossies.'

'He is a fool! Has as much brains as a coconut.'

Bates nodded. 'I'm going to buy myself a sports car out of the struggle for Algerian independence.'

'You are grotesque,' she said, 'and I do not wish to talk to you anymore.' She sat staring importantly at the map, her face stony with rage, and Bates said in English: 'Keep clear of politics, sport! She cooks well.'

Quinn squeezed her thigh and smiled at her; and her face cleared and she smiled back, making no effort to move his hand from her leg. He drove on for a little with only one arm at the wheel, feeling that the French Communist Party might have some virtues after all.

CHAPTER 4

The ride back was easier. On the last stretch the dawn began to come up and the sky was the inside of a seashell, throwing the country into savage relief like a landscape on the moon. They saw the town from twenty miles away, a honey-coloured pattern spread out on the desert below.

Quinn drove to the house and parked the truck next to the coach; then the three of them strolled back together to the hotel. Quinn tried lagging a little behind, and found that Leila stayed behind with him; and when they reached the gate to the hotel she turned to him and said, quite casually: 'Let's go and drink tea in the market.' She did not look at Bates. Perhaps she was still furious at his remarks about the Communists. He gave them both an unhappy stare, then waved and disappeared into the courtyard.

They both walked through the alleys, into the square where the ritual of Arab life was stirring out of the sleeping Casbah. It was the hour before the flies woke, when the minarets sent up their baleful calls to Mohammed, liked the necks of exotic birds; and in the souks the cupboard doors of the mud shops swung open and whole families climbed out into the new day.

The Arab merchants sat out on rugs and talked and prayed and sipped their mint tea, sweet and piping hot in the freshness of the morning. Leila and he sat down among them, and the Arabs paid them no more attention than if they had both been coming there every morning for years — even at the sight of a girl without a yashmak, wearing trousers.

They were sent over a plate of pastries by an elderly man who bowed to them without a word. Quinn watched her sitting on her heels, as he had seen her that morning by the stream, and said: 'You are very beautiful.' She looked at him, eyes steady, almost serious, but with the flicker of a sly smile. He said: 'I'm in danger of falling in love with you.'

She finished her glass of tea, never moving her eyes from him, stood up and they both began walking back across the square; and as they went he was imperceptibly steering her towards the place where he lived.

They walked on, hardly speaking, as though walking for the sake of being together. They reached the verandah steps and she said: 'So this where they took you when you were ill?' He led her up to the verandah, through the door, and all she said was: '*Ç'est bien sympathique!*'

The building was very quiet and the mesh door closed noisily behind them. There were no curtains and no windows; but the room had a silvery dimness which made it seem deep as a cave.

He put his hands behind her neck and kissed her on the lips, carefully at first, then more violently, feeling her mouth opening and melting and her body growing weak under his touch, backing into the darkness of the bed.

Then her hands slid from round him and she stepped swiftly out of her clothes, lying back naked across the blanket. He stood over her and kissed her on the eyes and mouth and throat, clumsily picking at the buttons of his shirt; bent down and kissed the hard dark nipples, groping at the clasp of his belt, his own body taut, sprung back like a bowstring.

He lay down beside her and her body moved gently, her small tender breasts with the points of the nipples pressed against him; and he was trembling, sweating, suddenly limp, whispering, 'Wait a little!'

She said, 'I love you! Love me well, please love me well!'

He was fearful of disappointing her, and the fear drained all desire out of him, and he began kissing her wildly, almost in panic, feeling her body fold under him, soft and eager, crying, 'Now! — please, now!'

'It will be dangerous for you.'

She kissed him. 'Make me a baby! I want a baby from you!'

'I love you, Leila. But just the first time — with someone who matters — it's difficult at first.'

'I know. I understand. We have all day — all next week.' She moved her knee between his thighs and he caught her rank animal smell, as he said: 'We'll go to the sea — to Mogador and Tangier. We'll stay a whole week.'

'The beach at Safi is very beautiful,' she whispered. 'I love you. Stay with me — don't ever go away.' She began to stir, very slowly, so that she was now lying beneath him. He slipped his hands down the curve of her spine, under the silken-cool buttocks, her smooth belly moving under him, as she cried out and arched and shuddered and lay moaning, the dusky face tilted upwards, eyes closed and sloping away. He felt her drawing the love out of him, scarcely moving at all inside her, until she writhed and suddenly fell quiet, wound round him with her eyes open and smiling, tiny drops of sweat on her upper lip.

She said, 'It has never, never, never been like that!' using the words *'jamais, jamais!'* as though they had some secret, sensuous meaning known only to herself.

'Have you loved many men?' he asked.

'A few. Not many. Only three. Only one was important. He was a boy in Algiers, a student. He was very sweet. He was rather thin, though — much thinner than you. He was a Communist. I don't know what happened to him after I left.'

'And the others?'

She smiled and said: 'Have you any cigarettes?' He fetched a packet from his trousers; and bent over and kissed the hollow of her navel which tasted of salt. He said again: 'And who were the others?'

She laughed: 'You're jealous!'

'Yes.'

'Good. The others were all American film stars. No, no! They weren't. They didn't mean anything, really.' He lit their cigarettes and she said: 'Well, one was another student who seduced me, and I liked him because he had very thick eyebrows like you — only yours are lighter. And the other was just a man I met at a party in Algiers — a Frenchman. He was very handsome, very physical. He went back to France — and anyway, we didn't love each other really. Now tell me all about your girls. How many have you loved? A hundred?'

He began counting on his fingers, then pretended to run out of fingers, and said: 'I can only remember the important ones.'

'Did you treat them very badly?'

'Terribly.' He looked at her, head in the crook of her arm, eyes shining. 'I can't remember any of them now,' he said, 'not after you.' Then he asked her seriously: 'Does Paddy love you?'

'I don't know. He is a strange man. I think he is very sad. You know, he doesn't mean all those cynical things he says about the war. He believes in it really, but he doesn't believe in himself, and he is terribly weak and he drinks so much.' She turned to him, her body wrapped close and warm round him. 'He likes you very much, you know. He was the one who saved you. The others wanted to kill you, and Paddy came and said that if they found you still alive and tried to kill you, they'd have to kill him first. I said so too,' she added.

'That was kind of you!'

'No, don't be angry. That's all forgotten now. Stay with me. Don't ever try to go away. Stay with me and give me a baby.'

'I'll stay with you,' he said, not knowing whether he would or not. There was a tiny pulse beating on the inside of her thigh. She said again, 'Stay with me always!' And as she spoke she drew him back into her, kissing him fiercely, her whole body moving with him, whispering to him, 'You must never leave me! Never!'

Later that morning the young Moroccan called to wake him, and smiled and went away, and they slept on till the day was beginning to lose its heat.

They washed under the pump outside, and Leila hung round his neck, laughing and sparkling with water, crying: 'God, how I love you!' She pranced round the pump, while he bid farewell to the Moroccan boy, who bowed them both all the way into the street.

They strolled to the square, down into the souks where they had coffee and kissed in the shadows, their bodies feeling light and at ease with each other. He went into a shop that smelt of cedar wood, where two little girls stood holding spools of thread which an old woman was winding on to a spinning wheel. He bought six metres of white cloth, scented with the musky cedar, and gave it to Leila who threw it over her hair and wound it round her arms and hips. He noticed with a catch of apprehension that it looked perilously like a wedding garment.

Later they meandered back to the hotel, where the tourist party was already gathered for the night-drive north to Asouf Mrimina. M. Beloued greeted Quinn with a little bow as if he were meeting him for the first time.

They found Bates muddled with wine, rolling dice with himself in the courtyard. He gave them both a cockeyed grin, and Quinn saw at once that he knew they were lovers; but he didn't say anything, and seemed resigned to the fact — almost relieved that they had got it over with. Later he took Quinn aside and said: 'Look after her well, sport. She's a good girl and she hasn't got anybody else. Don't ever foul her up — or you'll have me to reckon with.' The return journey took six days. The three German tourists were severe spinsters with iron-grey hair in tight sausage curls: just about the right age, Leila said, to have given schoolchildren lessons in 'Rassenschande'. There was also a middle-aged French couple and an earnest American boy who was studying Oriental languages and followed Leila about with doe eyes, trying to converse with her in Arabic whenever he had the chance.

There were no rebel agents on this trip; and nobody tried to steal Bates' keys, and there were no murders. Quinn did notice, though, that Bates had fitted a new lock to his holdall.

They reached Marrakech in the evening of the fifth day and drove straight to the Mamounia Hotel. Quinn booked a double room overlooking the Spanish orange groves and the Atlas Mountains; and Leila went into the heart of the hotel and bought an expensive plain black dress with a Rue de Rivoli label. Upstairs in their room they rang down for cocktails which they drank lying together in the bath; and she wound her legs round his shoulders and said solemnly: 'I will love you till I die!'

Afterwards she wriggled into her new dress and stood preening herself in front of the mirror, scooping up her hair and saying: 'My God, I am beautiful!' She called out to Quinn, who was sitting on the balcony: 'Darling, am I beautiful?'

'Yes!' he bawled.

The three of them dined in the Moorish dining room that had once been a stateroom of the Sultan's palace. As they came down the marble steps several European heads turned and watched her walk between the tables. Quinn watched her too, her neat little behind sliding under the Parisian skirt — and he thought of her helping to fight a foul desert war against the French, and having a walk like a spoilt girl in summer on the Champs Elysées, only better.

She took the menu and ordered herself the most expensive dishes she could find. (*Sound Marxist training*, he thought.) They had three bottles of champagne, with Grand Marnier to conclude, and she tried to smoke a Bolivar cigar with them, sitting up till after midnight, the last to leave. And back in their room Bates joined them for more brandy, where he became weepy and poetic, saying he could never have found two better friends and that he loved Leila but that Leila could never have found a better lover than Quinn.

They all broke up swearing each other eternal friendship; and Leila spun round, deliciously squiff-eyed, and collapsed across the bed; and between the sheets he tried to make love to her, but she dropped asleep beneath him.

Next day they took the afternoon train, first class, to Casablanca. Izard was anxious to see all three of them, especially Quinn. He met them that evening in the most famous restaurant in Morocco: a glass penthouse poised on a pencil-shaped skyscraper, like an aquarium above the flashing panorama of the port and Casbah. And inside Izard was the fish in the aquarium — small and old and dangerous, its spines drawn in, waiting.

He gave them an excellent meal, but did not order any wine, and they nursed their aperitifs through till coffee. The conversation was very formal; most of the time they concentrated on their food. It was not an easy meal, and towards the end a certain tension set in. Suddenly Izard signalled, almost rudely, for Bates and Leila to withdraw to the bar.

The old man faced Quinn across the table and began speaking in his careful English: 'Mister Quinn, I will say immediately that I was not pleased to learn what happened to you.'

'Thank you. I didn't like it much either.'

'You have no need to be ironical, please. This is a serious matter.' Quinn would have liked a drink. Izard said: 'I have discovered — no matter how — that your last employment was as a journalist. You did not tell me this when we met.' He paused; but Quinn said nothing.

"Did you come to Morocco to represent a newspaper?'

'No, I came to get away from one. What happened on that trip was an accident — I had nothing to do with it.'

Izard raised his hand: 'Please, I know what happened. Let me be quite frank with you. I will tell you, without humility, that I am a powerful man in this country. Morocco is not a Western democracy. The police here are not servants of the public; they are employees of the government. We are a young country and we are not ideal. There are many bad things, many political factions one against the other. The government must be strong, and not always scrupulous. For myself, Mister Quinn, I am not interested in government. I make money. I am a businessman.'

He paused again, and Quinn said: 'Well, that's something. I'd rather discuss money than political metaphysics.'

'You are a young man and you seem intelligent. I think you appreciate the situation? If you have any intention of communicating your experiences to a newspaper, or to the French authorities, I should be obliged to take action that would be disagreeable to all of us.'

Quinn called the waiter and boldly ordered a brandy. 'I suppose the Moroccan police wouldn't listen to me?'

'They would listen to me first.'

'But not the French? The government's even more frightened of the French than of you?'

'The government here has its interests to protect,' said Izard, unperturbed; 'we do not always like the French, but we must exist with them.'

The brandy came and Quinn warmed the tulip-bowl in his hands. Izard had a remarkable poker face, but Quinn knew that he was bluffing. He said: 'We're not in the Sahara now, sir. I only have to go round to the British Consulate. I can be on a plane to England in a few hours.'

Izard was silent. Perhaps he already knew that Quinn would not go round to the Consulate. Quinn wanted money and he wanted Leila and he wanted to be able to keep her. Izard took out a leather folder in which he wrote him out a cheque on an American bank in Tangier — the same in which Bates kept his account. The sum was for five hundred dollars. He pushed it over the table to Quinn and said: 'I must confess that you have forced me to employ you in a most unprofessional manner. I prefer to be the master of circumstances — but occasionally one must make expedient capitulations.'

Quinn thanked him and slipped the cheque into his passport; it was considerably more money than he had made at any one time in his life. If he were going to be a pillar of virtue, he should tear the cheque up, scatter it over Izard's plate and stride out, ready to be murdered between here and the Consulate. Leila was watching him from the bar, her foot propped on the rail under the stool; he caught a glimpse of her leg above the knee. A very nice leg. He inhaled the brandy. Izard waited; he seemed to have all the time in the world. Quinn said: 'I agree. On a strictly commercial basis.'

Izard nodded. 'You will receive the same sum through Monsieur Beloued on returning from each trip. And I must impress upon you that I am obliged to trust you completely.'

'I shan't betray you.'

'Please don't,' said Izard.

They discussed a few final details. It would be arranged that Quinn would have a flat in a few days. In the normal course, they would not be meeting or communicating unless something serious happened; any messages to Izard were to be sent through M. Beloued. They shook hands, and Leila and Bates returned to the table.

'It has been a pleasant evening,' said Izard, as he signed the bill. 'Good night to you all.' The waiter brought him his black cane and escorted him to the lift.

The three of them stayed on and celebrated, spending between them nearly twenty thousand francs. Both she and Bates seemed to have inexhaustible rolls of tissuey Moroccan money which they pulled out in handfuls.

CHAPTER 5

For the next couple of days Quinn stayed with Leila. Her flat was very small and personal, full of a kind of ordered shambles: piled with books and flowers and Arabic newspapers; and every inch of the walls pasted over with magazine photographs which even overflowed into the tiny bathroom, where Picasso stared saucer-eyed, and Paul Robeson and shadowy jazz quartets crowded over the bath and bidet. President Nasser grinned down above the bed, and across the door was the famous close-up of the three Hungarian AVH men dying at point-blank range in Budapest under rebel guns. Once Quinn commented on it and she said: 'Yes, those poor men were murdered by the fascists.' He nearly said something, then remembered Bates' advice. It didn't seem to matter, anyway. She made delectable cous-cous and soufflés and homard Belle Hélène.

He was given his own flat in a few days: clean and spartan, with three rooms and a balcony above the white-hot dazzle of the modern quarter. And within another few days Leila had given up her own flat and moved in with him.

The months that followed were lazy and idyllic; getting up late and taking more than an hour over breakfast on the balcony; then down to the beach and drinks before lunch in George's Bar, which was cool and panelled, hung with old English prints and notices from resident British ladies appealing for charities towards Animal Rest Homes: Please help old and infirm horses, donkeys, dogs and other unfortunate beasts to end their days in rest and peace. Leila always dropped a hundred francs into the collection box; and they stayed to drink chilled lager and watch the expatriates pretending that Casablanca was Bournemouth.

Most of the days they spent stretched out on the white sands under the fierce African sun. They went waterskiing and surf-riding on the beach just below Casablanca; hired an American drop-head and drove down the coast to Safi and Mogador; and stayed a week in Fez, that silver-grey city of canals and cypress trees, like a landlocked Arabian Venice sloping down the bed of a green valley.

They ate well and slept well, and their love-making was long and greedy, passions synchronized like a watch so that each time it seemed that it could never be as good again, and somehow it always was: at night, with sheets stripped off and the balcony windows flung open; and slowly, sleepily, in the hours before dawn. Then in the afternoon, fleeing together from the beach to the quiet of the flat, unhooking her skirt and peeling off her bikini, her slender dark body spread out sticky with oil on the white bed.

Once, when they had become too impatient, it had been on a dinghy a few hundred yards from shore, squirming against rubber and salt water and braving binoculars from half the penthouses in Casablanca. And for every time, she made a little proud mark in lipstick on the mirror in the bathroom.

Each month the run south passed without incident, although the heat increased and the flies grew bigger, and below the Atlas Mountains they were now able to travel only at night. Twice Leila left Casablanca before the others, going south to see the rebel agents over the border and returning with the Blue Men to meet the coach halfway down.

She and Quinn talked very little about the war. There was a tacit agreement between them that the less he knew about the FLN the better. In July there were rumours of peace talks, but

114

they came to nothing and the fighting dragged on, hundreds killed each week on the rebel side; while in Casablanca they were both living high and well, saving nothing, planning nothing, thinking of nothing beyond the next quick run over the border.

During that whole summer they only quarrelled twice. The first time was when he refused to let her become pregnant; he used cunning arguments, telling her that while she was involved in a war it was wrong to have a child; and when the first month was over and she found she was not pregnant she was at last persuaded to go fretfully to one of the family planning clinics which the government was setting up throughout the country.

The second row broke between them in a cinema. Leila was a passionate filmgoer, and for weeks had been dragging Quinn to a little open-air cinema where they watched the fireflies flitting across the grey images of exhausting Egyptian and Japanese epics. He had finally drawn the line, and deeply offended her, by walking out of Part Three of an Indian trilogy in the original version, with Arabic subtitles.

They were happy and loved each other evenly and well, although deep inside him he was not at ease. He knew that one day it would all have to end; but he tried to push the thought away, enjoying instead the sun and wine and clean white beach washed by the Atlantic rollers.

The idyll lasted until one afternoon late in the summer. It was the day on which they were due to leave on the next run south, and they had been drowsing on the beach under a huge umbrella, when he heard her voice calling to him, as though from a great distance, asking when he was going to marry her. He said casually, half-asleep: 'You know I can't marry you yet.

Things are too uncertain.'

'I can't live without you. We are one now. I would die without you.'

He said, with eyes closed: 'It wouldn't work — not at the moment.'

'It would work!' She rolled over and curled against him. 'I love you enough to make it work.' She stroked his face, and he kept his eyes closed, knowing that he loved her really, that if she left him he would never quite forget her. She said: 'Please, marry me. Take me to England. Please, take me!'

'I haven't got a job,' he said. 'I don't know what I'd do there. We're making a lot of money here, and it's good here. Why do you want to leave? Anyway, it rains in England,' he said. 'Let's stay here, Leila.'

A man in a blue suit with a baseball cap and a nibbled, evil face had come sidling up with a bag of newspapers. '*Herald Tribune*! You English? American? Like *Herald Tribune*, *France Soir*?' The French papers were yesterday's and the American two days' old. Quinn saw that all the headlines in the French ones were about Algeria. There had been a great offensive by airborne troops in the south-west; three hundred and sixty-eight FLN were dead.

He said: '*Allez, oust!*' but the man stood his ground, scowling, holding up the days' old *Herald Tribune*.

'*Fous le camp!*' Quinn yelled, and turned back to Leila. She said: 'I can't go on living with you like this.'

'Don't let's talk about it now.' The newspaper seller walked round them and spat leisurely in the sand, then moved off.

They lay in silence, and she began to cry. He said nothing, and later she went swimming and stayed out a long time; and when she came back she seemed gay and brittle, and they didn't speak any more about marriage.

Before taking the train that night for Marrakech they joined Bates for dinner at a pavement restaurant near the port in a street glistening with fish-scales where they drank wine to the run ahead, saying '*Merde!*' as they touched glasses.

It was a cool, pleasant evening and the city smelt of the sea.

CHAPTER 6

They had come to the spot marked by Leila on the contour map, twenty-five kilometres inside the border. This month they'd crossed a little more to the north than usual. The moon was in the first quarter, a thin slice of silver, and the night sky was like the bottom of a vast jewel case.

It had been just before midnight when they stopped. Quinn and Leila were sitting up on the front seat, and Bates was slumped asleep among the emergency petrol cans at the back. They waited one hour, two hours, and now it was nearly three o'clock.

Bates woke noisily. 'Haven't they come yet?'

The night was eyrie still. Quinn said: 'They've never been as late as this.' He was driving on the return trip; it was new country to them, and it would take at least an hour to reach the border. 'Something's gone wrong,' he said. 'If we don't start soon, we won't be in Morocco before dawn.'

As he spoke they heard a plane throbbing across the horizon; it took a long time to pass.

'Give them another ten minutes,' said Leila.

'Are you sure you marked the right place?' said Bates.

'Of course I'm sure.'

'They could have made a mistake.'

'They never made one before,' said Quinn. It was after three o'clock now. Dawn was at four.

A moment later they heard a machine-gun — a rapid knocking with echoes humming round them and the silence folding back in a deadly hush.

'Let's get out of here!' shouted Quinn. He started the engine and they turned, driving again on the fog-lamp. 'How far away do you think it was?'

'Five, ten kilometres,' said Bates; 'it's hard to tell.'

'It seemed to come from out there,' said Quinn, pointing out in front; 'we're driving slap into it.'

'You can't tell with the echoes. It might just as well have been behind.'

Leila said: 'It could have been a sentry shooting.'

'It could have been,' said Bates, 'but I'm not betting on it.'

Leila was examining the map; she told Quinn to turn down into a valley. The night was quite silent again. Bates leaned forward and peered out in front. 'It's a funny thing,' he said, after a moment, 'nearly a year of this war and that's the first shooting I've heard.'

'Encouraging,' said Quinn. Leila said nothing. They reached the end of the valley and began to wind up a rough track. Quinn put his foot down harder; they bumped into rocks and banks of sand. 'Careful!' she cried. The fog-lamp picked out nothing beyond a few yards.

They heard another plane, this time passing almost above them. There were no lights on it. 'That's no civilian plane,' Bates said.

'It's a Nord-Atlas transport,' said Leila quietly; 'they use them for parachute drops.' It roared over, perhaps three miles to the east of them. 'I wonder what they're as far down as this for?' said Quinn.

At that moment the silence exploded like a paper bag. The blackness flared white and purple and there came the boom and crack of heavy guns. Then it was over. In the dark a machine-gun opened up, much closer this time, hammering steadily through the stillness.

'That was no sentry,' Bates murmured.

The bumpers scraped against a shoulder of rock. 'We shan't make the border at this rate before daylight,' said Quinn again. He was beginning to sweat. Leila sat rigidly beside him, her lower lip curled in under her teeth. She said nothing, and Quinn switched on the headlamps. He put his foot hard down again and the truck began to career dangerously over the broken ground. The yellow beam streamed out for about fifty yards.

Suddenly, directly in front of them, they saw a group of figures. Quinn flicked off the lights and slammed on the brakes. The truck turned half in its tracks, and they were out of the doors before it had stopped, throwing themselves flat in the sand. A bullet shrieked and thudded above them. There were two more shots; both hit the truck. Bates swore. Quinn looked at Leila; her face was quite calm in the quarter moonlight.

Another bullet cracked into the rock. There was a tramp of boots and voices in the dark. Leila scrambled to her feet and shouted in Arabic. The voices stopped. The boots came nearer; she shouted again. Quinn and Bates began to get up, and a light went on.

Four men came towards them, two of them with rifles. There was a grisled Moslem leading them; he didn't have a gun, only a thin, nasty-looking knife, and wore a woollen khaki cap and gaiters with split straps. The other three were very young; two of them had fallagha capes and baggy cotton trousers, the third a denim uniform and olive-green helmet.

They approached the truck sideways, very slowly, walking half round it before they stopped. Leila walked up and spoke to them. Bates and Quinn came up behind, Bates with his revolver out. They looked at Leila, then at the revolver; the old

Moslem said something, and Leila and he began to talk for a full minute.

The other three stared suspiciously, two of them fingering the trigger-guards of their rifles. Leila turned and said: 'It is very bad. The French are coming — they're closing the frontier. There's a big retreat.'

They looked at the four Algerians, then at the truck. 'Let's get on,' said Quinn. The horizon flared again, and they heard the rasp and pop of mortar bombs.

'Why the hell didn't they say anything about this on the radio this evening?' said Bates. The mortars stopped. In the silence they heard a drip of water from the truck. Bates took the lamp from one of the Algerians and opened the bonnet.

Leila said: 'They say that paratroop units are being dropped in the north. It happened so suddenly. They lost a lot of men.' She looked very unhappy.

Bates began to fiddle with something in the engine; his head came up and he spat. 'These clowns have properly buggered us up!' He lifted out a twisted fan. 'They've shot the radiator to pieces too.' The Algerians stared at the truck. Quinn walked round it and saw that one of the back tyres was flat.

'Can you start her up?' he said.

Bates got in and switched on the ignition; there was a clatter and a backfire, and the motor went dead. He put his head down under the bonnet again. Quinn went to the back of the truck and took out the spare wheel and jack. He beckoned to one of the Algerians. The man didn't move. He said to Leila, still holding the wheel against his knee: 'Tell them to give me a hand.'

Leila spoke to the one with the helmet. He looked at the ground, then started sauntering away round the front of the truck. Bates looked up from the bonnet and yelled at the man, then brought out his revolver. The two Algerians with the rifles seemed to take no notice; Leila spoke again to the man with the helmet. He turned and came slowly back. He didn't look at Quinn, but took the spare from him, while Quinn knocked the hubcaps off the damaged wheel. They raised the truck on the jack and the Algerian helped lift on the spare wheel. It was very heavy, and twice it slipped off.

Bates closed the bonnet and came round, his arms smeared with grease. 'The engine's had it for the moment. We'll just have to push the truck off and hide it somewhere.' They had finished putting on the spare; Bates now climbed into the back and unscrewed the floor. Quinn asked: 'Are we going to dump the arms?'

'What, five thousand quid's worth! We don't get paid till the stuff's delivered.' He took out his bunch of keys and unlocked one of the crates; the machine pistols were packed tight in straw. He began to hand one out to each of them.

Quinn stood weighing the weapon in his hand; it was cool and delicate, beautifully made. He blew a shred of straw off the sights, which were sharp as thorns, and Bates said: 'Can you use one of these?' He had slung his own, guitar-like, round his neck, and took Quinn's and snapped off the circular magazine. Inside, the cartridges lay like fat brown insects. 'Forty rounds,' he said, 'air-cooled, dead accurate up to four hundred yards. Just point the thing and pull the trigger.'

Quinn hesitated.

'You're not funking out now, boy! We're in a spot. If we run into any French we're going to need these. They don't take prisoners down here — unless it's to make 'em talk.'

Quinn saw Leila watching him; he smiled boldly at her, worried that she might think he was afraid; then put the gun over his shoulder, wondering if he could go through with it.

Bates had collected several cartons of ammunition and screwed the crate back under the floor. He shouted at the Algerians in French, pointing at the truck and putting his shoulder against it. They pushed it as far as the slope, and Bates took the wheel and steered it down into the valley which they had just left. Leila thought there might be some rock clefts, even caves, where they could hide it well enough to prevent it being seen by an air patrol.

Down on the flat of the valley the pushing was hard work. The Algerians didn't seem very eager to help. The truck wheels hit a boulder and jammed. Bates went round the front and tried rocking it free. The four Algerians stepped back. Quinn and Leila went to help him. In spite of the chill of the desert night they were all sweating. As they worked they heard more firing. It was coming from several directions now. There was one gun that seemed to be very near, chiming in with the others in a furious crescendo that roared and bounced round the hills, the echoes dying like a slow cry.

The Algerians muttered something to each other and began to walk away. Bates shouted at them: Leila joined in in Arabic. The four of them kept going, their lamp swinging away into the dark. Bates took off his gun and levelled it, but Leila stopped him: 'Let them go if they want to. They're the only ones left out of a section of forty.'

'The little bastards!' Bates said quietly.

'We're better without them,' said Quinn. He looked at the crippled truck. 'Couldn't we try to pull the explorer stunt?'

Bates shook his head and heaved again at the truck. 'Not with the whole country crawling with FLN. No Frenchman's as stupid as that.'

'But if we jumped the guns?'

They heaved again and the wheels came free. 'Not unless we have to,' he said. 'Izard's paid for this stuff already. If we lose it, we lose the money.'

'I'd rather be safe and poor.'

Leila said sharply: 'We haven't been attacked yet. We don't leave the guns till we have to.'

Quinn decided to say no more.

They pushed the truck on down the valley, covering only a few hundred yards in more than half an hour. The dawn would be breaking soon.

The gunfire grew louder, and the sky was now full of aircraft. There was the slow thunder of the fat-bellied Nord Atlas transport planes; then the dive-bombers coming up behind, fast and low. The sky lit up with a spurt of flame, rolling over the horizon like a bright orange serpent. The explosion came a few seconds later. Leila cried out: 'Oh God, they're using Napalm! The filthy animals! They're the worst things they can use!' Her voice caught up in tears. Quinn took her arm, and she stared fiercely ahead of her. 'The poor men! They've got nothing. And the French have sent paratroops against them.' She used the dreaded phrase, *les paras*, known simply in Arabic as the 'Terrible Ones'.

Bates said impatiently: 'Come on, let's get this thing out of sight!' Quinn was badly scared now. He heard the zoom of more planes and the flames leapt out again, perhaps five miles away. At the same time he still couldn't grasp the full implications; the fighting seemed like a firework display, to have little to do with a rebel army in retreat, being blown up and roasted with jelly bombs.

Besides, the idea of the French being the arch-enemy struck him as slightly absurd. He began thinking about his student days in Grenoble. He'd been very young then and the war in

Algeria hadn't broken out yet. They were still fighting in Indo-China in those days, and he remembered the protest meeting organised by the Communist students one weekend, and how the police broke it up with firehoses. They'd knocked one gendarme off his bicycle and hurled his cap into the air; it had sailed across the Place Victor Hugo with the students chanting '*Chapeau! Chapeau!*'

A plane roared directly over them, a fighter with the jet singing in their ears long after it had passed. There would be Frenchmen up there, and French all round on the horizon, closing in. He thought of the Place Victor Hugo, shuttered and pigeon-grey, with the plane trees and the students drinking demis and playing cards under the café awnings. They were mountains beyond — skiing at Chambéry and Chamonix.

The mortars started up again somewhere behind the hill.

Dawn was breaking. The first light brought the quick advantage of being able to look for a hiding place. They were lucky. After another hundred yards or so they came to the edge of a gully. Bates got into the driving seat and slipped into second gear; they gave the truck a last push and it began to roll down the slope. At the bottom there was a cave under a ledge of rock. It could only be seen by someone coming down the gully; above all, it would offer some protection against the sun.

They put the truck as far back under the rock as it would go. Bates opened the bonnet again and began dismantling the front of the engine. The truck contained a competent supply of tools, besides the tinned food and cans of fresh water. He took off the radiator top and began hammering at a bolt, the noise slamming round the caves like a pneumatic drill. Quinn said: 'We ought to keep guard up there.'

Leila agreed to go with him and see what it looked like from above the gully. They darkened their faces in the sand, and rubbed on some engine oil for good measure, smearing Leila's képi as well. Quinn looked at her and thought she still looked as pretty as ever. It was the real test for any girl, he reflected, when she could remain appealing after a night in the Sahara, black with oil and under gunfire.

He gripped the machine pistol to his chest and followed her up the gully. The firing was all round them now: two separate volleys from opposite directions. They crept to the ridge, when she signalled him to get down. He whispered: 'Have you ever been in a battle before?' She shook her head. They peered over the ridge and watched the sun coming up — a blood-orange on the rim of the hills.

The firing stopped — both guns at the same moment. As the echoes whined away there came the grinding of machinery, like distant trains heard in the dead of night.

'Tanks,' she said; 'they've come down from Talifit.'

'But that's nearly two hundred kilometres away! They must have started out yesterday morning.'

She didn't say anything.

'Surely your friends could have given you some warning last night?'

She turned, suddenly angry: 'Rupert, this is a war! These people don't run a public relations bureau so you and Paddy can make your five hundred American dollars a month!'

'All right, I'm sorry.'

'It's been bad enough, anyway,' she went on; 'they use Napalm bombs against them. Do you know what Napalm does? You've never seen a whole village destroyed by it — women and children burnt to death because some French

126

officer hears a rumour that rebels are hiding there. You don't know about it, do you?'

'Perhaps not,' he said quietly.

The sound of the tanks continued for some minutes. While they listened they missed the padding of rubber boots at the foot of the ridge. It was Leila who saw them first — four men in the black berets and blotched leopard-camouflage of French paratroops, passing in single file about fifty yards below them.

They both lay flat behind the ridge, exposed only from the air. She whispered: 'There may be others.' They lay on their stomachs, quite still, the sand under them smelling dry and dead. The dawn was full of the crackling of gunfire. They both had their guns off their shoulders now, and Quinn felt his palms sweating against the blue-black steel. Forged somewhere in Czechoslovakia. He began to look for the markings on the gun. He wondered how they marked them over there.

Leila caught his arm. One of the paratroopers was coming back. He was a tall man with binoculars round his neck and a machine-gun slung at his hip: a stumpy weapon with the magazine jutting out at the side like an amputated limb. He turned at the bottom of the ridge and started up towards them. Quinn felt Leila stiffen beside him.

A loud barrage of artillery broke out over the hill and a column of smoke began to roll into the sky. He remembered thinking that it billowed like the folds of a fat man's neck.

The paratrooper came within about twenty yards of them and stopped. He stood sweeping the country with his binoculars. Leila clicked off the safety catch, her legs splayed out behind. The man turned and came on up, walking quite slowly. Once he looked at his watch. She put her head close to Quinn's and whispered: 'He's badly trained for a para.' The barrage over the hill kept up; at the same time several machine-guns began firing from the end of the valley.

Quinn knew they'd have to shoot. He heard Leila shift her legs to get more comfortable. He could see the man's face now: a little older than himself; rimless green sunglasses pushed up on to his forehead under the beret. He lifted the gun and sighted it, the hairline trembling over the webbing across the man's chest. He thought, *better the chest than the head or stomach*. His whole body was quite cold, trying to imagine what the sensation would be — the potency of this small mechanism ripping into living flesh.

In a few seconds the man would see them. Quinn could just make out the pricks of stubble on the upper lip and the angle of the jaw. His left eye had been squinting over the sights a little too long; it blurred over. The man was about ten feet away when he squeezed the trigger.

The gun leapt in his hands as though it were alive. Leila fired in the same second. He saw the bullets denting the man's uniform — across the chest, diagonally to the hip, and a second burst flattening the trousers above the knee. The body jerked as though it had been punched. Stumbled, then went flying over backwards and lay still.

They waited a full five minutes. The firing went on all round; the barrage boomed away behind the hill. The other three paratroopers did not return. Suddenly Leila got up and walked over to the body. Its eyes and mouth were open, the spittle glistening on the teeth. The face was very tanned and looked normal, except that the whole body seemed a little smaller. There was a soaking of blood round two of the five holes in the uniform over the chest, and a trickle down the leg, probably where the bullets had broken an artery.

The black beret and sunglasses had stayed on the head. Quite a good-looking young man: he'd have appreciated Leila. She looked down at him for a few seconds, then scooped up a handful of sand and threw it with all her strength into the dead face. '*Salaud*,' she said, calmly, still looking down at it.

The face had gone like a mask: the sand clogging up the mouth and nostrils, filming the eyes over, like throwing sand on to jelly.

Quinn looked at her and felt sick. She said: 'We must get him back into the cave.' She took off the man's machine-gun and slung it round her shoulder with her own gun, then lifted the dead hands. Quinn took hold of the feet by the rubber boots.

Her face was impassive. Looking at her now he realised for the first time how little he really knew her. He knew every inch of her, and yet nothing about her at all. The body slithered down the gully with the legs flopping loosely as though they might come off at any moment.

Bates came out and gave them a hand pulling it into the cave. 'So you lost your virginity,' he said to Quinn, nodding approvingly; 'with a para too!' Leila went through the man's pockets and unlooped the identification disc. Name of Jean-Pierre Hérault, born 1932 in Arles, private soldier, 24th Airborne Division.

'Better cover him up,' said Bates. They dragged him into the dark of the cave. Quinn walked round and collected some lumps of rock. No prayers were said. Leila was already shovelling sand and stones over the body. The head was half-covered. Quinn dropped a rock on to him, and it rolled off the chest and sagged into the belly. He went out again into the light. Somehow this crude burial brought out all the completeness of death. He sat in the early sun and rested his head on his knees.

Leila fetched some tins of corned beef and bottles of fresh water from the truck. They made a quick breakfast; afterwards Quinn helped Bates repair the truck engine, and Leila went back to keep a lookout. 'They'd have had us all,' said Bates, 'if you'd got up there five minutes later.'

'He had three others with him,' said Quinn. 'They might come back and look for him.'

'That's a risk we'll have to take.'

Quinn looked at the truck. 'Is it really worth all this trouble?'

'We're no worse off with it. If we get it back Izard'll probably throw in a bonus.'

As he stopped speaking they heard voices up in the gully. They both threw themselves under the truck, and Bates grabbed his gun down off the doorhandle.

Leila came down the slope into the cave, followed by the four Algerians they had met earlier. Bates groaned. She said: 'I saw them coming up the hill. They're completely lost. We can't just leave them.'

'They walked out on us,' said Bates; 'now they can look after themselves.'

The four of them had already crept to the back of the cave. The grisled man with the woollen cap stood looking vacantly at the truck. He might have been a herdsman if there were peace. The other three crouched sad-eyed against the rock wall. None of them looked more than eighteen, glum and dusty, staring at their boots. One of them started throwing pebbles in front of him, trying to make them all fall at the same spot, absorbed. Leila said: 'They don't know where they are, and they've hardly eaten anything for two days.'

Bates scowled at them; the one with the pebbles stopped playing and began picking his nose. 'We don't owe them a thing. They walked out on us.'

Leila turned to him: 'Don't be angry with them — they don't want to die.' She opened some more tins of corned beef and shared them round, and the Algerians saluted, scraping the tins dry with their fingers. She spoke to the old man for some time; then came back and said: 'I've explained that they can stay with us till tonight. We'll try and break out over the border after dark — and then they'll have to go their own way.'

'You bet they will!' said Bates.

She went up to the ridge again, while he and Quinn went on working at the truck. It was a long, tiresome job. The sun was coming up and the heat began to fill the gully and the cave.

As the morning drew on the fighting seemed to slacken and move south. Once she came down and said she had seen a helicopter patrolling the hills about half a mile away; and around noon there was the sound of more armour moving in the valley.

The inside of the cave was baking hot and full of flies. Quinn did an hour of standing watch, then Bates. One of the oddest things about the day was that they never saw anybody. There was shooting everywhere, and planes and tanks and smoke, but otherwise there seemed to be only Jean-Pierre Hérault. Once one of the Algerian boys went out and defecated in the gully; the stench seeped into the cave and made Quinn furious. He yelled at him, asking why he couldn't have gone up to the ridge; the boy muttered in Arabic and Leila said: 'He doesn't want to die without his trousers.'

Quinn felt the claustrophobia edging into him; closed his eyes, tried to concentrate on something else: on the beach and the big umbrella, at his worrying about her wanting to marry him. And he thought of Bates being so slap-happy, saying this sort of thing could never happen — and that if it did they were just a bunch of barmy Europeans on safari.

131

He began working out their chances. He could not calculate the military odds, but he knew that both he and Bates could just risk being taken alive. They might try bluffing their way out — pretending to be journalists, or even attempting the explorer stunt. And if the worst came to the worst they could always say they were madcap adventurers and throw themselves on the raft of the British passport to carry them to safety.

But for Leila it was another matter. She was an FLN agent and was clearly in peril. He thought, *if we ever get out of this together I'll marry her.* He would leave North Africa and take up another job in journalism, settle down and live with her in England. And while he worked at the truck he began to imagine how she'd look in English clothes, in a mackintosh in the rain, walking into a pub, seeing how the heads would turn. How he'd marry her in some nice stone church in the Cotswolds. She wasn't a Christian, of course; but the old vicar wouldn't have to know. He thought of her standing all in crisp white outside the church, posing before the shrouded photographer. Followed by champagne in the marquee, with Bates as best man in morning dress. He laughed aloud. Bates looked up and said: 'Are you doing your nut?'

'I was just thinking of you in morning dress at our wedding.'

'You are doing your nut, sport!'

It was late in the afternoon; the truck was almost repaired. Bates said it would do them at least as far as the border. Leila came down from the gully. She was beginning to look very tired. It was Bates' turn now to take the watch for the next hour; she said to him: 'The fighting's mostly moved off now.' He went on up the slope; and she sat down and leant against the rock. Quinn came and sat next to her; the four Algerians were looking at them across the cave. He kissed her on the cheek, but she didn't move. 'Please, not here,' she said, 'not while they're watching.'

'I want to marry you, Leila.'

She looked at him, puzzled. 'Why do you ask me this now?'

'I just love you.'

She didn't say anything for a moment. 'It's because you're frightened, isn't it?'

'I just want to get out of it — take you away and get out of the whole business, I feel as you did the other day on the beach before we left.'

She sat thinking about that day on the beach, her fingers steepled under her chin. He felt a little catch in the throat as he looked at her. 'I couldn't do without you,' he said.

She slid her eyes round to him, ironic and unsettling. 'You mean you could not do without my body. That's all you want really. You want me because I am the prettiest girl you know and I am exciting to show off.'

'That's not true.'

'I think it is. And when you say you want to marry me, Monsieur Quinn, you are a liar.' She said it smiling, in the nicest way.

'I'm not going to argue with you. We may not get out of here alive, anyway. It seems a bad time to quarrel.' He rested against the rock; it was still very hot in the cave. He heard a helicopter throbbing somewhere; it passed a couple of times, then went away. She said: 'I don't like those things. They're like wasps.'

One of the Algerians had begun tossing pebbles in front of him again. They dropped with small, sharp clicks. Quinn closed his eyes. He wondered if they could really make the border in the truck. He dozed off. Leila was still beside him.

Outside the sun was beginning to go down, and the cave was cooling.

'It's strange those three paratroopers never came back,' he said.

'He was probably going on a patrol over the hill; they wouldn't have missed him till later.'

'They might still come back, though. I'll be glad when we're out of here.' She didn't say anything. 'Leila, when we get out of here I will marry you.'

She took his hand and said, without turning, 'I love you too much. You are a liar, but if you ask me to I have to say yes.'

'I will,' he said. He meant it. 'As soon as we get back to Casa.' He wondered if she believed him. She was sitting half-asleep; he eased her head on to his shoulder. Her hand was still on his. Bates came down from the gully and said: 'It's your turn. There's a little bastard of a helicopter up there. I'm worried they may spot the wheel-marks down the valley.'

Quinn stood up, propping Leila's head gently against the rock wall; she was fast asleep now. 'I just hope we can get the truck up the slope.'

'We'll get her up all right,' said Bates. Quinn thought he was a good man to have at a time like this. He waved to them both and walked to the ridge. Except for distant gunfire, and the occasional plane, the night seemed normal.

He smoked a cigarette and watched the moon come up. A little later there was a sound from the gully and Leila appeared. She had left her gun in the cave, and sat next to him, her knees under her chin. 'I'm sorry I was angry with you down there.'

'I'll forgive you.' She kissed him, and they sat listening to the drone of a helicopter. It was cold and he shivered a little. She said, after a pause: 'We may have some trouble with the Algerians. They want to come with us.'

'Tell them they can't.'

'It's not easy. They say they don't know the way to the border, and if they don't come with us they'll die.'

'Well, there's not room for them in the truck.'

They both got up and began strolling down the slope away from the gully, stretching their legs and keeping warm. A flare fell about half a mile away. She said: 'When that patrol moves on we'll leave. I'll tell the Algerians to follow the stars to the west.'

The flare was drifting down very slowly, like something sinking through water. Then there was darkness; and a moment later the helicopter came chugging down over the hills towards them. There was a report and the sky burst into a bluish-white glow. They threw themselves down and for several moments it was as though the whole landscape were lit up with a strip of neon. The flare was falling almost directly above them this time; it seemed to take an interminable time to go out. They watched the helicopter hovering like a dragonfly.

Suddenly it opened fire. Quinn saw the sand spitting up with the bullets. A line of them came racing towards him, then stopped about six yards away. The helicopter swooped, just as the flare went out.

It was flying down, low and noisy, its blades flapping now like giant bat wings in the dark. About fifty yards away the engine cut out. They were both on their feet. There was shouting from the gully, and Quinn recognised the guttural Arabic accents. He said: 'The damned fools are running out of the cave!'

But she had gone. She was running back towards the cave, probably to warn them. He heard a pounding of boots and a searchlight came on. The beam swivelled and dazzled him for a moment. A gun opened up. The bullets passed very close, and he began to run too, but down away from the gully. There was more shooting — the whole sky bursting with noise — and he ran blindly, falling, cracking his kneecap. There were two explosions behind him.

Then he heard a motor. The firing had stopped, and there was silence now, except for the motor, which backfired and then began a steady grinding. There was a crash of gears. It was the truck trying to climb the slope out of the gully. The searchlight went out.

He had run perhaps three hundred yards, and stood panting for breath, his knee hurting badly. He realised that his gun was still round his neck. He hesitated an instant, then unslung it and started back, limping, dreading what he would find, knowing he should do something to help.

Ahead, the helicopter spluttered and roared into life. The truck was driving away down into the valley. Bates had made a good job of it. The helicopter swept once round, then flew off.

There was no sound ahead now. He came slowly up the slope and found one of the Algerians first, falling over him in the dark. The man was on his stomach at the top of the ridge, blood on the back of his neck. Two of the other Algerians lay close behind him, a little way down the gully. One had had the top of his head blown off, and the brains had fallen out like wet clay in the moonlight.

He paused, distracted and fascinated. The sound of the truck was quite a way off now, driving smoothly. His senses were jolted back by a scream from inside the cave. He ran down and found Bates. He was hunched up in a ball, eyes closed and hands pressed to his belly.

The scream came again. The body stirred and Quinn saw a coil of silvery intestine slip under the clenched fingers. The jaws snapped open and the teeth began to chatter. It had nothing to do with Bates. Quinn remembered thinking that the intestine looked oddly like a clock spring.

He leant down and said: 'Paddy! Paddy!' The place smelt of powder and burnt sand. There was nothing he could do. He stumbled round the cave and found the fourth Algerian, the old man with the woollen cap, with his chest and legs torn open with grenade splinters. There was no trace of Leila. He tripped over some maps and tins of food where the truck had been, and there were crystals of smashed windscreen. The paratrooper was still there under the rock.

When he got back Bates was dead. He tried to open his jacket and get out his passport and wallet. The body rolled over and he was terrified lest the whole stomach drop out.

Then he turned and ran out, up the gully, into the night.

PART 4: The Enemy

CHAPTER 1

Capitaine Lefévre, commander of the garrison fort at Talifit in south-west Algeria, sat up into the small hours drinking filter coffees and skimming through the latest military reports from Colomb Béchar. They made awkward, dismal reading; and after a time the captain laid aside the teletyped sheets and turned to a leather-hound copy of Claudel's *Partage du Midi*.

A corporal appeared in the door and saluted. 'Lieutenant Zimmermann's patrol will be back in half an hour, mon capitaine.'

'Tell him to report to me as soon as he arrives.' The corporal saluted and marched away. Left alone, the captain turned again to his book, occasionally marking in pencil a passage that struck him as particularly fine. The return of Zimmermann's patrol was not an event to which he looked forward with any relish.

Capitaine Lefévre had been a professional soldier all his adult life. A widower, childless, with a face like an old suede shoe, he had served in Algeria for more than five years. He was neither unintelligent nor burdened with imagination. The one thing he believed in, passionately, was France; and in Algeria he was convinced that she had a mission to accomplish: to clothe and feed and educate. He had little sympathy for the French settlers, whom he regarded as provincial and stupid, and like most of his breed he had the soldier's proper contempt for politicians — the corrupt, squabbling opportunists in Paris who swapped France's overseas heritage in shabby bargains in the Assemblée. (He had once been heard to concede grudgingly that Pierre Mendès-France might be superior to

most, but had added that he distrusted the man's intelligence.)
His only real faith lay with the military commander in Algiers.

At his post in Talifit the captain pursued his duties with
monastic devotion. He took classes at the infants' school run
by the army; his men supervised hygiene and hospital work;
and one of his conscripts, who had been called up before
completing his medical studies at the Sorbonne, and would
otherwise now be gallivanting about the Boul'Mich, gave
regular lessons in midwifery and childcare.

Towards the FLN Capitaine Lefévre's attitude was
uncomplicated. He did not hate them: they existed simply to be
hunted out and exterminated. He had seen the bodies of
Moslems mutilated for sending their children to French
schools; men with their lips and noses cut off for smoking
French cigarettes; a fifteen-year-old boy crucified on a tree for
having attended church.

But while prepared to devote his life to Algeria, privately the
captain did not much care for Algerians, tending to regard
them as deceitful children, often with unclean habits.
Nevertheless, they were citizens of France and it was his duty
to make them worthy of that privilege.

Apart from his own belief in French civilisation, Lefévre also
used his own conduct to justify certain other aspects of what
he liked to call 'the Algerian problem'. There were persistent
rumours of how rebel prisoners were treated at the hands of
the French Army. Now, after six years of war, atrocity stories
on the French side were rife. Usually, Lefévre managed to
accredit them to hostile propaganda — to Communists and
Radicals and Liberals (he made few distinctions) who
understood nothing of the war and enjoyed bewildering the
already dissipated loyalties of the French people. However, just
occasionally there came a report that could not be discounted

so easily. Such incidents disturbed the captain, but fortunately for him, and for those like him, there was always some counter-atrocity. Recently, there had been a particularly ugly report of how a Moslem suspect had been made to confess to a bomb outrage in Constantine. Then, a couple of days later, the captain was secretly reassured by an incident in the town north of Talifit: a pregnant Moslem woman, who had been consulting the local French doctor, had had her legs tied together by rebels and died during her labours.

But Lefévre found his confidence most shaken when he came in contact with other French troops in Algeria, particularly those from the battle areas and big cities. The most notorious were among the paras. Occasionally, when there was an offensive in the south-west, paratroops were stationed in the fort at Talifit. These were the crack troops of the Republic, the military elite who often refused to salute French officers back on Metropolitan soil, carrying about them an aura of vicious glamour that excited silly girls on the Left Bank — girls in green mascara and white lipstick, who kept *L'Express* tucked under their arms like banners and marched in rallies against '*la guerre en Algérié.*'

A unit of paratroopers had arrived at the fort three days earlier. There had been a breakthrough near Colomb Béchar, and a large offensive had been launched to cut off the escaping rebels from the Moroccan border.

Capitaine Lefévre had received the men with little enthusiasm; nor had his mood improved on finding that they included a young lieutenant already known to him by reputation — an Alsacian called Zimmermann who was officially on record as having kicked a man to death in Indo-China.

Earlier that evening the Lieutenant Zimmermann had reported back by radio that his patrol had found a consignment of smuggled weapons near the Moroccan border, and that he was bringing in a prisoner. Zimmermann and two of his men had been on a routine flight with a helicopter, had spotted some figures under a flare, and on landing had been attacked from a cave. One of them, who had been unarmed, had run straight into Zimmermann in the dark. He had felled the rebel with a scientific blow in the abdomen; the figure had dropped lightly, without a cry, and he had been pleasantly surprised to find himself hoisting over his shoulder the body of a girl.

She had remained unconscious till after they arrived back at the fort. They carried her across the parade square into the guard room. One of his colleagues laughed, jerking up his thumb, and said: 'Where did you find her, Lieutenant?' 'The stork brought her!' They laid her on a bench, and sponged down her face, which was like ash, and forced a brandy flask between her teeth. A corporal was told to inform the captain, who was now responsible for the prisoner. The corporal said: 'Capitaine Lefévre asked to see you as soon as you returned, lieutenant.'

'I'll see the captain here,' said Zimmermann; the corporal saluted and went out.

They left her on the bench under the naked light. Zimmermann hoisted off his webbing equipment and looked down at her. She was beginning to stir. *'Pas mal, hein?'* They had already taken her passport off her; he glanced at it again, nodding approvingly. She was even pretty in her photograph.

Lefévre entered. He looked at the body on the bench and stopped. 'So it's a girl?' He spoke with undisguised dismay. Zimmermann handed him the passport. He looked at the first page and frowned. 'Then she's not a Moslem? She has a

French name.' He looked closely at her face. 'Born in Oran.' He paused, and Zimmermann said: 'We stripped the truck down and found a pretty little collection of Red guns.'

'This girl must be sent at once to security in Algiers,' said Lefévre.

'We've plenty of time for that,' said Zimmermann. He did not bother to salute or address Lefévre as '*mon capitaine*'. 'First we've some questions to ask her.'

Lefévre looked at her and thought, *How does a pretty girl come to get muddled up in this war?* It was the sort of situation he dreaded; he was also worried about her being French. If she had been a Moslem it would have been slightly different. He looked again at Lieutenant Zimmermann — at the blunt face with blond hair chopped over a low brow — and said: 'Very well, the doctor will bring her round. When she's in a fit condition take her into the orderly room. I'll talk to her there.'

The doctor appeared in a dressing gown and took her pulse, then slapped her face and put a wet flannel on her neck. She revived slowly, her face twisted with pain. As soon as she was fully conscious she was very sick on the floor; he helped hold her head between her knees.

'Don't let the camel mess the place up!' yelled Zimmermann.

The doctor said quietly: 'Where did you hit her?' Zimmermann told him and the doctor felt her stomach and she screamed. 'You might have killed her,' he said.

'There's still time for that,' said Zimmermann. 'But keep her alive for the next few hours.'

The doctor eased her on to her feet, and said: 'You'll be all right soon.' She stared into the room, eyes glazed, trying to remember where she was. She mumbled a few words to him, and he said again: 'You'll be all right!' — helping her along the corridor into the orderly room.

He sat her in a chair and was about to give her a sedative when Zimmermann stepped between them. 'Leave that till later. We want to talk to her first.'

The doctor shrugged and snapped his case shut. 'Very well, I'll call Capitaine Lefévre,' and left the room.

The captain came and sat with his hands across the back of the chair, facing her. She noticed that they were well-kept hands, the nails cut to the quick.

'Mademoiselle, I have examined your passport. You are a French citizen of Algeria and have a visa de résidence in Morocco. We know why you are here, and it would now be in all our interests if you would answer my questions as accurately as possible.'

It was the old routine, and the captain repeated the words as though they were part of a catechism he no longer believed in. He knew from bitter experience that she would not answer — unless she were perhaps still too dazed to know what was happening. She said nothing; and he went on: 'Mademoiselle, who were the people who sent you? Who contacted you in Algeria? What are the names of the rebels here who contacted you and were to receive the arms? Who sent you?'

She said nothing. Zimmermann edged nearer and repeated: 'Who sent you? Who was to meet you this side? Was there anyone else with you?'

'Who sent you?' said Lefévre. 'Were there any others?' He felt almost disinterested, knowing it was useless.

'*Qui t'as envoye ici?*' said Zimmermann furiously. He looked at Lefévre, who was deliberately avoiding his glance, and said: 'There may be others in the area. We can smash every pocket of resistance down here if we just stop these supplies of guns.'

The captain ignored him. He looked steadily at her. 'If you do not answer me, you will be sent for trial. Do you understand that you can be shot for what you have done?'

She stared back at him, tired and terrified, the face still pinched with pain. He tried again, gently, feeling sorry for her, hating every minute of it, aware of Zimmermann's oppressive bulk close to him, knowing he should have the courage to tell the man to go to hell — that he was the commanding officer, and gave the orders.

Zimmermann took her under the chin, pulled up her head, and said: 'We haven't got time to waste asking you questions. If you won't be polite with us, we'll try something else.'

Lefévre flinched, ashamed; he could do nothing. There were standing orders forbidding torture, but they rarely questioned a few blows when a victory might be in the balance. It was not difficult weeks later to justify almost any action taken near the front. There had been a big battle in the south, and Zimmermann knew his drill. He was a useful soldier to have in Algeria.

The captain asked her the questions again, in vain. He knew that the credit would ultimately go to Zimmermann, but he was also aware that few things would damage his reputation more than failing to expose one of the arms' passages into Morocco, simply because he had been too literal to break a rule that had long been laughed at by half the French Army in Algeria.

She went on staring ahead of her. Lefévre called Zimmermann aside. 'She's still suffering from shock. Take her down to the cells and leave her there a couple of hours. Have her given some coffee and soup, and we'll hope she'll be sensible before morning.' He started towards the door. 'And I don't want her touched while I'm out.' Zimmermann watched him go, without saluting.

Back in his room Lefévre lay down and tried to sleep.

This was not the kind of war he understood. He had been trained to enjoy the trappings of an honourable profession. There had been the time, many years ago, when he had woken to a barrack square ringing with bugle calls, smelling of hay and horses; then later, evenings at the officers' club in Saigon, and parading in blue and white before the boulevard cafés in Sidi Bel Abbes. Then London in 1940, rallying with De Gaulle in the defence of civilisation. Even the terrible glory of Dien Bien Phu. And now here was this wretched girl downstairs, muddling everything up, throwing the mechanism of war into confusion and disrepute. He was exasperated with her, disturbed by her fragile prettiness exposed to brutes like Zimmermann.

He could not sleep. At four o'clock he got up, ran a dry razor over his black stubble, and went down again into the orderly room.

Zimmermann was sitting at the table drinking canned beer with two paratroop NCO's. One was a big man with an oily face and lips like bicycle pedals. The other was younger and smoked a curved briar pipe; Lefévre noticed with distaste that his nose was thick with blackheads. He looked sallow but tough.

They stood up and the two NCO's replaced their berets. Again neither of them saluted. Zimmermann said to Lefévre: 'The camel talks a lot, but not what we want to hear. She's been saying some very impolite things about us.' He grinned. 'She doesn't seem to like the French.'

Lefévre cursed and led the way down again to the cells. The big NCO with the oily face had a bamboo parade stick in his hand. Zimmermann called the guard, who unlocked one of the doors.

She was sitting on the bed, elbows on her knees, still staring in front of her.

'She didn't drink her soup,' said Zimmermann.

'Leave till I call you,' said Lefévre. The door closed and he sat on the edge of the bed.

'Mademoiselle, I understand you very well,' he began. 'I have been in Algeria now for five years. I am fully conscious of the problem here. You believe that you are helping to fight for a better life for the Algerian people. But I am a soldier. I see the other side of the problem. There will be no good life for anyone in Algeria until the terrorism is stopped. Nobody wants this war. We are here to help the Algerians.'

She turned her eyes slowly towards him. 'What do you want?' she said.

'I want you to answer my questions. I want to know who sent you into Algeria with these guns and whom you arranged to meet here.'

'I will tell you nothing.'

He leant a little closer to her. 'Mademoiselle, I speak in confidence now. The lieutenant who talked to you is not a gentle person. I want to prevent unnecessary unpleasantness for us all.'

She looked at him again, this time with a faint smile that was also a sneer. 'You are so respectable it is grotesque,' she said. 'All you want, old man, is to protect your little bourgeois sensibilities!' Her eyes had come alive. 'They kicked you out of Indo-China, they kicked you out of Morocco, and one day we are going to kick you out of Algeria! And now all you can do is threaten girls. What a nation!'

He had stood up, clenching his fists at the seams of his trousers, and opened the door. He called out: 'Lieutenant, here!' Zimmermann appeared with the NCO's. 'She's trying to play the comedy with us. I have tolerated enough. I want you to question her and get the answers.'

He suddenly spoke with an authority which impressed Zimmermann, who said: 'I'll have what we want in ten minutes.' He signalled to the big NCO, who handed him the bamboo parade stick.

'You are not to mark her,' said Lefévre quickly, making a futile gesture with his hand as though warding off a fly. Zimmermann smiled. *'Mon capitaine,'* he said, with mock respect, 'what do we do? Put her head in a bucket of salt water?' He turned to her: 'Would you like that, camel? Or shall we piss on you?'

'That's enough,' said Lefévre, reddening.

She remained impassive. Zimmermann went and stood opposite her. 'You had a nice collection of medicines with you on that truck,' he said. She didn't realise for a moment that he was referring to Bates' medicine chest. He turned to Lefévre. 'Enough to cure the whole of Pigalle. The little girl's a whore — a sick little whore.' She did not move. Lefévre stepped up to her and said bitterly: 'Why must this continue? Why can you not be more sensible with us?'

Zimmermann cracked the parade stick into the palm of his hand. 'We'll treat this as a private affair, *mon capitaine* — teach the camel a lesson she should have been given a long time ago.' He spat on the floor in front of her, treading the lob in with the toe of his boot.

Lefévre made a last effort. 'Mademoiselle, if you will tell us what we wish to know I can perhaps arrange for you to have a safe conduct out of the country. A French prison is not a pleasant place for a young girl.'

'I will tell you nothing,' she said.

He looked at her for a moment, his mouth sunk grimly, sorrowfully, suddenly wondering whether the leaders in Paris and Cairo really knew what it was all like. At his side Zimmermann stood watching him, waiting for him to give the order; but when Lefévre said nothing more the lieutenant signalled to the two NCO's. The big one grabbed her and threw her face down on the bed and sat on her shoulders. Zimmermann leant down and pulled off her jeans and cotton pants, swiftly and impersonally, as though he were undressing himself, while the younger NCO knocked out his pipe against the wall, then sat astride her naked calves.

She began to wriggle and beat her fists against the top of the bed. Zimmermann said: 'You're very immodest, little girl. And you're not going to be pretty when we've finished, unless you be good and tell us everything.' He suddenly brought the parade stick down with a loud dry crack across her buttocks. She let out a gasp and her body bucked violently under the weight of the two paratroopers, then began to shudder all over.

Lefévre had looked away and was fumbling for a packet of Caporals. 'Can you not be more delicate, lieutenant?'

Zimmermann lowered the stick. 'Then what do you suggest, *mon capitaine*? We don't have scalpomine in the fort. We don't have time to argue with her. And they won't show her arse to the magistrates, don't worry.'

Lefévre lit the cigarette unsteadily and looked down at her. She lay with her face and knuckles pressed against the blanket, the back of her head shaken with sobs. He watched the welt swelling and darkening across the curves of dear flesh, with pricks of blood breaking out under the skin where the notches of the bamboo had fallen. He wished only that he could feel the same detached ruthlessness as Zimmermann; she upset his conception of the FLN as a gang of bandits and savages. Looking at her he felt his career being sullied; yet he knew that before he reported her capture in the morning it was his absolute duty to find the source of the guns and the rebel contacts inside Algeria.

Zimmermann grinned at him and said: 'She has a pretty little body.'

Lefévre turned angrily away. 'I permit only the minimum of violence. And you are not to interfere with her.'

Zimmermann said: 'We wouldn't do that, *mon capitaine*. It might give her pleasure.' One of the NCO's laughed, and Lefévre walked out into the passage. As the door slammed behind him he heard the stick come down again and she cried out: 'De Gaulle has forbidden torture!' '*On s'en fou de De Gaulle!*' said Zimmermann, striking her again, and this time she screamed.

Lefévre walked quickly away. Her cries were now muffled. The big NCO on her shoulders had pushed a crumpled khaki handkerchief into her mouth. She tried to spit it out, when the next blow fell, slicing into her, flesh hot and cracking, searing up her spine and rippling out through her whole body, with her belly crushed against the coarse blanket and the breath forced between her teeth into the lump of damp khaki. The Zimmermann's voice was saying: 'Who sent you here? What are their names? Do they belong to the willaya? He always repeated the questions three times, in a slow flat voice. Then there came a pause. She struggled to take a deep breath and her shoulders and chest ached under the weight of the big NCO;

150

she tried to move her legs and felt the muscles growing numb. Zimmermann repeated the last question, and she thought frantically whether any of the men did in fact belong to a willaya; here in the south FLN organisation was very bad. The stick came down again with a noise like a high wind, and the air burst red and black before her eyes, and she felt as though her legs were being slowly severed from her body.

Zimmermann said again: 'What are the names of the people who sent you here?' He stood with the bamboo poised a few inches above her, absolutely steady.

Outside, Capitaine Lefévre had walked to the end of the passage, up into the corridor above where he passed the radio room. There was music coming from behind the closed door; he recognised Smetana's suite, *Vltava*. He stepped in and saw a very young conscript sitting by the two-way set, earphones on the table, listening to a portable transistor. The boy came clattering to attention and Lefévre shouted: 'What happens if a message comes through, and you're listening to a concert?'

The soldier switched off the music and mumbled something, handing Lefévre a piece of paper with a scrawled note in pencil. One of the Mystère fighters had been hit by rebel fire and was losing fuel; the pilot was trying to get back to Talifit. 'If he radios that he's going to make a crash-landing,' said Lefévre, 'report directly to Lieutenant Marziou. Now put on those earphones and keep awake!'

There was no sound now in the passage outside the cells. Lefévre went in and saw that she had fainted. Zimmermann was forcing the brandy flask between her teeth and she began to choke. The younger NCO had got off her legs and was relighting his pipe, and the little cell quickly filled with the dense smell of black shag.

'She won't say a word,' said Zimmermann, almost sadly. She came round moaning, and he lifted her head by the hair so that Lefévre could look at her. Her nose was running and the handkerchief lay soaked where her head had been lying.

The captain looked steadily at the wall above her and began his catechism of questions over again. She lay below him and said nothing. Zimmermann had flogged her with precision, laying on the strokes exactly one against the other, careful never to split the skin. Her body was now splayed out like a rag doll, swollen and shivering and racked with little spasms which the captain tried to ignore as he went on through his questions. As he finished she turned her head and spat across his trousers. He took out a handkerchief and flicked off the little globules, then said thoughtfully to Zimmermann: 'This girl is not going to talk.'

The lieutenant's face was heavy and furious; he muttered something and brought the stick down with all his strength diagonally across the ridges of flesh; she shrieked and writhed, and he watched the beads of blood seep slowly up where the welts crossed. Lefévre said quietly: 'This is useless.'

The two NCO's were standing now, and the four of them made an awkward little squad round the door. Zimmermann spoke to the two NCO's who saluted and left the cell. The he turned to Lefévre and said casually: '*Mon Capitaine*, there is no reason why you should trouble yourself until this matter is finished.'

Lefévre said: 'I want to be informed as soon as she is ready to talk. And it is essential that none of my men hear of what is happening.'

'You can rely on me,' said Zimmermann, and for the first time he saluted. Lefévre went back to his room, to his military reports and old group photographs from the academy of Saint

Cyr and his bound volumes of Claudel and Barres; while Lieutenant Zimmermann rejoined the two NCO's at the top of the stairs. The big one was carrying a black metal box with two lead terminals and a handle on one side. The second paratrooper, his curved pipe still between his teeth, had a coil of wire in his hand. Zimmermann gestured back towards the cells. Inside she lay just as they had left her, eyes closed and crying. Zimmermann hoisted her up and sat her painfully on the edge of the bed.

The three of them went to work with an efficiency that suggested professional routine. The metal box was placed on the floor between her legs. The second NCO unravelled the wire, broke it into two strands which he screwed to the terminals on the box, then took from his pocket a pair of serrated crocodile clips, which he fastened firmly to the other two ends of the wire. Then he handed the clips to Zimmermann.

At the same moment the younger NCO leapt on to the bed and grasped her fiercely under the throat; she tried to struggle, but he increased his grip until she grew limp. Zimmermann was holding one of the crocodile clips; he leant over her with the care of a doctor, swiftly parting her thighs and clipping the wire between her legs. She flinched and twisted under the grip at her throat; then he picked up the second clip and lifted her shirt.

She opened her eyes wide and began to scream. Zimmermann looked at her sternly, without any apparent viciousness; he said quietly: 'You know what will happen. This is the worst thing that can be done to you. The Germans did it to members of the French Resistance — to people much braver than you.' She did not seem to hear him. 'They always talked,' he said; then added, close to her ear: 'This can stop you ever having children.'

Her hands flashed down to her groin, but Zimmermann was too quick for her. He grabbed both her wrists and handed them to the big NCO. Then he leant down and took hold of the handle of the black box.

He began to turn it slowly and methodically. At first she closed her eyes and gave a little low moan, and her body stiffened and trembled. He started to turn the handle faster.

He turned it three times, very quickly, with a whirring noise, and suddenly her body arched and sprang forward, knocking him backwards against the wall, dragging the two NCO's half across the cell. The one with his arm round her throat was pulled over her shoulders, his pipe knocked to the floor; and the one holding her wrists slipped and fell against the side of the bed.

Her screams were trapped and amplified in the tiny stone cell. Both the clips had been torn from her body and lay trailing on the floor. 'Hold her fast!' yelled Zimmermann. The two NCO's were now lying almost on top of her; she writhed and screamed, while Zimmermann picked up the clips and fastened them back on.

This time, after he began to turn the handle, it was soon over. The NCO's were at first swung backwards and forwards like men trying to hold on to a bucking horse. It always amazed Zimmermann how strong a fragile human body could be. Then suddenly she slumped forward, shaking with hysterics, screaming for them to kill her, promising that she would tell them everything.

Zimmermann ordered the younger NCO to send for Lefévre and the garrison doctor. They laid her out on her back, and the big NCO scowled down at her and said, 'She's fouled up the bed!' Zimmermann dragged the blanket from under her and tossed it into a corner.

The doctor came in behind Lefévre, glanced at her and winced, then looked at the captain, and the expression between them conveyed nothing. Zimmermann began collecting the equipment off the floor. Lefévre took out his pocketbook, and the doctor sent for a bowl of hot water and some cotton wool. Then the captain began to put the questions to her once again, this time very slowly, almost kindly.

As soon as she began to talk she told them everything, even things that they had not asked her for: she told them about Izard and the trips south and the name of every FLN agent she knew in Morocco and Algeria; and she gave them Quinn's name, and said that she thought he was still alive and down in the desert, and then she became hysterical again, begging them to kill her.

Lefévre was exhausted. His collar was clinging with sweat as he wrote down every detail in his small neat handwriting, trying to ignore the doctor who was taking swabs of blood and discharge from between her legs and putting dressings on her buttocks. Then, when it was all over, they wrapped her in a towel and carried her up to the sickbay, where Lefévre ordered her to be confined under guard. The doctor gave her a sedative and joined Lefévre in his room. Zimmermann was already having the information sent on the teleprinter to Algiers.

The doctor said that she would be ready to be moved in about twenty-four hours.

'There's a convoy going north tomorrow night,' said the captain. 'She can go on that. And I'll recommend that she gets a safe conduct back to Morocco. There are enough people in gaol up there already, without adding to them.' The doctor made no comment.

Later that morning a squad of officers in the air-conditioned block in Algiers, which contains the headquarters of internal and military security for the Department of Algeria, were preparing orders for the arrest of several FLN agents known to be operating in the south-west of the country.

The officers also drew up a report on a Moroccan industrialist, Sebastien Izard, to be handed through diplomatic channels to the Moroccan Government in Rabat.

CHAPTER 2

Rupert Quinn was lost. Struggling to the top of a hill, on to a plain that stretched through the first pallor of dawn to a line of hills twenty or thirty miles away.

He had been going for more than five hours now: running, slowing to a walk, running again, collapsing to rest, moving in a great circle. At first he had been too confused to care where he was going. Later he had tried to follow the stars and could make no sense of them. Then the sun began to come up and he found he was running east, away from the border, further into Algeria.

But at least he felt better now without the gun. Somehow the moment of flinging that evil gadget away seemed to have cut him loose from the shock of the killing. He stumbled on, not thinking about it, deliberately driving his body to exhaustion, forcing his mind away from Bates and Leila.

He knew the French had taken her. They'd put her in prison to await decent trial. Here he allowed him imagination to stop: to remember only that the French are a civilised nation. Subtle, logical, with a flair for good taste and good living. If it had been the other way round, of course — a pretty young French girl falling into the hands of the FLN. But the French were safe. They were allies. He wondered if it would be any good trying to help her through the British Consulate, in Casablanca. Write to *The Times*; appeal to the Foreign Office; stimulate some popular newspaper to come haring out to the aid of a retired gun-runner trying to rescue his rebel bride-to-be from the hands of the French paras.

The plain was lighting up, brown and empty, seared with the stony beds of rivers that would trickle a few weeks of the year, every year for millions of years, and Quinn was just a tiny speck moving wearily across the plain, caught in a moment of history, in a cruel conflict between nationalism and pride and ignorance and delusions of grandeur.

He sank on to a rock. A smudge of smoke drifted slowly, almost imperceptibly, across the edge of the sky. In the night he had run again and again through the ugly smell of burning, past whole hills charred cinder-black with Napalm. Once he thought he had seen a ditch full of bodies. And now the planes — the low-flying bombers and the swift little singing Mystères — were all around on the horizon, where the fighting still flared; but here on the plain everything was a primeval nothingness.

He sat on the rock, with his head dropping between his knees.

The sun was hot on his neck when he woke. He had dreamt about Bates, alive and kicking, with his bush hat and bottle of booze. He would be lying now in the sepulchre under the rock: four Algerians, one Australian and Jean-Paul Hérault from Arles. He wondered how long it would take to find them. Who would bury them. Would it be the rebels who came, or the French? Or just the creatures of the desert?

Proud soldiers in their white képis, he thought. Young pilots in the Mystères, pushing buttons, watching the bombs flame and crackle — high and fast and away from it all. And the well-groomed political PRO's on the Quai d'Orsay, ankle-deep in carpet, sipping iced water in front of the resident correspondents, giving the routine bulletin. A new French offensive in the south-west. Three, four, five hundred FLN dead. French losses as yet uncertain. And who cleans it up?

Buries them? Keeps the stench down before it blows across the Mediterranean and upsets the bikinied beauties on the Riviera?

Above the far-off drone of aircraft he now heard another sound. Two or three miles behind him the dust was rising against the sun. He stood up shielding his eyes, watching it come gradually nearer, moving about a thousand yards to his right. He began to run towards it, suddenly desperate. If he missed them he would be alone here forever.

He kept on, and the more he ran, the faster the dust seemed to move. He reached them just in time: an armoured car out in front, two jeeps and an ambulance with red crosses on its sides, back and roof. He stood waving for a moment, then wobbled and sat down. A helmet popped up from the armoured car; below, through the slats, a machine-gun barrel swivelled and lined up his head in its sights. The armoured car came within a few yards of him, then ground to a halt, its engines throbbing across the desert. One of the jeeps came round the side to it and two soldiers jumped down. They were both bareheaded with their belts off. One was very fat, his stomach sagging under the sweat-soaked khaki like cheese in a bag. The other was a dark pleasant-looking boy carrying a Sten gun.

They helped Quinn to his feet. He managed to get his passport out and muttered, 'I'm English. I'm lost.' The fat man took the passport, glanced through it without interest, then wiped the sweat from his face.

'Englishman, *hein?*' He spoke with the accent des faubourgs, like boots crunching on coke.

'I'm a journalist,' said Quinn; 'I got lost. Where am I?'

The fat soldier laughed. He called to the young one: 'He wants to know where he is!' He flipped back through the passport, looking as though he'd never seen one before. 'So you're a journalist?' he repeated. 'You write, *hein?*'

There was a shout from the second jeep: 'We can't stay here all day. Get him aboard!'

The fat one said: 'Which newspaper do you write for, Englishman?'

'*The Times*,' Quinn lied, '*Le Temps*.'

'*Le Temps*,' the soldier repeated, pulling a stupid face. There was another shout; they took him by the arm and led him over to the jeep. He sat between the fat one, who was driving and was called Gaston, and the young man, Maurice, who came from the Midi and was in high spirits because he had only three weeks more of his military service. Neither of them seemed interested enough to discover that he had no Algerian visa or military pass. Maurice offered him water and dates and cigarettes, talking with the twanging Midi accent. They treated him as though they'd all just met at a football match. Gaston kept turning to him and slapping him on the arm: '*Un beau pays, l'Angleterre, hein?* Churchill, brave type!' He gave a mock salute, spitting out a charred stub of cigarette from his lower lip. 'So Englishman, what do you think of this sacred country, Algeria? *Putain d'endroit! Tous les arabes, rat-tat-tat, comme les Allemands!*' He mowed them down with his forefinger. 'Give me Paris every time.'

Maurice grinned. 'The Midi's better. In Paris the life is too fast.'

'Paris is all the world,' said Gaston, breaking into the first two lines of a song. Maurice sat with his gun on his lap. Gaston broke off and said: 'When we get into the hills, Englishman, we have to pay attention to the road. You're a journalist — you keep your eyes open. The Arabs put down bombs and traps. We hit one of them — pouff!'

Maurice said: 'War's a dirty business.'

They didn't enquire how he happened to be so far south, but they were also canny enough not to tell him exactly where they were going. They just said they were driving to a post in the north, then later making for Colomb Béchar. Quinn asked them if they had anything to do with the paras. Gaston made a rude face and thumped his elbow: 'They're swine, *les paras*! Gestapo.' Maurice smiled: 'You stay with the poor conscripts like me. We're a nicer lot.'

They had reached the end of the plain; the sun was now high and the boulders shining white. They began to climb into the hills, then into rust-red mountains. Far out to the east they heard the occasional boom of artillery and planes flashed in the sunlight. Quinn began to fall asleep between them, but Gaston prodded him. 'Keep awake, Englishman! We have to watch the road.'

At noon they stopped in the mountains and lunched out of tins. And as they sprawled in the shade of the jeep Quinn thought about Leila. He closed his eyes, letting the talk of the soldiers drift away and seeing her coming in off the balcony, dusky-brown out of the sunlight with a scarf knotted across her breasts.

Gaston touched him with his boot. 'You sleep all day! There's a war on.'

Maurice was saying: 'Twenty days and I'll be drinking Ricard and have a good roll with a little Niçoise.'

'Maurice is a randy dog!' laughed Gaston, and cuffed the boy over the ear. 'He doesn't get it out here in Algeria.' Later they passed two veiled women on mules, and he waved at them, and they kicked at the beasts and jogged away. 'Disgusting women out here,' he said, 'never wash — full of microbes!'

They followed the winding roads, with the flanks of the mountains growing richer, now speckled silvery-green with olive trees; and there were villages on the slopes, and donkeys and birds and white jellabahs down in the valleys. They began to leave the mountains late in the afternoon. Quinn lay back and basked in the slanting sun, and thought of how he would go straight to the commanding officer of the nearest French garrison and demand to be taken to Algiers. There he'd plead that he loved Leila and wanted to marry her. He began to enjoy the doubtful hope that the French would be sympathetic; as a people they were reputed to be more imaginative in dealing with matters of the heart than most nations. After all, Leila wasn't going to lose them the war.

Maurice and Gaston were singing an obscene ballad out of tune. Quinn dozed off, and this time Gaston let him sleep. When he woke twilight was falling and they were well beyond the mountains, driving along a straight road across the Bled. There were more planes flying near, and the smell of trees and dung and petrol. It was like coming to the end of a sea voyage and catching the first scents of dry land.

The convoy turned off about a mile in front of the town. They passed a notice marked 'RF Zone Militaire'. Beside the road stretched rows of tank-traps, regular as concrete teeth, and tangles of barbed wire scattered across the sand like tumbleweed. Ahead rose the silhouette of a fort with the tricolor flag high above the crenellated tower. There were sentry boxes and nests of mortars and machine-guns walled up in sandbags. The soldiers saluted idly. There were more sentries at the gate, where each vehicle had to surrender its papers. A group of soldiers gathered round the jeep, examining

Quinn's passport. Gaston shouted to the NCO: 'He's an Englishman — a journalist. We picked him up in the Guir.'

The NCO called Quinn down. A bar swung up and the convoy was waved through. They led him aside, not even giving him enough time to thank Gaston and Maurice. He was taken through a side door to the fort. The passages were brightly lit with bulbs in wire cages. They came to a guardroom where De Gaulle stared severely down at them from a colour photograph over the door.

The NCO now disappeared with Quinn's passport, and for a moment he was left alone. He felt tired and grubby, with a bad taste in his mouth; and was just thinking of asking someone where the washroom was, when three men marched in.

He recognised the familiar leopard uniforms. One of them was strapped across with a belt of sharp machine-gun rounds, gleaming golden under the electric light. Without a word they grabbed his arms and hustled him out of the door, down a corridor. 'What's happening?' he cried. They came to a room with chairs round the wall, and sat him down and stood close round him saying nothing.

'What am I here for?'

'You'll find out,' said one of them.

An officer came in. He signalled to the paratroopers to draw back, then stood for fully ten seconds studying Quinn, balancing the passport between his finger and thumb as though it were something not quite clean. Finally, he sat astride a chair, facing him.

'Rupert Quinn?' He spoke quietly. 'I understand one of our convoys picked you up in the desert this morning?'

'I was lost.'

'It's a bad place to go wandering about in. People should be more careful when they come to a country like this.' He began turning over the pages of the passport.

Quinn said cautiously: 'I'm very grateful to your men. I might have died if they hadn't found me.' He tried a small laugh, and the Frenchman said: 'You might indeed, Monsieur Quinn.' He suddenly put the passport away. 'You are a journalist, I see. With which newspaper, please?'

Quinn repeated the lie about *The Times* and the officer gave him a thin smile. 'Have you credentials to prove this?'

'I lost them.' He was beginning to sweat now.

'And your entry permit into Algeria.' The officer raised his eyebrows. 'Did you lose that too? Or perhaps you never had one?'

'I was working in Morocco. I went down to the border to write a story and I got lost.'

The officer watched him coolly, his fingers aligned along the top of the chair-back. Quinn added: 'There's no proper border down there. Anyone can get lost.'

The officer nodded. 'You are lying. You are not a journalist. You work for a Moroccan called Izard. A racketeer. A gangster.' Quinn sat studying the shiny holster on the man's hip. 'How do you know all this?' he asked.

'We have one of your colleagues with us.'

'Where is she?' He started up from his chair, but one of the paratroopers pushed him roughly back. 'What have you done with her?' he shouted.

'She goes to Algiers tonight to stand court martial.' The officer did not look at Quinn as he spoke. 'I tried to arrange a safe-conduct for her to leave the country. Girls like that should not get involved in war.'

'What happened?'

'The authorities refused.' He suddenly rounded on Quinn, his face stiff with controlled fury. 'Why don't you damned foreigners keep out of our affairs? We don't interfere with your problems. You British and Americans are not so perfect. What makes you want to support the rebels? What do you know about Algeria? Do you think we send out French to help your enemies in Cyprus and Kenya? What has this war got to do with you?' He paused, shaking slightly. 'Or perhaps you do it as a quick way of making money? Selling guns so that decent young men can get killed! Your type are below any rebel — below vermin!' Then he called Quinn a name that was not part of his usual vocabulary.

'I'd have helped the girl,' he added; 'she at least had courage — she did it for something she believed in. What do you believe in?' Quinn stared at the floor and said nothing. 'I'll see you get a minimum of five years. And don't think the British will help you. They won't!'

He turned and strode out of the room. Quinn yelled after him: 'What have you done with her? Where is she?'

'On your feet!' said one of the paratroopers. They lifted him under the arms and marched him briskly out, holding him so that his toes skimmed the floor, down a flight of steps into a passage lined with cells. They barked his shins purposely on one of the doors as they opened it, tipping him in on his face.

There was a bed with one blanket, a bucket in the corner, and a high barred window with a light beyond that shone into the cell. Crouched at the top of the bed was a Moslem, his head shaved and his body wrapped in what looked like pieces of grey rag. Quinn saw that one side of his face was swollen with a bruise like a plum. The man was staring silently at him,

165

obviously puzzled that a European should have been made to share his cell.

Quinn picked himself up and sat on the tip of the bed away from the Moslem, who cringed further into the corner.

He looked round the cell. Almost every inch of the stone had been scratched with slogans, mostly in Arabic. Next to his head someone had written in tall capitals, '*SALAN ENCULE-TOI!*' He realised that all he had left, besides his clothes, was his watch and belt containing seven thousand Moroccan francs. Hardly enough to bribe his way out.

The Moslem on the bed had not stirred. Quinn glanced at him again, noticing now that the man's nostrils were dark with blood. He thought of Leila, wondering vaguely how they had made her talk. There had been no reason why she should have told them about him; they need never have known his name if she had only kept her mouth shut. *Stupid bitch*, he thought.

The Moslem's eyes never left him. He got up and began walking round the cell, his sandals clacking on the stone. He thought of England: rain and rush hours and the smell of gasworks. *You wanted adventure, Quinn. Escape from tired crumpled people drinking tea and queueing up whey-faced for buses that splash out into suburbs of black brick and wet washing.*

The Moslem shifted his legs suddenly and groaned. His eyes were closed now. Quinn thought of prison. Five years. Nearly two thousand days and nights, being banged up in the grey of the morning, shaving with a pebble of soap and rusty blade, and the stench of the buckets after a whole cell had used them, and long grim lines of men in corridors of white tile, with no girls or cafés or theatres for five years. No Leila, sleeping with her knee tucked between his thighs; combing out her black hair with a crackle in front of the balcony windows.

He stopped and began pounding on the cell door. There were footsteps outside and the spyhole clicked open. A voice said: 'What's the matter with you?'

'Where is the commanding officer?'

'You go to sleep,' said the voice. The Moslem had opened his eyes and was staring terrified at the door.

'I want to speak to the commanding officer!' Quinn shouted, and the footsteps went away. He went on hammering and yelling, and a few moment later the bolts were shot back and a soldier stood in front of him swinging a ring of keys. 'Young man, go to sleep.'

'I can't sleep with that light on.'

The soldier looked up at the light, then at the Moslem on the bed, and said: 'The light stays on all night. It's always on.' He turned round. 'Now go to sleep.'

'I want something to eat.'

'I can't give you anything,' said the soldier; 'it's not my job.' He began to close the door.

'I demand to speak to the commanding officer!'

'You cannot speak to him now,' said the soldier, and closed the door.

'I want to telephone the British Consulate!' He banged and shouted, but this time nobody came. He had just begun to kick the door when he heard a noise behind him.

The Moslem was standing up, swaying slightly with one arm outstretched. Quinn stopped kicking and went slowly back to the bed. After a moment the Arab sank down on to the floor in the corner next to the bucket.

Quinn waited perhaps ten minutes, but the man did not move again; his eyes were now closed and he was breathing heavily and unevenly. Quinn pulled the blanket over himself, but it was too short to cover his feet. It became very cold in the cell. He lay exhausted but wide awake, longing for sleep and unable to sleep, taut and strained and waiting for something to happen.

He turned his face to the wall and listened to the Moslem's thick, broken breathing.

CHAPTER 3

It was past one o'clock. There were more footsteps in the corridor. The bolts shot back once again and two paratroopers came in. 'Get up!'

'Where to?'

'Get up!' They pulled him off the bed and he rolled on to the floor, his legs tangled up in the blanket. 'Don't be so bloody impatient!' he muttered. They led him down the passage and out into the parade square. There were arc lamps lighting up the walls and he saw the ambulance and one of the jeeps that had come with the convoy the day before. In front of the ambulance was an army truck. The tailboard was down and the two paratroopers on either side of him pushed him up into the back. A couple of soldiers climbed in after him. He looked round and saw Gaston and Maurice. One of the paras slammed up the tailboard and secured it, and the motor started.

'I thought you were both with the jeep,' he said.

Gaston grinned. 'They thought we'd have more fun travelling with you.' He turned to Maurice. 'So our English journalist's a friend of the Arabs.'

One of the paras called from outside: 'He was running guns in for the rebels.'

'*Espéce de con*,' said Maurice.

'And I get told off by the captain for not having been more careful,' said Gaston, shaking his head. 'If I'd known I'd have put a bullet through his head.'

The truck began to move. Quinn sat between them in the middle of the floor. At the front, against the driver's cabin, were several jerrycans of petrol which began to rattle noisily.

'Running guns in for the rebels,' repeated Maurice thoughtfully. '*Ç'est un vrai salaud!*' They passed through the gates, out on to the concrete road. The ambulance was following at about fifty yards.

'Where are we going?' said Quinn.

'*Ta gueule!*' Gaston growled, and got up and pulled the canvas flaps shut, while Maurice turned up a hurricane lamp.

'All nice and cosy, Englishman,' said Gaston, sitting down again. 'Now tell us about it! What's the life like with the Moslem swine?'

'Where are we going?' said Quinn again.

'You're very curious, Englishman.'

'He's dumb,' said Maurice.

'I'll tell you where you're going. Up for the tribunal. For the firing squad.' Gaston smiled and took out a pair of handcuffs.

'Those aren't necessary,' said Quinn, 'I'm not going to escape.'

'Put your hands behind your back.'

'Put them on on the front,' said Quinn.

'Turn round!' He started to turn and Gaston hit him on the side of the face. He fell against the sideboards of the truck, and they hit him again, three times. The handcuffs were snapped on and he heard Gaston say, softly and distantly: 'You do what we want, Englishman! Now tell us about the rebels. What's it like down there with the scum of the earth?'

He didn't speak for a moment. The side of his face was blowing up like a balloon. He lifted his head. The truck was moving fast down the flat, straight road. Gaston said: 'Tell us about life with the rebels, Englishman!'

'Did you see them mutilating French soldiers?' Maurice asked. They both edged a little closer. 'I didn't see anything,' said Quinn. He turned away from them, and they spun him round and Gaston hit him hard in the left eye.

'Did you help them ambush a few convoys?'

His legs were out in front of him and his head down near his knees. Blood was dribbling on to his trousers.

'Perhaps you killed a few Frenchmen?' said Maurice. Gaston lifted his head and hit him again.

He screamed: 'My eye! You put my eye out!' The words sounded odd, as though he was speaking through layers of rubber. His left eye was closing up. 'Are you a Communist?' said Gaston, after a moment.

He managed to say: 'You bastards have put out my eye!'

'You're not blind,' said Gaston.

His good eye was weeping down his face and there was a salty taste of blood and mucous in his throat. 'Where's the girl?' he asked. 'There was a girl too.'

'She's in the ambulance,' said Gaston. 'She goes to the firing squad with you.'

They both laughed.

The inside of the truck suddenly smelt of Gauloises: the raw, gritty smell even penetrated the blood-choked ducts of his nose. 'Give me a cigarette,' he said feebly.

'He asked for a cigarette!' said Gaston.

'What happened to the girl?'

'Never mind. The paras took care of her.'

'What did they do to her?'

'They gave her what she deserved. Now shut up! We're tired of you.'

'Tell me what they did to her.' They didn't answer. 'One thing I will say to you,' he said; 'you give your prisoners a sporting chance. First a girl, then someone with handcuffs on.'

'Be quiet,' said Gaston. He winked at Maurice. 'He's very talkative, our English journalist.'

'He's not pretty,' said Maurice.

'We ought to do his other eye for him, too.' Gaston poked at the weeping eye with his forefinger. Quinn flinched away. 'You fat bastard!'

'Listen to him! Now he's insulting me.'

'You're too fat to be a soldier,' Quinn went. 'I thought they had their best men out here in Algeria. And they get specimens like you…'

'You're being a bore, Englishman,' said Gaston. He took his cigarette from his mouth and stubbed it out on the floor. 'You talk too much,' he said, and shifted up and swung his fist. Quinn ducked and the blow caught him on the shoulder. He tried to move again but Gaston was too quick for him. He threw his weight against him and banged Quinn's head against the floor. Then he hit him in the mouth and again in the left eye. Somewhere he heard Maurice say: 'Better leave him.' Gaston hit him once more, in the stomach. His knees hunched up and breath went out of him, making a creaking sound between his teeth like an old door being slowly eased open.

It was over. For a moment he was suffocating. He couldn't get the breath back into his lungs and his chest felt as though it were going to burst. He tried opening his good eye. There was a spear of light and blobs rising and falling like bubbles. He moved the muscles in his face and the blood cracked and flaked off.

They were both talking about bicycle racing. He listened for what seemed a very long time. Gaston was complaining that

Bonnard was sure to win; he had better wind. Maurice disagreed; there was still no one to beat Metz. Quinn muttered: 'I never heard of either of them.'

'*Ta gueule!*' said Gaston. In his opinion Bonnard was better on the longer stretches; that's where he had the advantage over Metz. Maurice still disagreed. Quinn said: 'I thought Coppi was champion.'

'Coppi's Italian,' said Maurice.

'What, with a name like that! I thought he was Chinese.'

'Don't talk to him,' said Gaston. 'He's a fool.'

'Whoever heard,' said Quinn, 'of a people who had bicycling as their first national sport?'

Gaston lifted his fist, and Maurice said again: 'No, leave him. His head's going.'

Gaston shrugged. '*Mais il est bien barbant!*'

'You're not being friendly,' said Quinn. 'You were much nicer yesterday.'

'We're bored with you,' said Gaston. 'You're not very interesting to talk to.'

'But I thought you both wanted to hear about life with the FLN?' They didn't answer. 'It's a terrible pity you put these handcuffs on. If I ever get you alone without them —' He broke off and felt dizzy. His head was filling with pain and his eye felt as though something were sticking through it.

The truck was grinding into low gear; they were turning sharp bends and there was a heaviness in his legs which told him that they were climbing steeply. Gaston and Maurice were still debating the virtues of Bonnard and Metz.

'Do you like horse racing?' he asked.

'Shut up,' said Gaston, without much force.

'No, really, I'd like to talk to you both. Pass the time. I'd like to discuss this sport of bicycling.'

'*Il est cinglé*,' said Maurice.

'I'm being serious with you. Perhaps I could learn something from you —'

There was a shuddering crack. The air seemed to be blown right out of the truck, then came blasting back, sucking the canvas roof in with it. He lay half-stunned, his head in the lap of the canvas, his back against the sideboards. One arm rested against a wooden wall. It was the floor of the truck. He tried to move. His back felt bruised and his handcuffed hands were numb. He sat up. At first he could hear nothing but a loud humming inside his head. The truck had stopped.

He began to shuffle sideways and his foot touched something soft. It was a body. He stepped carefully over it and pulled up one of the canvas flaps. With his good eye he watched a jeep burning briskly; the ribs of the hood were buckling in the heat. One of his ears popped and roared with noise.

He dropped the flap shut and tried to move back along the narrow sideboards; but with his hands locked behind him he lost his balance and toppled into the canvas hood. It caught him like a safety net.

The inside of the truck was full of dust and petrol fumes. At the back the hurricane lamp was still alight. He struggled up and crept on a few more feet and touched the body again. It was Maurice. He was upside down, one leg against the tilted floor, the other twisted underneath him. The foot poked out at an odd angle, as though it belonged to someone else. Quinn thought he heard the boy give a tiny groan.

He moved further inside and found Gaston. His fat body lay against the driver's cabin, broken under the weight of the jerrycans. One of them had split and drenched his legs with petrol.

Quinn knelt down and tried to fumble for the keys of the handcuffs. Somebody was tapping on the little window into the driver's cabin. He looked up, just as a volley of bullets ripped through the canvas, striking blue sparks off the steel wall. He stumbled hurriedly back along the boards, coughing with dust. The petrol fumes were making his head reel.

He fell through the canvas flaps. The ground was trembling, the night full of flashes and shouts and bangs and dancing figures, like a fiesta. He picked himself up and began to run. The handcuffs made him feel bent and crippled, waddling clumsily down the road. The truck was perhaps twenty yards behind him. He turned his head in time to see a little man in a turban coming at him with a knife; his mouth was open as though he were laughing, and his eyes had a wild, happy look. He jumped. Quinn did a half-somersault, crashed painfully on to his shoulder, and the man sprang at him again. Quinn kicked out and caught him hard on the thigh, and the man went spinning sideways.

At that moment the truck exploded. There was a boom and a pool of yellow flame splashed out across the road, and the heat hit him like something solid. Vaguely he saw two French soldiers running near him, lit up by the blaze. One of them tottered and fell, the other had his képi dashed from his head, going over backwards after it.

The rebels were all round, leaping like released schoolboys, waving guns and knives and green-and-white flags. Quinn went on running. There were hills out in front. The shadows moved strangely with the flames, which swept showers of sparks far into the black sky, crackling luxuriously.

He came round a bend behind the burning truck, and saw the ambulance. There were men coming after him. He thought, *I'm a European. As conspicuous as a leper with a bell. If I try and shout at them in French it'll only be the worse. If I shout in English I'm still a European — one of the enemy, the colons from the other side.*

He tripped. There were faces all round him, some shouting, some smiling, others dark and purposeful, all closing in on him. There was one tall handsome boy with an American-style forage cap.

It happened very quickly. Someone grabbed him and he was pulled from behind; the ambulance tipped on its side and went flying into the sky; the faces spun round, and the face of the handsome boy moved down on him. There was a knife in his hand. Quinn tried to yell.

Then the crowd rolled back and he was hauled to his feet, and there were arms round him and all over him and someone was crying his name over and over again. He felt her face, wet and sooty, crying and kissing him, and her hair was blown back by a breeze that seemed to be sucked in by the fire. It was a cool breeze singing in his ears. The shooting had stopped and they were leading him away. He stumbled and dropped on to his knees. They had the handcuffs off him, and she was saying: 'Darling, your eye! What did they do to you? Poor, poor love!'

He saw two French dead lying near the cabin of the ambulance. One of them had had his throat cut and his trousers were down to his knees. Quinn caught only a glimpse of what they had done to him. It was senseless savagery. Leila glanced at the body and looked away. One of the rebels was grinning at her. Quinn noticed that she was walking slowly and stiffly. The ambulance doors were open and they were both helped into the back, and he lay dazed on the floor. The engine started and they began to drive down the winding road.

Leila was cleaning his face with a handkerchief, kneeling awkwardly beside him; then she began tying the handkerchief carefully over his eye. He peered at her and smiled: 'We have the luck of the damned!' She put her mouth against him, her lips quivering like butterfly wings, while the rebels sat bouncing about on the floor, cheering them both and singing nationalist songs.

She told him that they were driving towards Morocco, which was a bare twelve kilometres away. It had been a border raid to sabotage the railway track to the east; half the rebels in the ambulance were FLN, the others hired guerillas from the Moroccan Armée de Libération. She told him how they had wrenched open the ambulance doors and come at her with knives, thinking she were a French girl, and how she had just managed to shout at them in time in Arabic.

The singing in the truck grew wilder. They were all clapping and chanting in Arabic, 'Long live Algeria! Long live Ferhat Abbas!' She spread herself on her stomach beside him and whispered silly, adoring things in his ear, trying to drive out the patriotic fervour of the rebels, remembering that she had betrayed them. He asked her what the French had done to her, and she told him, her face averted, saying miserably: 'I couldn't help it. It was so horrible!'

'You're going to forget all about it,' he said. 'This war's over for you now. He smiled at her with his good eye, saying: 'I must look a dreadful sight!'

'I love you very much, Rupert. Did they hurt you badly?'

'I'll survive,' he said. 'We both will.' She suddenly began to cry. 'Darling, it's all over now. There's nothing to be sad about.'

'You don't understand. I betrayed you.'

He told her that he didn't give a damn now whom she'd betrayed. 'Izard will just have to think up a new way of making money.'

'It isn't so simple,' she said. 'It wasn't only Izard. I betrayed my people. Some of them will be shot. I betrayed you all. You as well!'

He said gently: 'I don't care what you did. All I care is that we're alive and free.' Then he told her about Bates, and she cried a little more, and said: 'Poor Paddy!' He added that any one of them would have talked if they'd fallen into the hands of the paras.

'No,' she said, 'most of us don't talk. But I couldn't help it — all I wanted was for them to kill me. It was like being cut in half.'

'You're much braver than all of them,' he told her.

PART 5: The Killing

CHAPTER 1

They were out of the hills now and had left the road, jolting over the Bled towards Morocco. Quinn's bruised back and arms ached against the rattling floor, and there was a deep stabbing pain in his eye.

Suddenly the bumping ceased. They were again on a proper road, and he lay listening to the whirr of tyres on concrete. They were driving very fast. The ambulance began to sway, almost soothingly. One of the rebels then shouted that they were in Morocco.

Leila was lying with her face away from him, and at first he thought she was asleep; but when she turned he saw that her eyes were open and that she was crying again.

About an hour after crossing the border they came to a small town. The dawn was breaking and goats were being driven down the one street. It was a very poor town, with the mud walls gnawed away like bits of broken biscuit. The truck stopped and the rebels piled out in search of food and wine. Old women peeped at them from doorways, their eyes flitting fearfully behind yashmaks. They broke into a bakery, strewing the toadstool loaves across the street, and one of the Armée de Libération discharged his burp gun into the air, sending birds screeching out of the dome of a tiny mosque.

But there was no wine there, and they drove on to the next town, which was larger, and had a clean white market and a café with chairs outside and a Coca-Cola advertisement. Here they were luckier; they found two huge jars of wine, filling their water cans with it, and this time several of them released their guns, watching the bearded merchants scatter across the market. More than half the rebels stayed in this town to get drunk. Quinn noticed that the local militia did not appear, lying low like cowardly sheriffs while the gunslingers rode through.

The next town was three hours away, and now there was only a hard core of the Armée de Libération left in the truck, drinking freely and noisily, and the steering was becoming perilous. Quinn was glad to find that there was a bus in the next town leaving for the north in less than an hour.

It was a rusted carcass of a machine made in Birmingham; the roof was piled with goats and trussed fowls, and the inside packed with Arabs who seemed able to relax in extraordinary positions, as though their bodies could be twisted and left like pieces of wire. They were very gracious to Quinn and Leila, crushing up to make room for them on the wooden seats.

They drove through the full heat of the day, stopping at villages to pick up more passengers, climbing again into mountains where the bus swerved at terrible speeds round the rims of precipices, with the wedge of Arabs inside rocking like clothes on hangers. They reached the next town at sunset. Leila was cramped with pain and crying, and she hardly spoke after they left the bus. Something was worrying her badly, but she refused to tell him what it was, sweeping her hand over her face and saying it was nothing.

The town had a single-line railway track and a pleasant white station with a platform decorated with flints arranged in the shape of flowers. There was one train going north at six in the morning. They traipsed away down the main street, and found the only hotel in the town, a house with a tower and a garden solemn with cypress trees. They were given a room up a spiral staircase at the top of the tower. There was a bed like a small sofa, and in one corner a tap that didn't turn on. It was very quiet. Their footsteps rang round the tiny room, and Leila took her shoes off and lay on the bed facing the wall, and said: 'Please leave me alone for a little.'

He went down and asked a servant boy to take her up some mint tea and pastries. Then he found a pump at the back of the hotel, where he washed and bathed his eye which was still closed up.

Outside, gusts of wind were driving chaff down the main street. A man came up and asked him to have a drink. 'I'm not paying for it,' Quinn said. The man told him that he wished to invite him. They went to a café near the station, where the Arab said they had cognac.

When it came it was a sticky brown liqueur that tasted like nutmeg; but it was strong, and cleared some of the furriness out of Quinn's mouth.

The man smiled and asked him if he would like a girl. Quinn laughed.

'*Pourquoi tu ris?*'

'No,' said Quinn. 'Not tonight.'

'I know some very pretty girls,' said the man. He ordered him another drink. Quinn swallowed it and stood up. 'I don't want any of them,' he said, and left the Arab sitting in the café.

Back at the hotel the proprietor called him aside and asked him to fill in the police questionnaire. He did not seem interested in their passports. Quinn wrote that Leila was his wife. Afterwards, it seemed a curiously perverse gesture, as though provoking fate.

She was still in bed when he got upstairs. The tea and pastries lay untouched on the floor. She turned her head from the wall, and he saw that there were shadows under her eyes, and the face was haggard, making the eyes look huge and unnatural. He sat beside her and stroked her hair. 'You'll feel all right, darling, when we get back to Casablanca.'

She nodded, unsmiling.

Under the blanket she was still fully dressed, and when he tried to put his arms round her she shrank against the wall. He kissed her softly, but her body was straining away from him. He lay and watched the room grow dark, and on that small hard bed he suddenly felt no longer the same with her — that something had snapped between them and that she was now slipping inexplicably away from him.

Some time in the small hours she sat up shrieking in Arabic, backing against the wall; he woke her and she began shivering all over. 'I dreamt they were attacking me!'

'You're safe now. The French are a long way off.'

'It wasn't the French.' She lay with her eyes open. 'It wasn't the French this time. Darling, I don't want to go back to Casablanca. Please, don't let's go back!' She turned and faced the wall. 'I'm afraid.'

'Darling, you've nothing to be afraid of now.' He tried again to pull her closer, and again she flinched away. He kissed the nape of her neck. 'It's all over,' he whispered, 'you're safe now.'

He didn't try to touch her again. The room was very close and he lay tossing and sweating, kept awake by the pain in his eye. A few hours later he got up and stood under the window, watching the sky grow light over the town.

When it was at last time to leave, she walked behind him to the station almost without speaking a word. Once, while they waited alone on the platform, she smiled at him, but it was a distant smile and seemed to have nothing to do with either of them.

The train ran on logs, with carriages built of honey-brown wood; and the engine had a funnel like a Puritan's hat turned upside down. They travelled in the only first-class compartment, with wine-red seats and mirrors and brass fittings. He found a plaque on the door saying that it had been built in Paris in 1911 — perhaps to serve on the old Orient Express.

They slept most of the morning, and some time round noon they had to change trains and wait about on a dusty platform where boys in skullcaps hawked peanuts. The next train was made of steel and was very crowded. All the windows were open, but the steel trapped the heat like a glasshouse. In their compartment a veiled woman suckled an infant opposite a bearded man who sat under the hood of his jellabah reading a *roman policier*.

Late in the afternoon they changed trains again, taking the express to Casablanca which would arrive just after nine in the evening. There were four American engineers in their compartment — rangy men with shorn heads and loud laughs — who had been on a bridge-building contract in the south. They kept passing round hipflasks of whisky, always offering them first to Leila, who disliked whisky, and when she refused it, they screwed up their big brown faces and cried: 'Aw, c'mon, sister, c'mon!' Quinn mentioned that they had both lost their passports, and one of them said: 'That's bad! I got my passport stolen here once — cut clean out o' the back pocket of my pants. It was just standing there and some little rascal came up, then slit it right off my arse!'

During the last hour of the journey Leila became fidgety and nervous, and kept going to stand in the corridor. While she was outside, the Americans, who were all getting entertainingly tight, would nod towards her and say to Quinn: 'That's a very charming young lady you have there, boy!' Then one of them took the opportunity of her being away to tell Quinn how he'd recently taken a cinefilm of two camels making love. 'A really fantastic and beautiful sight! No, really. All kissing and licking each other. Really beautiful!'

Just as they were coming into the outskirts of Casablanca she beckoned him into the corridor. She seemed quite calm now; and it was this sudden calmness that first alarmed him. 'Darling, I don't want to go back to the flat. I'll wait for you in the station, and you go and fetch everything. Don't worry about my things — just bring a few clothes. And there's a lot of money in an envelope in a drawer by the bed.'

He said: 'Yes, but why? We can surely stay till tomorrow?'

'No. Let's go on to Tangier. Darling, please.'

'But the passports…'

'We can settle them in Tangier just as well.' Her eyes held him, beseeching him.

'All right,' he said at last. 'You wait for me in the station. We'll stay tonight in a hotel.' She squeezed his hand, then hugged him like a little sister. 'Thank you, darling!'

They drew into Casablanca. The central station was packed with the crowds who always travel at night in Morocco to avoid the heat. Porters scrambled through the scrum like centre-forwards, while women wailed and children wept and old men squatted impassively on the ground as though they had settled there to die.

The porters set on the Americans like bear-baiting dogs. The biggest of the bridge-builders shook them off his arms, calling them all 'Jackson', and soon he had five Jacksons getting their luggage out; and as Quinn and Leila waved the Americans goodbye one of them toppled drunkenly and disappeared under the yelling crowd.

They had given Quinn a sense of the warm, well-fed side of humanity, untouched by flies and hunger and war; and they had even made Leila smile.

He left her in the buffet drinking coffee among the bundles of waiting families, and promised to be back in less than an hour. He took a taxi straight to the flat. It was in a residential street lined with parked cars.

He went up in the lift and pressed the minuterie. The key was always kept through the letterbox on a string; he opened the door and switched on the light.

The flat appeared just as they had left it. The bed was unmade and there were some stockings hanging in the bathroom. He took down a couple of suitcases and began throwing in his own clothes, which weren't many, then folded in her dresses and petticoats as carefully as he knew how; and when he was almost finished he went out on to the balcony and stood for a moment looking into the winking lights of the city. The cars down in the street were silent.

He went back into the room, collected her toilet things, and was getting out a few of her underclothes, which screwed up in a silken ball, when the door-buzzer sounded. He thought wildly that it was the police. He hesitated an instant and there was a sharp rap on the door.

'Who's there?'

'Please open, Monsieur Quinn.'

He went over to the door, put on the chain and eased it open six inches. Outside stood M. Beloued. The face showed its nickel teeth. 'May I come in, please?'

'What do you want?'

'I would like to talk to you.'

Quinn let him in, then walked away to the table and poured himself out the last finger of a bottle of brandy.

M. Beloued strolled through the flat, looking into each room. He paused by the bed, his eyes on the open suitcases. 'Where are you going, Monsieur Quinn?'

'I'm leaving. Leaving Morocco.'

'I see.' He lifted out one of Leila's flared underskirts. 'You know then that our affairs are terminated?'

'Yes, I know,' said Quinn. He swallowed the brandy. It was good brandy and made him feel warm and less tired.

'How do you know?' asked M. Beloued. 'Monsieur Izard only made the decision today.'

'I guessed. You heard what happened on the run. Paddy was killed. Leila was taken by the French.'

M. Beloued looked narrowly at him, then turned his eyes back to the cases. 'Where is she, Monsieur Quinn?'

'I don't know. I told you — the French took her.'

'We heard a report — quite unofficial — that she had escaped.'

'I don't know anything about that,' said Quinn. 'I haven't seen her.'

'Then why are you packing her clothes?' He dropped the underskirt back in and smiled. 'Well?'

'I can't just leave them here,' said Quinn feebly; 'I can give them to a charity or something.' He went back to the empty brandy bottle. Unexpectedly, M. Beloued did not press the point; instead he said: 'You were very fortunate to have escaped. Monsieur Izard congratulates you.'

'Where is Izard?'

M. Beloued did not answer. He walked over to the balcony windows. 'Monsieur Izard would like to have seen you before you left. You ought to treat him with more courtesy.'

'I don't know about that,' said Quinn. 'But the business is finished now. I'm getting out.'

'When do you leave Morocco?'

'In a few days. When I've got a new passport…'

'You have no passport?'

'No. Now please, I want to finish packing.'

M. Beloued stood watching him with a deep, quiet gaze; then he roused himself and smiled: 'Can I offer you a lift?'

'That won't be necessary. I'll get a taxi when I'm ready.' Quinn held out his hand and M. Beloued took it in a hard scaly grasp that felt as though the inside of his fingers were crusted with callouses. Quinn realised that it was the first time they had ever shaken hands, and he hoped passionately that it would be the last.

M. Beloued turned towards the door; he moved swiftly, like a dancer. 'One last thing, Monsieur Quinn. If Mademoiselle Soissons is still alive, you would do best to keep away from her. They do not like traitors in the National Liberation Front.'

He disappeared into the passage. Quinn heard the lift-gates snap shut and the cage clicking down past the floors. Then he remembered the money that Leila had told him about in the drawer; the envelope contained nearly sixty-thousand francs.

He telephoned for a taxi, and tossed some last things into the cases — a few paperbacks of Leila's, of Camus and Aragon. The intercom with the front door sounded. He carried the two cases downstairs and told the taxi driver to make for the station as quickly as he knew how. The Arab grinned, and the car leapt forward, throwing Quinn back into the springy American seats. There was a glimpse of wobbling bicycles; tyres squealed, skidding round a corner, hooters howling, neon signs swerving and flashing past: 'Fly TWA to Five Continents': plate glass and nyloned air-hostesses; promises of the cool insulated smell of the pressurized cabin humming through the purple darkness: escape from sand and bombs and flat lonely villages, and Moslems crouching in French cells bleeding from the nose.

Quinn missed the pair of sidelights racing and bobbing behind the taxi. They screeched to a halt outside the station, the driver smiling like a mouth organ; Quinn patted him on the shoulder and told him to wait. He disappeared into the station, up to the buffet.

She was sitting where he had left her. She said: 'Did you get everything? You've been very quick.'

'I had a taxi driver like Fangio. He's waiting outside.'

'Was it all right?'

'I think so. Beloued came up to see me. He wanted to find out where you were — he seems to know that you escaped.'

She had turned very pale. 'He was waiting there for you?'

'Well, he arrived just after I got there.'

'Did he follow you here?'

He paused. 'I didn't see anybody. The driver was going very fast.'

She said. 'Rupert, there's a train leaving in half an hour for Tangier. We can be there in the morning.'

He sat down opposite her, and noticed now that her hands were trembling. 'Listen, darling, it won't make any difference whether we go tonight or tomorrow. I haven't had a decent sleep for three nights, and I need a doctor to look at my eye.'

'Damn your sleep!' she cried; 'you can sleep on the train. And damn your eye! I need to see a doctor too. We can do all that in Tangier. You only think of yourself!'

He stood up wearily and said: 'Very well, if you want to go on to Tangier tonight, go.' He threw down the envelope with the sixty-thousand francs and started towards the door. He did not look round till he reached the station entrance, but knew that she was following him a few yards behind, walking lamely

189

after him into the square outside, where she caught him up just as he was getting into the taxi.

She climbed in beside him and put her head on his shoulder. 'Please don't leave me alone!' He took her hand, and gave the driver the name of a hotel near the station. He kissed her on the forehead and she closed her eyes. Neither of them looked out of the rear window.

'You think I'm being stupid, don't you?' she said at last.

'No. But I still don't see why we should have to go to Tangier tonight. Nobody's going to hurt you now.'

She shivered slightly and hunched up her shoulders. 'You don't understand. I don't feel safe in this city. They know all about me here, and they don't like people who tell things to the French.'

'They won't touch you while I'm here,' he said. She nestled against him and squeezed his arm. 'I know, darling,' she whispered. The taxi drew up in a side street outside a modern hotel studded with the discs of European motoring clubs. 'I'll just see if they have any rooms,' he said. She leant out of the window and kissed him. 'I won't be a moment, darling.'

The receptionist was a thin European with rimless glasses. He examined Quinn from the feet upwards, his eyes becoming colder as they passed the flecks of dried blood on his trousers and shirtfront, the three day's beard and the bandaged eye. '*Monsieur désire?*'

'I'd like a double room for tonight.'

The man took out a ledger and began studying it. 'Are you French?' he asked, after a pause.

'No. English. My wife's French.'

'Have you luggage?'

'It's outside in the taxi.'

'May I see your passports, please?'

'Our passports are in Tangier. But I can give you all the details.'

'I'm sorry, monsieur.' He closed the ledger. 'We cannot give guests rooms without having their passports.'

'But I have a residence permit here — I work here.'

The man's eyes remained as negative as celluloid. 'I regret, monsieur, but without a passport…'

'Oh, damn you!' said Quinn in English. 'Damn all you bloody French! Why don't you go back where you belong!'

The man picked up the ledger and turned his back on him. 'Please leave the hotel,' he said; 'there are no rooms for you.'

'*Vive les Algériens!*' Quinn shouted, going to the door; '*vive les Allemands!*' He went out and got into the taxi. 'They won't take us because we haven't got passports,' he told her.

'There's still time to catch the train.'

'I don't know,' he said, taking a deep breath. 'Bloody little French bureaucrat!'

'Darling, it'll be the same in all the hotels here in Casa. Let's get the train to Tangier.'

'All right. Take us to the station,' he called to the driver.

The ticket hall was crammed with long patient queues. Quinn had the ritual fight with the porters who seemed to exert their entire energy on Europeans, leaving their fellow countrymen burdened like mules. He chose one who seemed the strongest and noisiest, and gave him a tip to buy them first-class tickets on the sleeper to Tangier. They watched him skipping ruthlessly to the head of the queue.

There was still twenty minutes before the train left; they went into the bar and drank two large brandies each, and bought a bottle of wine for the journey. The porter met them grinning at the barrier, and bowed them through to the wagon-lits, looking like an armoured coach with its shuttered windows and uniformed attendants.

He gave the man a handful of grubby notes, and they were shown to their cabin with its stainless steel basin and laundered beds, hygienic as a clinic.

They opened the wine and drank from the tooth-glass, kissing each other's mouths messily red, feeling suddenly safe again, as the train lurched and began picking up speed, skimming through the night towards Tangier and the gateway to Europe. They drank the whole bottle, and it was good wine, without the pewter taste most North African wines have; and he pulled her down on the bed and began caressing her slowly, lovingly; trying to bring her back to him. The train vibrated beneath them; he slid his hands down the curve of her back and touched her buttocks, but she shuddered and straightened up, staring away from him into the mirror. The air smelt metallic and electric. He said softly: 'Come to bed, Leila.'

She stood still and said nothing. They heard an attendant coming down the corridor ringing a bell for dinner. Suddenly she began to laugh, then spun round to face him, her eyes bright with a hard, dry glitter, and threw her head back with mock gaiety, and cried; 'Darling, take me in to dinner!' She seized his arm, and he saw a smear of wine on her chin; he said quietly: 'Your shirt's undone.' She giggled and began doing up the buttons, while he opened the door into the corridor.

The restaurant car was crowded, mostly with Europeans. There was a five-course meal, swiftly served, with the white-jacketed waiters flitting up and down the coach like relay runners. He thought of the snoot and snarls he had grown to endure on the London-Manchester; then suddenly, for no reason that he could explain to himself, he began to feel uneasy.

Next to them two French businessmen nibbled their food and discussed prices on the Paris Bourse for Sahara oil. Leila had set to with an almost improper appetite, tearing at a leg of duck between her fingers, showing the Frenchmen her little white teeth, grinning when they turned away and pretended not to notice her.

They drank a bottle of Chateau Neuf du Pape, and the hard look in her eyes grew brighter, and she laughed more, and talked quickly, recklessly, about anything that came into her head. He squeezed her thighs together under the table, forgetting about the two Frenchmen and trying to drive out the sense of malaise. 'I've always wanted to make love on a train,' he whispered. She leant over, licked the tip of his nose and purred, '*Moi aussi!* — to the rhythm of the wheels.' She laughed loudly, but her eyes were not looking at him. 'Especially when we bump over the points!' The two Frenchmen dabbed napkins to their lips and called for the bill; and as they both stood up, she turned to them and stuck out her tongue, saying with a smile, 'Cretinous French!' They left the table, ignoring her.

The car began to empty. He felt himself growing groggy with wine and sleep; and he gripped her thighs more tightly, saying: 'I'm going to make love to you all the way to Tangier.'

'Liar!' she growled; 'you've drunk too much wine'; then added, 'you can't make love to me tonight.' There was a sharp finality about the words, as though they were suddenly strangers together — she a sweet, self-possessed girl to whom he'd just made a drunken pass.

He started to say something to her, but she put her finger against his lips and said: 'Sshhh!' — kissing him across the table, while the waiters shook out tablecloths and whisked away empty glasses.

The corridor was deserted. He swayed along behind her, steadying himself with his hands on the soft shelves of her hips, feeling quite drunk now with the motion of the train.

Most of the compartment blinds were down; he peered into the others and saw the passengers sitting asleep under the blue nightlights. At the end of one of the first-class coaches he stopped while Leila fumbled to get the communicating door open. He looked sideways and saw Izard's face looking at him a few inches away.

He looked again, and there was nothing. Just the drawn blind. He tried the door of the compartment, but it was locked. Leila tugged at his arm: 'Darling, you're tipsy! That isn't our cabin.' He followed her, thinking that it had been like an image at the back of some dreadful dream: the grey face swimming fleetingly up and looking at him through the glass of a dark fish tank, then vanishing.

He was sweating when he reached their cabin, but he decided to say nothing to her. Perhaps it had been the wine after all. The cabin was moving round him and he sank on to the bed, drawing her down on top of him, helping to peel off her clothes, convincing himself that it had only been his imagination.

She switched off the light, so that he would not see her wounds, and under the cold papery sheets he touched the dressings that the French doctor had put on. She flinched at the ridges of pain underneath, and he heard her whisper, 'No, darling! No, you're too drunk.'

'I'm not drunk at all,' he said crossly. His body was hardening against her in the narrow bed, but she pushed him away, saying again, 'No, darling. I want to sleep. I'm too tired.'

He began to kiss her, but her lips were dry and still, and kept sliding away from him. For a moment he lay quietly beside her, feeling the rails throbbing past beneath them; then he tried angrily to pull her under him, but she struggled and screamed out: 'Go away! Leave me alone!' Her hands went up to her face, and she curled away from him against the wall.

He said gently: 'What's the matter, darling?' He could hear her sobbing in the darkness, and her cool naked shoulders quivered against him. 'What's the matter, Leila?'

'I don't want to! I don't want to ever again!'

He lay on his back listening to the rails, thinking, *It's just the wine. We've had too much wine, and she's tired and still suffering from shock. It'll pass.* He had forgotten about Izard now.

Those bloody French, he thought.

He woke suddenly about an hour later. The train had stopped He looked under the blinds and saw that they were in a country station with palm trees beside the platform. Two men were walking across the tracks towards the train. He got back into bed and heard voices near the window talking Arabic. Leila stirred next to him, her body rank with sleep.

There were more voices, this time in the corridor, then a sudden knock at their cabin. He jumped up and she stirred again, half-awake, murmuring: 'What is it?'

He pulled on his trousers and opened the door. The controleur of the train stood outside with a small Moroccan in a sausage-brown suit, who said: '*Pièces d'identité, s'il vous plaît.*'

'What is all this?' Quinn was still feeling muzzy with wine.

'*Passeport!*' snapped the little man.

'I don't have it here.' He thought of the French concierge in the hotel. Somebody must have told them. The man in the brown suit said: 'Come with me, please. And bring your luggage.'

'But why? This is ridiculous!'

'Come with me!' said the man. He had the trim, narrow face and smudged moustache of the pedigree official, as though the French had bred them into the Arab race during generations of colonial rule. Leila was sitting up now, blinking with sleep. Quinn put on his shirt and sandals, kissed her and said: 'I shan't be long!'

They led him across the tracks to the far platform, not bothering to help him lug his two cases after them. They took him into an office and closed the door. The controleur sat down importantly behind a table and said: 'Have you your ticket?'

Quinn took the tickets out of his belt-pouch. The man in the brown suit said: 'Where is your passport?'

'I lost it. Who are you, anyway?'

'Police de sécurité,' said the man impassively. 'You're British?'

'Yes. How did you know I didn't have a passport. Are you checking the whole train?'

The man didn't answer, just said: 'Please fill out this form with all your personal particulars. You have a visa de résidence for Morocco?'

'How did you know? Who told you about me?' Quinn was too angry for the moment to be worried.

The man said again: 'It is no matter. Please fill out your particulars.'

They searched expertly through the two cases, examining in particular the books and the inside of his shaving kit. He said: 'I'm an international spy. I work for Hitler.'

'Fill out the form!' said the plain-clothes man.

He began to work at it, scraping at the questions with a pen that refused to flow. He had got down to the names of his father and mother, when he heard a car crash into gear and roar off into the night. He thought quickly: *A very powerful car — too powerful to find out here in a little country town.*

In a flash he leapt up and sprinted through the door, across the tracks with the two men yelling after him.

The train lay in the moonlight like a long grey caterpillar. He jumped aboard, ran down the corridor and threw open his door. The light was out, and for a moment he thought it was the wrong cabin. Then he saw Leila's clothes over the rail. The bed was empty.

CHAPTER 2

He collided with the controleur and the policeman in the corridor. The policeman had a revolver out; he said: 'Stop, or I shoot!' Quinn shouted: 'She's gone! They've kidnapped her!' He began waving his arms and the little man came up gripping the revolver; 'Stand where you are!'

Quinn leant limp against the windows. 'They've kidnapped my girl!' he said again. It seemed to make no impression on the man, and the two of them stood facing each other stupidly.

The controleur, who had gone to speak to the sleeping-car attendant, now came running back talking excitedly in Arabic. The policeman turned, and Quinn followed them both to the end of the corridor. The attendant lay in his narrow cubicle, slumped on his belly among the wreckage of spilt coffee cups. He had been hit over the back of the head and the coffee had scalded the side of the face. They lifted him and he groaned, and the controleur splashed water on his face. Quinn said again: 'Please understand — they've taken my girl!' The words were desperate, and at the same time faintly absurd.

The policeman still looked at him suspiciously, but he was now puzzled and had put away his revolver. They carried the attendant out and laid him on the rumpled bed in Quinn's cabin. Quinn saw again, with a feeling of panic, Leila's clothes still hanging over the rail. He took the policeman by the arm and tried soberly to explain to him. The attendant was still unconscious. The policeman and Quinn got down and walked over the tracks to the station entrance. It was deserted. There was a pair of fresh skid marks in the sand.

Quinn said: 'How far are we from Casablanca?'

'Nearly two hundred kilometres,' said the policeman, frowning.

'Could a car have got here as quickly as the train? — if they both left at the same time?'

'It would be a very fast car,' said the policeman.

'What happened?' asked Quinn. 'Why did you have the train stopped here? Who told you about me?'

The man looked worried. 'There was a telephone call in Casablanca — they said you were to be stopped here and held. They said you have no passport...'

'Who said?' cried Quinn.

'That I do not know. It was a police matter.'

'How a police matter? Come on, tell me!'

'Monsieur, I do not know. I had my instructions. I was told to stop you here and hold you for questioning.'

'The police told you?'

The man turned and said unhappily: 'Please, monsieur, this is a police matter. I cannot tell you. We will return to Casa and make full investigations.'

Back in the train the attendant was just regaining consciousness, murmuring about being attacked by bandits. He had seen nothing. They looked in the compartment where Quinn thought that he'd seen Izard. It was empty. There was no sign of anybody having just left it.

Quinn folded her clothes over his arm, climbed down and walked back over the tracks. He thought of her being driven away, helpless and naked, across the flat empty Bled. It was all quite clear now: M. Beloued had followed them to the station, where Izard had boarded the train after putting through a call to his friends at security police, while M. Beloued had driven on to intercept the train at this small wayside halt.

It seemed a curiously elaborate way of punishing a young girl for treachery; but they had made up their minds, and now they would kill her. He knew that he should be doing something to help; but all he did was sink down on a bench under the palms, gripping the pitiful bundle of clothes, and watched the train start up and slide away into the darkness.

The plain-clothes man had disappeared into the hut to telephone his superiors in Casablanca; he now came out and asked Quinn if he would prefer to wait inside. There was a slow train to Casablanca in two hours' time. The man had become quiet and courteous, and back in the hut he opened one of the cases and helped pack Leila's clothes.

Quinn sat and looked at the timetables in Arabic, at the old-fashioned telephone with its detachable earpiece hooked to the wall, and waited in despair.

The train had wooden seats and took over seven hours to reach Casablanca. Quinn slept on in snatches, dreaming that he was back again with Leila in the sleeping-car heading for Tangier, then waking to find the plain-clothes policeman opposite him, hands on his sausage-brown knees.

They arrived in the mid-morning, with the streets glaring white and choked with the stream of bicycles and American cars. The plain-clothes man took him by taxi to central police headquarters where he was examined for nearly two hours by three detectives. They were very polite and attentive, sitting round him in their shirtsleeves, with all the windows open and the fans whirring.

His eyes stung with tiredness and his head was slamming. There was a building going up in the street opposite and the air shuddered with drills and steam-hammers. It felt as though the room were being pumped full of compressed air. He found it very difficult to concentrate. He had no papers to identify him, and they wouldn't let him telephone the Consulate until he had finished telling the whole story. They watched him carefully as he spoke, one of them jotting it all down in shorthand, and at one point they allowed him to break off, while an officer brought him in a cup of coffee and a glass of water on a tray.

He told them everything, from the time he arrived in Morocco, to the moment when he thought he had seen Izard on the train, and then the kidnapping. The chief detective, a cadaverous man who spoke immaculate French, asked him casually if Leila had any private enemies. Quinn was certain she had none. He remained adamant: she had been kidnapped by Izard who would now arrange to have her murdered. He had already told them about M. Bloch. Didn't they realise that exactly the same thing would happen to Leila?

The chief detective held up his hand. 'Please, monsieur, listen to me.' For a moment the din from the street seemed to recede. 'The facts concerning Monsieur Izard are already known to us.' He paused. 'You know, of course, that this girl, Mademoiselle Soissons, was a prominent agent of the National Liberation Front. She had many contacts here in Casablanca. By giving information to the French' — he gave a dismal gesture with his hands — 'she will have made for herself many, many enemies.'

The noise from outside came crashing back. Quinn said dully: 'Where is Izard now?'

'We shall be getting in touch with him,' said the detective. 'Monsieur, you have been most co-operative. This is a delicate matter, and for the moment we would prefer that you do not leave Casablanca without our permission. I must therefore ask you to report here each day. It is possible that later we shall require you as a material witness.' He stood up.

'But this is fantastic!' Quinn cried. 'I'm not the one who's guilty! That man of yours who brought me here told me that Izard had arranged for me to be stopped and taken off the train. Izard knew I hadn't got a passport because I told his assistant, Beloued.'

'That is all being looked into,' said the detective, turning to the door.

Quinn shouted: 'It's a fine thing when a criminal can rope in the police as his accomplices in the murder of an innocent girl!'

The detective wheeled round. 'Young man, you are talking recklessly. It will do you no good.'

'Then why don't you arrest Izard?'

The detective drew in his breath and placed his hands on the table. 'Please understand,' he said; 'we have nothing against this man, Izard, except what you have told us, and that is not enough to arrest him. On the other hand, we know you worked for him and that yesterday you were trying to leave Casablanca without even telling him, and without a passport. Monsieur Izard, as your employer in Morocco, is partly responsible for your conduct here. He was certainly entitled to report any suspicions he had to the police. It is an offence for a foreigner in this country to be without a passport. You had made no attempt to inform the police that you had lost your passport. Monsieur Izard did so instead — as was his duty.'

'You seem to have forgotten,' said Quinn, 'that Izard is a smuggler and a murderer.'

'We have no proof of murder,' said the detective; 'again, there is nothing besides your own word, and that would be disputed. As to the other matter, the Moroccan police are not employed to work for the French colonialists in Algeria.'

'You imbecile! I saw Izard on the train. He kidnapped my girl!'

The detective came a step forward. 'We have no reason —' he began, but Quinn broke in: 'I told you, I saw him on the train!'

'You also told us you had been drinking,' said the detective, with a small, deprecating smile. 'I'm sorry, but on the evidence we have there is no reason for us to believe that Monsieur Izard was directly responsible for the disappearance of this girl.'

'Then who the hell was?' Quinn was half out of the chair. 'Just tell me that!' he shouted.

'I will tell you,' said the detective, patient as ever. 'I will tell you for the second time, after which I hope you will be more intelligent. This girl worked for the FLN. She gave vital information to the French. I have it on authority that perhaps as many as ten men will be shot as a result of what Mademoiselle Soissons told the French. The FLN has its own code, even in Morocco, and what this girl did was treason. They would kill her.' He looked at Quinn with slow black eyes. 'Monsieur, I could name to you now as many as fifty people in this city who might kill Mademoiselle Soissons.'

He turned again towards the door, and Quinn sprang up and bawled: 'It was Izard! How much did he pay you to keep your mouth shut?' His voice sounded hoarse and broken, not his own voice at all. One of the other detectives laid a hand on his shoulder. 'Quietly now,' he said; then they led him out to the duty room. A policeman came in with a folder marked 'Soissons L'; inside was a single typewritten sheet in Arabic and French, and a blurred snapshot of Leila that was not a good likeness. They asked him for more details: height and weight, colour of eyes and hair, shape of nose and state of teeth. He said at the end: 'She was very beautiful.'

'I am sure she was,' said the policeman.

The duty officer then dialled the Consulate, and after a few words in French, handed the receiver to Quinn. A high, reedy voice the other end said: 'British Consulate. Weatherby here.'

'I want to see the Consul at once.'

'Oh. Tricky. Is it urgent?'

'Very.'

'Well, look here, you'd better come over. The Consul's away in the mountains fishing…'

Quinn hung up and asked the duty officer to ring for a taxi. The police were holding his luggage for a few hours, but he still had Leila's envelope with the sixty-thousand francs, and nearly a hundred pounds in his Tangier account. He felt that he was going to need it all.

The Consulate was a plain white house with a garden full of singing birds and a portrait of the Queen in a lobby that smelt of leather and floor polish. The man at the door was a little old Scotsman with the knotted face of a boxer who dodged his head about as he spoke as though avoiding imaginary blows.

Weatherby came down in a few moments. He was a tall callow youth with flat hair and not much chin, probably just down from university and on his first post in the foreign service. He was dressed as though he'd just come from a wedding.

'Hello, what can I do for you, old boy?'

'When does the Consul get back?'

'Not till this evening, I'm afraid. Can I help?'

'I doubt it,' said Quinn rudely. 'I've had my passport taken away by the French. They want me on a charge of gun-running. That's just for a start.' Out of the corner of his eye he saw the old Scot ducking about trying to listen. 'Then I want you to help me investigate a kidnapping and a probable murder.'

'I see,' said Weatherby slowly. 'Perhaps you could do with a drink?'

'I could do with a dozen.'

'Righty-oh! Mac,' he said to the doorman, 'I'm down in the Bodega if anyone calls.' The Scot grunted and parried a volley of left-hooks. Weatherby drove Quinn to a bar down on the beach outside the city. It had a tang of salt and seafood and was very quiet.

'I'd have taken you to the club,' he said apologetically, 'but I hardly think you're quite dressed for it.' He laughed. 'Still, this is a jolly little spot. What happened to your eye?'

'Beaten up by the French.'

'Hard lines. They can be blighters, those French.' They sat in a corner under a fan and Weatherby ordered Bacardi cocktails with crushed ice and the rims frosted with sugar. 'Well, now,' he said, suddenly serious, 'fire away and tell me all about it.'

It took Quinn a full hour to get through the story for the second time that day. He drank altogether five Bacardis, with a couple of brandies just to help him over the last stretches. Towards the end he was having some difficulty with his diction and the chronology of events became confused. He was also aware of how fantastic the whole story sounded. At least the police had had their own reasons to believe him — they knew as much, and perhaps even more than he did. But this green young man from the Consulate was another matter.

'You don't believe me?' he slurred. 'You think it's a lot of balls?'

'No, I don't at all.' Weatherby was frowning and looking unexpectedly astute. 'I'm just wondering where we ought to start. You think the police are being awkward?'

'I think they're in on it,' said Quinn. 'In fact, I'm bloody sure they are.'

Weatherby, like the detectives, then went through each point of the story. 'It's this gun-running business I don't much like,' he said at last. 'The old man can be pretty touchy about that sort of thing.'

'I don't give a damn about myself,' said Quinn. 'I just want to find the girl.'

'Yes, of course. But if she's French it's not really our pigeon.'

'Oh, f — that! I told you what the French did to her.'

'Yes, I know,' he said dubiously; 'rotten business. But I still don't quite see how we can help. Directly, that is.'

'I want to marry her,' said Quinn. He called for another brandy.

'I should go easy on the drink, old boy. Have you eaten yet?' He ordered them both baskets of lobster and salad. 'Don't think I'm not on your side. In fact, if you'll excuse my sounding a bit callous, I rather jump at the chance of helping you. We don't get much excitement out here. Most of the English are just the gin-and-tonic types.' They began to eat, and Quinn repeated, through a mouthful of lobster, 'I want to marry her!' He called again for more brandy.

'I'll do my best,' said Weatherby. 'Now first of all, are the police after you?'

'I have to report each day like some bloody juvenile delinquent.'

'Well, I think I can get you out of that. And I can fix you up with a new passport. But what about the French? Will they try to get you?'

'F — the French!' The brandy came and he emptied it and was suddenly very drunk. Weatherby said: 'I think the best thing for you is to get a good sleep. What's the address of your flat?'

'I can't go back there!' He tried to focus on the long pink face. 'You've got to help me find her.' He slipped and dashed his glass to splinters. 'I want to marry her.'

'We'll find her,' said Weatherby. He paid the bill. 'Now be a good chap and go to bed. I'll ring you tomorrow morning. Where do you live?'

'I can't go back there!' said Quinn again. 'That's where we lived for five months. That's where she used to sleep. It's her bed. Everything there's where she used to be.'

Weatherby helped him out into the sun. 'You'll feel better after a sleep.'

'But the sun's all shining!' He stumbled into the car.

'You'll sleep,' said Weatherby. 'I'll call you in the morning. Now, what's the address?'

'I can't go back!' yelled Quinn. 'Not if they've killed her. I can't face it. I loved her! D'y'unerstand?'

'Steady on, old boy,' said Weatherby humorously.

'I've got to talk to somebody. I can't go back there alone.' The car had started and he heard Weatherby say: 'That's all right. I'll put you up in my flat.' On the way they stopped at a chemist where he was given some pills and his eye was dressed with stinging ointment and a bandage. They drove on and he burbled something about Englishmen all sticking together. Weatherby got him out of the car and up some stairs, and he was undressed with the help of an Arab manservant. As they dragged off his trousers he muttered: 'The good old British Consulate…!' The sheets were pulled over him and Weatherby said: 'I'll get cracking now on your new passport.'

He had gone and the sun shone deep orange through the drawn curtains. Soon a muggy torpor crept up from his toes, and Leila and the train and the police headquarters all slipped away, and he woke with the sound of someone banging about in the bathroom. It was just after nine o'clock next morning.

Weatherby appeared in black silk pyjamas, his upper lip frothy with shaving cream. 'Slept well, old boy?' Quinn looked around and the memories stole painfully back. He rubbed his eyes. 'I'm sorry about yesterday,' he muttered. 'I was a bit sloshed.'

'Sloshed!' Weatherby laughed; 'you were stark staring bonkers! By the way, I've got news.'

Quinn sprang up in bed. 'What news? Where is she?'

'Oh, not that sort, I'm afraid.' He paused. 'But I have got you a provisional passport. The Consul was pretty sticky about the French business.'

Quinn had sunk back on to the pillows. 'Nothing else, then?'

'Well, I managed to see somebody from the police headquarters, and found out that this chap Izard and his assistant left for Madrid yesterday on the four o'clock plane. I also arranged that you don't have to report to the police each day. But don't leave Casablanca, because I more or less guaranteed you, and it would put me in the hell of a spot if you skipped out.'

'I shan't leave,' said Quinn. He got up and shaved and showered, and Weatherby made coffee and fried some eggs which they ate almost in silence.

When they had finished Weatherby said: 'By the way, I brought your cases over from the police.' Quinn went and looked through them, and saw that all her things lay just as he had left them. He wondered hopelessly what he would now do with her dresses and hairclips and Camus' *La Peste*, with an inscription inside in Arabic. It was from the student in Algiers who'd been her first lover.

'Is there no other news?' he asked at last.

'Apart from Izard going to Madrid, nothing. And I'm afraid the police don't seem very keen to chase him up. They prefer to put it down as an FLN job.'

'Why?'

Weatherby looked sorrowfully at him. 'Search me, old boy. This is a funny country. I'm afraid they don't always do things as we do.' He began to collect up the breakfast plates and take them into the kitchen. When he came back he said: 'I'm awfully sorry about all this, you know. It must be bloody for you.'

Quinn said nothing. He stared out of the window and for a moment thought he was going to cry.

'I wish I could do more to help,' said Weatherby.

'You've done all right.' He shook himself and went over and picked up the two suitcases. 'I'd better hang on to these. She might still turn up.'

'Yes, she might,' said Weatherby, taking one of the cases from him. 'I'll run you down to a hotel I know. It's a very decent little place.'

Outside in the street Quinn turned to him and said: 'You'll keep trying, won't you?'

'I'll do what I can. I've got one or two contacts here with the police.' He threw off the remark with a modest assurance that made Quinn suspect that the boy might not be such a sap as he looked.

As they got into the car Weatherby smiled and said: 'Not to worry, old boy! We'll hear something.'

CHAPTER 3

But for eleven days they heard nothing. Each time he spoke to Weatherby it was the same answer: 'Sorry, old boy, still a blank.' Then, late on the night of the eleventh day, he arrived back half-drunk at his hotel and found two policemen waiting outside in a jeep. They stopped him and told him he was to come with them to headquarters. They refused to say anything more, and during the drive he became cold-sober, his stomach tight with excitement.

The detective who had headed the first day's questioning was there to receive him in an anteroom. He seemed ill at ease, hastily offering him a cigarette, and when he spoke he avoided Quinn's eyes. 'We've been trying to contact you since noon,' he began; 'I regret, monsieur, but we have a disagreeable task for you. You must identify a body.'

A teleprinter clacked busily away in the next room. The metal ashtray on the table contained the squashed stubs of three French cigarettes. The detective said: 'We found it last night. It fits the description.' He led him out to the jeep and they started down towards the port. Quinn was very frightened, like someone about to undergo an operation that has to be performed while the patient is still conscious.

They turned into a street full of fish smells and garbage and cats springing about in the shadows. The jeep stopped at a low building with a policeman outside; he saluted as the detective led the way down a cement passage to a door with a second policeman on guard. As they waited for the door to be unlocked the detective turned to Quinn and said: 'Monsieur, this will not be pleasant. I ask you to have courage.' The words had a curious elegance, like the words of a priest to a condemned man on the scaffold.

Quinn said: 'All right, let's get it over with' — and they stepped into the room. It was bare and very bright, with a fetid stench of fish. Against the back wall was a marble platform with steel lids along the top. The detective led Quinn over and suddenly gripped him by the arm; then the policeman who had been on guard outside lifted one of the lids.

Inside lay a long shape wrapped in a tarpaulin; the material was frosted white and a blast of cold air swept up, carrying with it a smell that made Quinn step back for a moment. In doing so he noticed that the policeman had gone grey and had closed his eyes; then he opened them again and took hold of the edges of the tarpaulin which creaked under his fingers. The detective nodded to him, holding Quinn more tightly by the arms, and the tarpaulin was whipped back.

They only showed it to him for a few seconds. He felt his eyes grow dim and the room swayed, while the policeman and the detective supported him. The policeman's hands were very cold. The detective said distantly: 'Did you recognise it?'

At first Quinn could not speak. They made him look at it again, and this time he gazed at it, fascinated. The tarpaulin had been pulled down below the breasts, which were not like breasts at all, but huge dark tumours; and there was no face and no eyes, and the throat had been cut as though a slice had been taken out of a melon, full of tiny yellow insects instead of seeds. A liquid had flowed out of one of the eye sockets like a frozen tear. And he noticed that the hair was long and black and fine, and it was Leila's.

They showed him the lower half, and he said, with a voice a long way outside himself: 'It's her.' The stomach had shrunk and the pubic mound was like moss on the grease-paper flesh.

The detective helped him outside, where he choked out: 'It must have been her, mustn't it?' They told him that the medical report put the time of death at approximately the right date. Then they led him to the end of the street, where he broke away from them and was sick all down the promenade.

He stayed for some time leaning over the palisade listening to the sea. After a while the detective came up and said: 'This has been a bad shock for you.' Quinn said: 'It was those bastards, Izard and Beloued. They killed her. And I'm going to get them, if it's the last thing I do.'

The detective led him back to the jeep without answering, and during the drive Quinn began to shake all over. Back at headquarters they wrapped him in a blanket, but he went on shaking until the police doctor gave him a jab in the arm. Then they made him sign a formal identification paper and told him that he would have to give evidence at the inquest. Afterwards, the police drove him back to his hotel.

The inquest was held two days later in a modern court like a schoolroom, and was all over in a few minutes. Weatherby accompanied him, after they'd both consumed nearly a whole bottle of brandy on the beach; and Quinn tripped on the stand before answering a couple of questions in French from the Arab magistrate. They would not allow him to make any statement of his own, and a verdict of murder was given against a person or persons unknown.

Afterwards, he and Weatherby went into a bar and discussed burial arrangements. 'There are three normal classes of funeral out here,' said Weatherby, almost cheerfully as though explaining the rules of a game. 'First-class, Moslem ceremony, and pauper. The pauper costs only about five bob, but it's pretty sordid.' He paused, and Quinn said nothing. 'The

Consulate always expects a first-class one if it's a British subject, but it comes damned expensive.'

'She wasn't British,' said Quinn thickly.

'Oh, of course not. Well, the Moslem-do isn't too bad…'

'She wasn't a Moslem,' said Quinn. He drew wet rings on the table and muttered, 'I suppose you'd have called her some kind of romantic Communist camp-follower.' He gave a humourless laugh and pushed back his chair. 'I don't care what they do with her. I don't care if they put her in Westminster Abbey. Nothing's going to do her any good now.'

But a couple of bars further on they decided that she should receive discreet rites in the Anglican Church for a fee of some forty-thousand francs. 'It's the best we can do for her, old boy!' Weatherby called, as he jumped into a taxi and headed back to his desk at the Consulate.

Late that night the telephone rang beside Quinn's hotel bed. It was Weatherby; his high voice squeaked with excitement. 'Can you get round here at once, old boy? I've just heard news for you.' Then, exasperatingly, he hung up.

Quinn was at the flat in less than ten minutes. Inside, Weatherby first made him swear an oath of secrecy. 'If they find out I've been letting on, the Moroccans'll chuck me out on my ear, and our chaps'll probably post me to some oil-blister in the Persian Gulf.'

'Don't worry,' said Quinn impatiently. 'Tell me.'

A look of impish cunning crept over Weatherby's smooth face. 'I did some snooping after I saw you this afternoon. Heard a spot of gossip.' He leant close to Quinn and said: 'I think I've found Izard for you.'

He paused. Quinn said quietly: 'Where is the bastard?'

'Well, I heard that he and his chap Beloued have gone to Rome. Izard apparently has some kind of business there. I gather he's lying low until the whole thing blows over, then he plans to come back to Morocco.'

'Not if I get to him first, he won't. Where's he living in Rome?'

'Well, that's the point. He's under another name, and I shan't be able to find out exactly where he is for a few more days. Meanwhile, I'm afraid, old boy, I also heard that the police here are about to throw you out. So I'll just have to let you know by post.' He stared innocently over Quinn's head. 'The flights to Rome at this time of year can be rather booked up — but I dare say I can wangle you on to a plane. We don't want to find you rerouted to somewhere in France, do we?' He gave a little chuckle. 'Have a Cointreau, old boy. I'll look forward to reading about it in the papers — as long as you keep me out of it.'

'Just get me on that plane,' said Quinn. He felt a sudden sense of release and excitement.

PART 6: The Inferno

CHAPTER 1

Quinn had been in Rome for exactly one week, and was sitting on the Scala di Spagna watching the girls tripping up the steps past the flower-sellers, waiting for the American Express to open for the afternoon.

He had arranged to have his mail, together with what remained of his savings from his Tangier bank, sent there to the poste restante. The money had arrived; but each day he had been calling in to see if there was any word from Weatherby. There had still been nothing that morning, and he was now beginning to feel foolish and despondent. The role of lover bent on the vengeance of his murdered mistress does not easily survive the Anglo-Saxon temperament; and here in Rome there was none of the remote, hidden violence of Africa.

The October days were cool and dear, scented with charcoal and new bread, the ancient streets infested with cats and widows and tiny children. All along the noble Corso the crowds strolled, dark and dapper, in dove-grey; and on the Via Veneto the café tables were packed with girls like tulips, idling over Strega and empty coffee cups with golden-haired degenerates from the film studios: with poets and dancers, tourists and painters, acrobats and aristocrats and fragile roués who spent half the day having their hair permed and the wrinkles smoothed out around their fine, exhausted Roman eyes.

And Quinn saw that the girls now passing on the steps were all very pretty, and they seemed to come in shoals, with oval faces and lovely figures, and they reminded him that he had not as much as spoken to a girl since leaving Leila that last time on the train.

The girls walked up and down past him, and none of them looked at him and he felt no desire for any of them. At the foot of the steps sleek young Romans hung about whistling and capering after them, and the girls swung haughtily past, heads high, while the boys ambled away and laughed and played games in the air with their eloquent hands.

Quinn knew that he looked like a tramp. One day he had caught a glimpse of himself in a street mirror: he was tanned copper-brown, with a scrub of blond beard, and his drill trousers and khaki shirt were stained an indeterminate colour somewhere between the desert and the swamp. A more generous people might have put him down as an explorer back from the wilds; but to the Romans, who are vain, beautiful and provincial, he was just a badly dressed nonentity.

He basked in the sun and waited for four o'clock, when the American Express would re-open. There might be something from Weatherby. It was a peevish pleasure, this hanging about waiting for word to strike down a cruel old man; but it was the only thing that kept him from brooding and drinking and cracking up altogether.

The noise of traffic throbbed up from the piazza. Once a Volkswagen got into the wrong lane, started down a one-way street, spun round and stopped in front of a rostrum, where the policeman lowered his baton, shouted '*bravo!*' and applauded.

At four o'clock all the clocks and belfries began to chime together, as though the city were some huge musical box. Skeins of pigeons flapped up from the piazzas, and Quinn strolled down to the American Express office on the corner.

These visits had become a ritual to break up the monotony of the day. Inside, he joined the queues of diet-starved American women nervously waiting to collect their month's alimony.

'Kveen?' said the Roman clerk. He riffled through a stack of letters under 'Q', extracted an airmail envelope with a stamp bearing the head of Mohammed V. It contained a single typed sheet with no address heading. At first Quinn thought that he had opened the wrong letter. He read:

Dear Dick Hannay,

Your quarry run to earth. Name of De Sanctis, 19 Viale Piemonte off Via Scrofa. Don't do anything I wouldn't do. Here is hot as Hell. Regards to Signorinas.

Sandy Arbuthnot.

Quinn had not read his Buchan for some years, but the roles ascribed by Weatherby seemed a little presumptuous. *Postgraduate wit*, he thought. Or perhaps the more asinine the better. If anything happened, Weatherby had certainly stuck his neck out.

He took a taxi at once to the Viale Piemonte. Number 19 looked like some ministry or bank. There was an iron grille over the door, and the façade was late baroque, covered with pillars of bluish marble like sausages wrapped in cellophane. It was just the sort of house, Quinn thought, that Izard would choose to live in — full of stone rooms and empty passages, impossible to heat in winter; and somewhere in the heart of it the old man would sit over his collection of mountain flowers, thinking of new ways to make money which he would never enjoy spending.

There was no sign of life from inside. He went to a bar with a telephone and hunted through a street directory. No. 19,

Viale Piemonte, was listed under the name of a limited company. He dialled the number and after some time a voice said: '*Pronto!*' It sounded very distant. He asked for Signor de Sanctis and the voice started to croak out a string of words that he could not understand. He repeated, loudly and impatiently: 'De Sanctis! — De — Sanc — tis!' He gave up and called the woman over from behind the bar, who bawled fluently into the mouthpiece, and after a pause, while the telephone made a sound like a trapped wasp, she turned and said: 'Signor De Sanctis is away — *fuori!*'

'When does he get back?'

The woman began again, then said: 'Returns tomorrow morning — *domani mattina.*'

'*Grazie!*'

All he could do now was sit and wait. There was still a chance that the man identified as De Sanctis might turn out to be somebody quite different. He went into a shop opposite number 19 and asked if they knew anything about Signor de Sanctis. They had never heard of him. He was tempted to go over and try the house, but decided that it would be wiser to be seen by no one.

He passed the rest of the afternoon in the Albergo Diurno under the central railway station, where he soaked in a hot bath, was shaved, had his hair cut and shampooed and his face massaged, and bought himself a silk shirt, a dust-coloured linen jacket, and a pair of pointed black shoes like the prows of gondolas. When he emerged he looked quite dashing in the mirrors round the Diurno café, and the girl at the cash desk pinged the register with her beautifully manicured finger and gave him a flashing smile. He was feeling almost respectable.

CHAPTER 2

That evening it rained — heavy, almost tropical rain, splashing across the streets, with the waiters battling to get the awnings down and the tables stacked inside. It was the first real rain Quinn had felt for many months, and he walked luxuriously through it with his head back, letting it trickle into his mouth. When it stopped it left the city smelling fresh and steamy, like a garden after a storm.

He walked on through the streets, thinking only of tomorrow. A horse-drawn fiacre clopped round the Trevi Fountains. The ruins were floodlit, standing out paper-white from the darkness like structures in a film studio. A girl called to him from the shadows. She was very small, in a black leather jacket, with a cat-face and hair up in a beehive. 'Y'wanna make love, mister! Ten thousan' leery!'

He walked on and the girl vanished. He began thinking about Leila again, and found that he couldn't remember exactly what she had looked like. The image in his mind was blurred, and as soon as the features began to form he had to fight out the other face that came swimming up — the one on the marble slab, with the tarpaulin pulled down below the breasts.

He stepped into a bar and had a strong drink. There were neon signs winking down the street, and he meandered on, past the nightclubs with the kerbs lined with English sports cars. He went down into one of the clubs, which had black mirrors and couples swaying to jazz violins. He was shown to a corner table as small as a coffee stool, where he ordered a bottle of iced white wine, drinking it alone, wanting Leila badly; and the more he drank the more he wanted her, and the more he felt his hate rising against Izard. He tried to imagine what he would finally do when he faced the man. The thought of that meeting gave him a twinge of pleasurable suspense.

A girl pressed past his table and upset his glass. She was holding a furious-faced boxer dog straining at a leash, and Quinn noticed that a zip at her hips had come several inches undone. He stood up to wipe the wine off his trousers, and she said hastily, '*Scusi!*' then shouted something in Italian with a strong English accent at a man who was already disappearing up the stairs.

Quinn said: 'Did he walk out on you?'

She swung round: 'Who are you? Oh, I spilt your drink…'

'Come and sit down.'

'These damned Italians! Sit, MacGillicary!' she yelled at the dog. 'That chap walked out just because I've got another date for tomorrow night. They're all like children. Lie down, MacGillicary!' she fastened the leash to the table leg and smiled suddenly: 'So you're English?'

'Let's drink to it. The name's Rupert Quinn.'

'Oh, that's a good name! I'm Juliet — Hillary-Burnett. Awful, isn't it? I want to change it to Savonarola. They roasted him alive, you know, hanging in a cage in front of the Palazzo Vecchio in Florence. And this,' she said, patting the boxer's head under the table, 'is Mister MacGillicary. He's still only a baby, so he doesn't have to wear a muzzle yet. Isn't he sweet?' The beast rolled its rheumy eyes lovingly up at her, and Quinn ordered more wine.

She was plump and pretty, with a nose turned up like the spout of a teapot. 'How long have you been in Italy?' she asked. 'I've been here all summer studying in Perugia. I think it's just blissful!' She gabbled on, drinking the wine in gulps, smiling brightly, telling him how she had come down from

Cambridge in June and was now working in some branch of UNO.

'I do research,' she said gaily, 'so I don't have to go back to England. Because if I go back they'll put Mister MacGillicary in quarantine for six months. Gosh, I love it here! — only the men are so silly. What do you do?' He smiled to himself. 'Come on, do tell me! What do you do?'

He told her about Morocco and the war, and shot her a swashbuckling line about being a gun-runner, and her eyes went as big as half-crowns and she cried: 'Gosh, how super!'

'The English are all so dull here in Rome,' she added; 'just a lot of dreadful cretins gaping at ruins. They're pretty dull back in England too, aren't they? All that Affluent Society stuff — kills the spirit of adventure!' She laughed and emptied her glass. 'I think capital punishment's so awful too, don't you?'

They went on to the dance floor and shuffled about cheek-to-cheek, and she felt warm and voluptuous against him in a puppy-fat way. 'Your zip's coming undone,' he whispered; 'first thing I noticed about you.'

She giggled: 'My hips are too big. But I've got a lovely figure, you know!' She had big malleable breasts, and when he squeezed one of them she just giggled again and made a mooing noise. Then suddenly he had an evil image of that face on the slab, and stopped dancing and said: 'Let's sit down.'

'But it's a Charleston!' she cried.

'I don't care what it is,' he said, starting back across the floor. She was following him to the table when a young Italian shouted: '*Ey, ciao, Giulietta!*'

'*Ciao, Guido!*'

'*Bella mia!*' he heard. Somebody doing the Charleston collided with his table. The club was very full now and he saw Juliet in

222

the middle, kicking up her heels and spinning like a top. Her zip was again coming undone.

Under the table Mister MacGillicary shifted his belly and growled. Quinn finished the wine, thinking that tomorrow Izard would be less than a quarter of a mile away. He got up and went through to the telephones. An old crone sold him a jeton and he dialled the number of the house in the Viale Piemonte. It was past midnight and there was no answer. He left the receiver dangling off, the line still ringing, and went back into the club, where Juliet and her Italian were sitting at his table.

She waved to him, one hand on the Italian's lapel; the man looked like a male model. 'Ruperto,' she said, 'this is Guido!' and the Italian stood and bent stiffly from the waist.

'This is my table,' said Quinn. He called a waiter: '*Il conto!*'

'You're not going?' she cried, her face falling like a child's. 'Please don't go.'

The Italian remained standing. There was barely room for even two at the table, and there were only the two chairs. They stood looking at each other for a moment, then Quinn said: '*Ciao, Guido!*' snapping his fingers at him, and sat down.

She said quietly: 'You don't have to be rude to him.'

'Why not? I'm with you, aren't I?'

She looked at him, then at the Italian, and said: 'He's a friend of mine.'

'I'm not in the mood for your friends. Now get rid of him — or I shall!'

She made a pleading gesture over his head and the Italian took hold of his shoulder. Quinn swung round and snarled: 'Scram! F — off! *Vai!*' The girl gasped and the Italian slapped him hard on the cheek.

What happened then gave the impression of film in slow motion. Quinn kicked at the Italian who howled and sat down heavily on the table, then gradually sank to the floor, bringing down with him a heap of glass and linen. People scattered with shouts and knocking of chairs, and for a moment the Italian lay still on the floor.

Suddenly Mister MacGillicary, goaded by the noise and confusion and the falling body, went berserk. He bounded from under the table, tearing his leash free with a further crash of glass, and began to savage the inert man, biting deep into his ear.

There were screams and blood and Juliet Hillary-Burnett's well-bred voice crying rebuke at the incensed hound; while Quinn felt himself rushed towards the door, up the stairs, with men round him yelling '*Polizia!*'

There were five white-coated waiters outside in the street, all very small and holding on to him panic-stricken. His head cleared a little and he said: 'O.K. I go! I pay and I go.'

'Twenty-thousand lire!' they cried, still clinging to him.

'Too much.'

'Twenty-thousand lire or police!' There were people coming up the stairs from the club. He opened his belt-pouch and took out a crumpled ball of one-hundred bills.

'Twenty-thousand!' They repeated. He threw the notes into the air. They let go of him and scrambled for the money across the pavement, and he started down the street. He heard them shouting behind him, and there was a clatter of high heels. He turned and saw Juliet, running far too fast, her bottom thrust out and the zip coming down further, with Mister MacGillicary panting at his leash. Just as she reached him her shoe flew off into the gutter, and she cried: 'Wait! wait! — it was all my fault. They've called the police. We'll take my car.'

At the corner she stopped beside a white beetle-shaped sports car. She fumbled with the keys, and he said: 'Is this little monster yours?'

'Yes. Get in!' He caught a glimpse of carabinieri mingling with the crowd outside the club. Mister MacGillicary had leapt into the 'occasional' seat, and she was wagging her finger at him, saying: 'You're a bad dog, MacGillicary!' Quinn slipped into the bucket-seat beside her, and she said: 'He bit half Guido's ear off!' The boxer had begun greedily licking the nape of her neck, just as the carabinieri started to chase down towards them. The engine started up behind their seats, whined like a jet, and the car swung out across the piazza, down a side street.

He said nervously: 'Are you all right to drive?'

She laughed: 'There's no one about — no witnesses.' They were driving along the Corso at just over seventy miles an hour. The car had a right-hand drive, and there was a luminous green aero-compass screwed to the dashboard. They turned through one of the original city gates and started along the Aurelian Walls, with the speedometer needle flicking up to a hundred.

'Did Daddy give you this?' he asked.

'Yes. For my twenty-first. Goes like a bird.'

'What is it?'

'Porsche.'

'Like the one James Dean was killed in.'

'Don't be morbid! You're mad, you know. I think you knocked Guido out. At least you kicked him in a horrid place. You're not a gentleman.'

'Glad to hear it. Now be a good girl and run me back to my hotel.' He gave her the address and she braked the car to a stop with a shriek of rubber, and lunged over and gave him a big wet kiss, as though she wanted to swallow half his face. He mumbled into her teeth: 'Come back and sleep with me.'

She broke away. ''Ere, 'ere, 'ere!' she cried, in mock Cockney; 'and who do you think I am, Rupert Quinn?'

He heard a menacing growl behind him, and said: 'All right don't.'

She started the car angrily, and they drove back without another word, scraping through the streets near his hotel, the engine sending a high moan among the medieval houses.

Outside the hotel she suddenly threw her arms round him and said: 'You're very masculine. Not like these soppy Italians.' He didn't say anything, and she put her head on one side and said: 'My special Algerian gun-runner!'

He opened the door. 'I'll give you a ring some time. What's your number at UNO?'

She said: 'Can I come up and sleep on your sofa?'

They passed the old porter in the hall, asleep like a mole with his wrinkled snout against his waistcoat. She tiptoed after him, with Mister MacGillicary bounding up the stairs three steps at a time. He held the door open for both of them, then stripped off his clothes and got under the sheet. The room was very close. She said: 'It's pretty small in here.'

'There's no sofa,' he said; 'you'll have to come and sleep in bed.'

She hesitated, while the boxer leapt up and lay across his legs; then she turned out the light and he heard her picking at little hooks and clips in the dark. She climbed in next to him, and he found her still strapped up with bits of elastic and whalebone.

'You're not getting undressed?'

'No, I mustn't,' she whispered.

He turned his back to her, and as he dozed off he could hear Mister MacGillicary busily licking his private parts.

He dreamt that he was lying alone in the little room and the door opened and somebody came in, and he switched on the light and saw Leila standing beside the bed. Only it was the other Leila, with the tarpaulin round her like a cloak; and he woke up sweating and half out of bed, to find himself staring into the brutal black face of Mister MacGillicary. He slept badly for the rest of the night.

He got up at about ten, dressed and shook her awake: 'When do you have to be at work?'

'Not till after lunch,' she said yawning. He looked at her lying there with the sheet clinging to her rump, and had an idea. 'Your Italian's pretty good, isn't it? When you're dressed could you help me make a phone call?'

She sat up, rubbing her eyes and frowning. 'You didn't want me last night, did you?'

He shrugged: 'I always take no for an answer.'

'I didn't say no,' she said.

He watched her crawl out of bed and begin fumbling for her skirt and slip. 'I'm going down for breakfast,' he said. 'There's a café outside — meet me there.'

There were some little boys walking slowly and reverently round the Porsche, which glinted diamond-white in the sun. She came down about ten minutes later, with Mister MacGillicary nosing eagerly about for somewhere to relieve himself. Her hair was like a bird's nest and her face still creased with sleep. 'You've got nowhere proper to bath,' she said grumpily.

'What's your exact job with UNO?' he asked.

'Oh, I just look things up. About India and the Congo and things.'

'Well, I want you to ring somebody up for me and ask for a Signor de Sanctis. Say you want some information for UNO.'

'Is that all?'

'Just make it sound natural. If he's not there, ask when he'll be back. Say it's urgent. If he is there, don't speak to him — just hang up.'

'Mystery man,' she said. 'Is this all to do with your gun-running?'

'Never mind.' He stood with her in the booth and watched tensely as she dialled the number and waited while it rang. Her Italian was very confident. She asked several questions, then put her hand over the mouthpiece and said: 'He'll be in about lunchtime, then he's going away again. He won't be able to see anybody.'

'Ask where he's going.'

She spoke some more, then turned and said: 'They don't know. It's some old bitch speaking — doesn't sound very pleased.'

He thought quickly. 'Right, that'll do.' She hung up. 'Now listen, *Giulietta amore*, I want you to do me a great favour. A matter of life and death!' Her eyes goggled excitedly. 'Lend me your car until this evening.'

'You won't get it shot up by a lot of Algerians and gangsters?'

'I'll take perfect care of it.' He kissed her briskly on the cheek and bolted down his coffee, urging her to leave before she'd even finished hers.

She drove him back to her pension, explaining the controls of the car; and as she got out and let him move into the driving seat she kissed him sloppily and said: 'You're a super chap, you know! *A presto!*'

He took the car into the Via Aurelia, getting the feel of the gears and the dangerously light throttle; in third gear the acceleration gave a thrust like an ejection seat. He drove to the American Express and drew out twenty-thousand lire (almost the last of his resources), then stopped to refuel and have the tyre and oil pressures checked, while the garage attendant shook his head and said adoringly: '*Bella macchina!*' Then he headed back to the city centre, turning into the Viale Piemonte.

It was a quarter to twelve. He backed the car into a side street, allowing plenty of room to draw away; then positioned himself behind the bead curtain of a bar-tabacchi, commanding a view of the front of number 19.

He drank several espressos, chewed a prosciutto sandwich; watched, and waited.

CHAPTER 3

The iron grille was now open, and during the next hour several people called at the house, mostly squat, bald men with briefcases.

By one o'clock there was still no sign of Izard. He was just about to make a further phone call to No. 19, when a car like a propelling-pencil slid up in front of the house, and a man in chauffeur's cap and gaiters got out and went inside. Quinn could not see his face. Several people in the bar moved to the window and stared wondrously at the car. Someone said it was a Ferrari Gran Turismo 250.

There was a crowd collecting round it, when the chauffeur appeared again at the door. He wore dark glasses, but even under the peaked cap Quinn knew at once that it was M. Beloued. Behind him a small man emerged, pushing himself on a black cane. He was wearing spats, like little white hooves, and M. Beloued held open the door and helped him in. Quinn threw down a thousand lire, not waiting for the change, and hurried into the street.

The Ferrari was facing away from him, so there was little risk of his being seen as he ran across the street and jumped into the Porsche. M. Beloued returned to the house, brought out two cases, put them in the boot, then got into the driving seat and Quinn pushed the starter of the Porsche. The engine grunted and roared, as the Ferrari glided off from the kerb with a sound like a summer breeze, to vanish at the end of the street.

Quinn accelerated after him, cutting dangerously in front of a lane of cars, and there were shouts and gnashing of teeth, as he spun round the corner and opened up along the packed Via Nazionale. The Ferrari seemed to slip away like an arrow, without sound or effort; and Quinn had to shoot a traffic light on the Piazza Venezia, sliding round the Colosseum, opening up in the Porsche's third gear, flying under the grey-green Roman pines into the three-lane avenue through the hideous granite Nuova Citta.

The tarmac shimmered, the white lines swerving, breaking away, running together again like tracks of a railway junction. Modern tenement blocks swung past, scattered over the hills like monstrous chests of drawers. They reached an intersection where the Gran Turismo floated out to the left, a white arrow and the word Napoli flashing from under its wheels. Quinn pointed the Porsche's sloping bonnet down a road as broad and straight as a runway.

The Ferrari was now doing over a hundred miles an hour. Quinn positioned the Porsche and flicked down the overdrive. The high whine of the engine behind his seat took on a steady rhythm, the oncoming traffic leaping past the corners of his eye. The speedometer needle quivered on the 110 mark. The luminous aero-compass gyrated slowly, then settled down pointing south-southeast.

He pushed in the cool-air button and turned on the radio, imagining himself in a cockpit closing on the tail of an enemy aircraft, tracking it down and destroying it. For a moment he had the idea of crashing the Ferrari. At this speed it would require only to nick a bumper and they would all be spattered for hundreds of yards. But it seemed too easy. The car was fast and light, and the radio now came up with the crackle and throb of jazz, also fast and light and loud enough to drown the sizzle of tyres, and Quinn felt suddenly relaxed and exhilarated, watching the strip of hot grey road racing under him, slowing down into Latina — all concrete and pylons, designed by Mussolini to be Italy's model town. The Ferrari swept through at fifty miles an hour; the Porsche stayed three hundred yards behind.

Outside the town the road straightened out again and ran down along the sea. Bubbles of pumice-grey rock began to swell up on either side. The road swerved; the sea opened up. They ducked into tunnels, and the sudden pitch-darkness after the sun was full of the pounding roar of the high-compression engine. Out again, shrieking round the coast road, narrow and fenced in with white-painted granite slabs, he saw the Ferrari about a mile ahead.

He still had no clear idea of what he wanted to do. Occasionally it did occur to him that Izard and M. Beloued might become suspicious at the sight of a white sports car persistently behind them. He also remembered, with only a prick of conscience, that he had promised Juliet to return the Porsche by evening.

They came into Gaeta, and the road became slower, twisted among rocks, and once, at a complicated flyover, he thought he had lost the Ferrari; then, about a kilometre away, he saw the slim grey bullet-shape on the horizon shoot out behind a finger of rock, still on the Naples road.

Thirty kilometres from the city the Ferrari drew into one of the spacious Supercortemaggiore service stations, with the seductive sign offering a bar, café, restaurant, showers and barber's shop. Quinn pulled into the side of the road a few hundred yards ahead and sat smoking and waiting for the Ferrari to pass. For a moment he considered taking the crankshaft and going back to the filling station and bludgeoning them both to death over their cappuccinos. But that would be too untidy. Besides, quite probably M. Beloued had a gun. He was a killer — it was no doubt his hand that had drawn the knife through Leila's throat. Quinn decided that if he was going to do anything it must be done in style, with pleasurable anticipation. And just for the moment he was enjoying the chase.

He almost missed the Ferrari as it passed. By the time he'd drawn out it was a good kilometre away, entering the road that cuts down into the Bay of Naples. The dark flat-topped pines like wide umbrellas stretched along the border of the road, and behind lay the stony track of the original Appian Way winding off the shoulder of the hills.

On that last stretch into Naples the Ferrari suddenly drew away into the heat haze and vanished. Quinn had his foot flat on the floor and the needle struggled up to nearly 120, when the car began to shake. He held his foot there perhaps twenty seconds. The speed made his body vibrate, and his mind slowed up, happy, almost mesmerised.

Suddenly, about a mile ahead, a haycart lumbered out, blocking half the road. He brought the car down to 90, had his hand down on the horn and swung out to pass the cart, when he saw a car coming straight at him. He aimed at the gap, kept his hand still on the horn, then closed his eyes.

It was a tiny Fiat, buzzing along at a fair speed. It reached the gap perhaps three seconds after the Porsche. The man inside was yelling, and Quinn opened his eyes to see the car skid round, hit the grass verge and bounce on to its back like a rubber ball.

He had instinctively slowed down further and was sweating. Ahead there was no sign of the Ferrari. He eased the throttle down again, knowing that he had to catch up with the car before it disappeared into Naples.

He snaked round sharp bends through a village; swooped and roared into the mouth of the six-lane tunnel under the hills. Tail lights glimmered ahead of him like hot animal eyes in the darkness; and when he came out he was bumping along a noisy street, the sky cobwebbed with tram wires. The traffic charged and weaved like dodgems. There was a square with roads striking off in the points of a star. He was just in time to glimpse the Ferrari disappearing down a narrow street at the far corner. He accelerated, missed a tram by less than a foot, ignoring the horns and bells, and followed the street down into the port.

He kept the Ferrari close in sight, driving past huts built of packing cases and mud and corrugated iron patched up with newspaper. The smell was warm and fetid. There were bomb ruins and clusters of masts and rusted smoke-stacks. The bright ragged crowds stood and gaped at the cars; and there were whistles and sneers. The Ferrari turned at the dock gates, up a steep evil-smelling street leading to the south side of the city. Quinn knew now that he was staying dangerously near his quarry, but he dared not risk losing him again in the confusion of the traffic. He cursed the English number plates on the Porsche: they would be the first thing to attract attention.

They passed a cinema showing *The Last Days of Pompeii*. Blue-chinned Neapolitans, saddled with shrieking bambini, crowded in past the peeling posters on the tenement walls where Steve Reeves, tripped and flexed, heaved his sword against a chaotic background of toppling temples and molten lava. A hundred yards further on the white-laundered policeman pirouetted on his rostrum and deftly directed the Ferrari on to the Autostrada to Pompeii: twelve miles of hoardings for Fiat and the six-legged black dog of Supercortemaggiore flipping past, counting off the kilometres. Arrows on the tarmac marked off the flyover turning towards the excavated town of Herculaneum, and to Vesuvius.

The volcano moved past on his left: a truncated slagheap rising out of the sea haze with the chairlift creeping up its flanks like a line of tip-trucks. The Ferrari kept straight on, at over a hundred miles an hour, two miles ahead of the Porsche.

It slowed down past the entrance to Pompeii, where the deluxe diesel coaches stood parked up against a crumbled wall. The guides prowled about armed with postcard racks, waiting for the trippers to come crowding through the turnstiles with their cameras and transistor radios.

Quinn kept his eyes on the Ferrari as it turned up on to the road for Salerno.

Twilight was falling fast. They were well beyond Salerno now, winding down the spine of southern Italy, with the road looping away under the moon like a ribbon of tinfoil, the windscreen clouding over with green insects.

For more than an hour they had not passed a single house and hardly another car. The headlamps of the Porsche threw a hard white light through the darkness, and the valleys grew steeper, the curves of the road sharper, the two cars alone in the night.

The fuel gauge of the Porsche had suddenly dropped almost to the empty mark. Once Quinn glimpsed some pinpricks of light far on the horizon, but they came no nearer, then disappeared altogether. The aero-compass gyrated steadily to the singing of the road; the gearbox howled with the double-declutching at each bend; and the radio played grand opera throughout the evening, the arias roaring into the night.

It was just before eleven o'clock when he at last saw below him the lights of a town. He followed the Ferrari into a tree-lined square with arcades and a brightly-lit petrol station. The Ferrari had stopped to refuel, and all round the crowds strolled out to examine Izard's splendid machine. Quinn saw the danger at once. He turned the Porsche into a side street, drove round behind the square, edging back into it from the far side. But the Ferrari was still there, with the crowds pressing round, and he pulled into a quiet street with a bar where he ordered coffee with cognac.

He was now beginning to feel the tension and tiredness. He bought a cheese sandwich as big as a spade, and some chocolate to last him later on, already suspecting that Izard was making a night of it; there was no large town now before Reggio Calabria in the toe of Italy, still more than three hundred kilometres away.

The Ferrari drew away at last, and it was now Quinn's turn to take petrol and submit to the awesome worship of the Italians, as they closed round the Porsche, stroking its dust and fly-spattered wings as though they were the flanks of some beautiful woman.

After paying for the petrol he realised, with some dismay, that he was left with little more than twelve-thousand lire — now eight hours from Rome, and still no idea of where he was going.

He stayed at the filling station barely three minutes, but it took him nearly an hour of hard driving before he caught sight again of the Ferrari's lights. Tosca and La Bohème encouraged him till midnight; then Musique Pour les Routiers took over through the small hours, when he was steering round perpetual hairpin bends over nearly two hundred kilometres. It was a long, stiff, weary night.

CHAPTER 4

He reached Reggio Calabria just after dawn through a thin rain. He had lost Izard some hours back in darkness, but a policeman outside the town remembered seeing the Ferrari streak past about twenty minutes earlier.

Quinn drove straight to the port. There, alone on the cobbles in front of the gates of the Messina ferry, stood the Gran Turismo. It was empty. He stopped the Porsche in a side street, and imprudently got out and walked round the Ferrari, noticing that the front seat next to the driver was folded down into a bed that still bore the imprints of Izard's frail body. There was also an open cocktail cabinet with a coffee machine and a half-full decanter of orange juice.

There seemed to be no one about. It was a grey morning with a squall blowing off the Straits of Messina that made Quinn shiver under his linen jacket. His eyes stung with lack of sleep, and his back and buttocks and fingers ached with cramp. He went into the port office and bought a one-way ticket on the first ferry of the day, which left in just under an hour, then settled to wait in a café across the square where he drank three coffees and a couple of fierce glasses of grappa. Then, under the brooding eyes of the waiters, he began a series of press-ups in the middle of the floor.

When he jumped up he saw a man watching him from the door. He was very thin, standing spindle-legged under a rucksack that bristled with picks and spiked boots. Quinn returned to his table and the man came sidling up to him, saying, with a thick accent: 'Excuse me, but are you the Englishman with the white car, please?'

Quinn asked him to sit down. The man bowed and began depositing his load on the floor, introducing himself as a Swedish geologist called Pettersson who wanted a lift over to Catania. Quinn said he wasn't sure where he was going in Sicily, but he would take him as far as he could. Pettersson joined him in a grappa, and then began hurriedly explaining that he was a specialist in 'volcanology' and planned to explore Mount Etna — 'the Great God Etna' as he called it. 'The largest and most dangerous volcano in the Northern Hemisphere.'

He had a long bony face like a sheep. Quinn listened to him patiently, waiting for the hour to pass. He was worrying about the trip on the ferry. If the Porsche were the only other car on board it would probably attract Izard's attention.

Pettersson was saying: 'The mountain has killed more than sixty-thousand people since Christendom.' His pale eyes narrowed with a terrible passion behind scholarly spectacles. Quinn asked him suddenly: 'Can you drive a car?'

'I can. Do you wish me to drive?'

Quinn explained that he wanted him to take the Porsche on to the ferry, then drive it off again. He invented a tale about following a man who was his wife's lover. The Swede shook his head gravely. 'That is not good,' he said.

Quinn took him outside and began showing him the controls of the car, gave him the car ticket, and told him to stay at the wheel until the ferry had started, then join him at the stern of the boat. The man seemed to accept the conspiracy as quite normal; but while being shown over the car his eyes continually wandered to the line of hills along the Sicilian shore. Once he looked up and gave Quinn a wolfish grin, showing a row of crooked, dark yellow teeth. 'The Greek,

Pericles, made suicide into the crater of Etna,' he said; 'and one sandal was thrown out.'

During the choppy crossing Quinn kept well down near the canvas-hooded lifeboats at the stern. The sun had not come up and it was still very cold. Pettersson joined him after they had put out and began muttering distractedly about the history and phenomenae of volcanoes. He had some theory that if a man could be lowered down the 'chimney' of a crater in a fireproof cage he would be able to descend almost to the centre of the earth.

Quinn smoked and nodded and looked out to sea. When they reached Messina Pettersson duly took the Porsche ashore, and Quinn leapt in on the landing ramp and drove furiously after the Ferrari which he nearly lost in the narrow streets off the port. The big car had turned off towards Catania. Even along this wretched, almost Arab coastline of eastern Sicily the road was broad and fast, and once again Quinn had to brace his worn-out muscles for the chase.

The Swede, meanwhile, kept bobbing about next to him, trying to catch his first glimpse of Mount Etna. He had taken out a fat Swedish guidebook which he was now translating aloud, reading with some difficulty for Quinn's benefit about the splendours of the volcano. "'The head-crater is more than one kilometre wide and one thousand metres deep..."' The Ferrari was approaching the 100-mile an hour mark, the wind shrieking under the Porsche's wings. "'...The ascent to the head-crater is heavy, but once arrived, it is an unforgettable sight..."'

They rounded a promontory along the shore, and across the horizon in front of them they saw the great pyramid of Etna disappearing into cloud. Pettersson became positively unhinged with excitement. He bared his bad teeth, fingers clenched to his knees, straining forward to study the charcoal-black lava slopes humped with hundreds of subsidiary cones like smoking beehives. The sky was discoloured with storm cloud, and presently he swore and said in English: 'Blardy weather! It will be like night up there.'

Quinn saw the Ferrari's tail flick off to the right, up the steep road to Taormina. Pettersson was saying: 'Did you know that in the seventeenth century Etna threw out one million cubic metres of lava?'

The Porsche screamed up to the turn; Quinn did a frantic racing-change, braked hard and felt the back wheels slide round like a pair of skates, the light bodywork slither and bump and scrape along the embankment of lava bricks. Pettersson cried: 'Oh blardy hell!' — and the car stopped. One side was dented and rubbed black, and the front wheel was buckled. Quinn restarted the engine, but the car would only limp up the mountain road, and by the time they reached the ancient town of Taormina the Ferrari had vanished.

Quinn drove under a walled gate, across a piazza full of cafés and shops bursting with bright junk for the tourists. There was no sign of the Ferrari. He drove down the main street, which was littered with placards saying, *Zimmer Frei* — English Breakfasts, and stopped the Porsche in a square that looked out over the sea and the rising sweep of the volcano. There was a tourist office opposite that was just putting up its shutters. Inside were photographs of ruined temples and the crater of Etna. A blonde wide-faced girl stood behind the desk and smiled. She spoke English with a slight German accent. Quinn said: 'I'm looking for two people in a Ferrari Gran Turismo. They're Moroccans. One is an old man. He's called de Sanctis. The other is younger, has dark glasses…' He paused and the girl smiled and shrugged. 'I do not know everybody here,' she said.

Pettersson, who had been moving along the rows of photographs of Mount Etna, suddenly bounded up to the desk and cried: 'When is the excursion to Etna?'

The girl, still smiling, said to him: 'There is no excursion from Taormina today. The weather on Etna is not good.'

'But when is the next?' cried the Swede, his mouth hanging slack, showing the full extent of his decayed denture.

Before she could answer Quinn had interrupted. 'These two men have only just arrived here. They've driven down all night from Rome. De Sanctis — a Moroccan…'

'I cannot help you,' said the girl. 'There are so many strangers here. Behind Taormina are more than three hundred villas.'

At that moment Pettersson leant out and grabbed her wrist. She tried to withdraw it, but he held on like a man possessed. 'When is the next excursion?' he yelled. Her smile had faded now. 'There is no excursion up Etna today,' she repeated, her little hand squirming free. 'I cannot tell you about tomorrow. The weather is bad and there have been many explosions on the crater.'

'Explosions?' roared the Swede.

'It is dangerous up there,' said the girl firmly. She turned to Quinn. 'Do not try to go up now. In Catania the people are lighting candles in the churches because they are frightened that it will erupt.'

Pettersson had run to the door and was staring out at the volcano. 'Your friend is very strange,' said the girl to Quinn. He looked gravely at her, and said: 'Listen, it's most important that I find these two men. They came in a Ferrari. Perhaps you could make some enquiries.'

'You can try the hotels here,' she said. 'But if they are not in Taormina itself it will not be easy.' Her smile had fully returned now, when Pettersson came striding back in. He faced the girl and said: 'I must get up that mountain! How do I do it?'

'There is a bus every morning from Catania,' she said, with secretarial efficiency; 'but it only goes as far as Nicolosi at the bottom of Etna.' She turned back to Quinn and said, 'I hope you have luck and find your friends.' She had a beautiful smile, with square white teeth, and her face was broad and brown and healthy. As he was leaving he called to her: 'Perhaps we'll see each other again. Where do you come from, by the way?'

'I am from Vienna. I come to Sicilia to work in the summer.' He waved to her and joined Pettersson outside. 'What are you going to do now?' he asked him. The Swede spread out his hands and scowled: 'What can I do with this blardy weather?' He followed Quinn back to the car, and they drove round all the hotels in the town, but no one seemed to know anything about two Moroccans with a Ferrari.

Quinn stopped, exhausted, and had breakfast with Pettersson on the terrace of a hotel with a notice on the wall announcing, Dancing Cha-Cha-Cha Tons Les Soirs All Evenings Jeden Abend. There were some English tourists with shorts and gym shoes on the terrace reading the *Daily Mail*; Quinn saw a black headline about an unofficial strike in the car industry. Next to him Pettersson fidgeted and sulked, and finally glared at him and said: 'You have lost this man. You will not find him. So you come down to Catania with me, yes?'

Quinn had no energy to argue; he stared into the pale sea haze and thought about the Viennese girl, seeing her up in the hotel that evening dancing the cha-cha with the English boys in their gym shoes. The memory of Leila seemed suddenly remote and dismal.

He paid the bill, then took the Porsche to a garage and had the wheel changed. The Ferrari could be almost anywhere in eastern Sicily by now. A good country for a vendetta, he thought, as he drove wearily into Catania.

Up in the tall stone bedroom of their hotel he flung himself down fully dressed on the bed, ready to sleep through till evening. On the other bed Pettersson sat for some time studying his guidebook and preparing his assault on the volcano. Quinn could hear him rummaging about in his rucksack, laying out ropes and boots, special goggles to fit over his spectacles and a leather helmet and gasmask.

'And don't forget your thunderbox!' he called to him, 'in case you're taken short with terror!' The Swede nodded thoughtfully and began dressing for the expedition. Quinn was asleep before he left.

When he woke it was already evening. Pettersson had burst in and was standing in the middle of the room, zipped up in a tracksuit, swearing in soft, trembling Swedish.

Quinn swung off the bed and said: 'So you've had a hard day on Etna?'

'It was impossible!' the Swede cried, tearing off his goggles and helmet. 'The guides halted me.' He zipped open the tracksuit down to his groin, as though he was committing hara-kiri, then sank down on to the bed in his underpants, his face thin and miserable. For a moment he sat staring at his long white toes, then suddenly he looked up and said loudly: 'Tomorrow I will climb that mountain. I come all the way from Stockholm to do it and nothing will prohibit me!'

Quinn glanced at the pile of gear on the floor and said: 'But why do you need all this stuff just to go up Etna? Tourists go up it every day?'

As he spoke the Swede sprang from the bed, his eyes lit with an unnatural fire as though a pair of red-hot saucers were glowing somewhere far back in his narrow skull. He spoke slowly, controlling his emotions:

'I intend to go down into the crater. I shall be the first man to do it.'

'And what will you do down there?'

Pettersson shook his head, as though he were talking to some heretic or fool. 'I shall look,' he said. 'I shall regard what is at the bottom.'

'Come on, I'll buy you a drink,' said Quinn.

Pettersson shrugged, then put on a shirt and jeans and loped out after him into the street. At the door he noticed for the first time that their hotel was called the Hotel Etna, and was in the Via Etnea, which is an avenue down the centre of Catania with Etna framed impressively at one end. They went into a bar that happened to be called the Bar Etna, and most of the wine they drank that evening had a name coupled with that of Etna, nourished on the lava slopes.

Pettersson drank quickly and without pleasure, soon lapsing into Strindbergian gloom. He moaned and banged the table, riling against the weather and the volcano — while all round him the name of Etna goaded him with temptation like that of some infinitely desirable girl who was eluding him.

Quinn drank in silence. His enthusiasm was sinking. He thought of the girl from Vienna smiling at all the tourists and wondered if it wouldn't be better to forget about the whole business, and go back and marry Miss Hillary-Burnett for some of her daddy's money.

Pettersson had broken his glass and was yelling: 'I am the first man in the centre of the earth!' Quinn led him shouting and stumbling, back to the Hotel Etna where he laid him out on his bed and promised to drive him in the morning to the foot of the volcano.

When Quinn woke, the Swede was already climbing into his equipment like some preposterous bomber pilot before a mission. He was twitching slightly, either with a hangover or nervous excitement.

The morning was clear, but there was a high wind in the streets and the summit of the volcano was capped with a fuzz of brown cloud. Pettersson peered anxiously at it, muttering to himself. On the way out of the city Quinn stopped to send a telegram to Juliet Hillary-Burnett, telling her that he would be back in Rome the next day. Then they followed the winding road up to the volcano.

All around Etna the land is lush and green, with vegetation bursting out of the crusts of lava with an unhealthy vigour like the greenness round a graveyard. The trees have heavy leaves, even after a scorching summer, and the lower slopes of the mountain, where the lava fields spread out like a stain across the parched land to the south, are rich with clusters of burnt-out cones terraced into vineyards.

They drove up to where the road finishes at a concrete hotel at the foot of the funivia. Pettersson had got out and was examining the rusted pylons of the chairlift that disappeared up the mountain face into a broken ceiling of cloud.

But Quinn's attention was held by something else. Standing, as though by fatal obedience, on the tarmac outside the hotel was the Ferrari Gran Turismo.

In that moment he had the strange sensation that it was suddenly not he, but Izard, who was now the hunter. Pettersson had turned to say goodbye to him, but Quinn simply said: 'I'm coming up with you.'

They went into the hut at the foot of the lift, where a man with a flat square face like a Red Indian sat behind a window marked: All'Inferno del Cratere Centrale. He seemed reluctant to sell them tickets, warning them about explosions and high winds, adding lugubriously that last year part of the chairlift had been blown down. 'Five Germans gravely injured,' he told them, with false solemnity.

Quinn asked about the people who had come in the Ferrari. Yes, he remembered them. Two of them. They had gone up the mountain about a quarter of an hour earlier to collect wild flowers. Then he led them out to the shed behind the hut where the chairlift began. They could hear the wind moaning in the cables, and a few seconds later a pair of chair-brackets came swinging over the pulleys, looking alarmingly fragile. They swept Quinn and Pettersson out into the wind, hurtling them up the lava slopes. Over the first pylon there was a loud clank and they could see the supports wobbling in their concrete bases far below. Once over it the chairs dropped like a switchback.

Quinn turned his head and saw stretching away behind him a landscape that was illogical and frightening: a vast lunar wasteland full of swellings and scars and smooth cones that were almost beautiful. The lava was whipped up by the wind and imparted a strange sense of death, black and gritty like bomb dust. Then suddenly in the midst of this desolation there would appear frightful flowers more than six feet wide — spongy thistles with white spines and fat leaves as soft as velvet.

They lurched past another pylon, out over a smoking crater that gave off a smell like fireworks. On either side the cones were rising higher, charred black with streaks of red and raw yellow: monstrous cankers thrown up through the crust of the earth during the Creation, full of steam holes and pits and heaped lava flows like petrified avalanches.

Suddenly the cloud closed round them and they were jerking up through a dark fog, bitterly cold, with the smell of the volcano growing strong and sickly. Then the shape of a hut loomed down towards them, and they were on the concrete platform with the guides closing in, whining at them in a polyglot jargon gleaned from half a century of Baedekers. Pettersson tried to shoo them off, but they grinned wickedly and pursued them both into a bar behind the chairlift, where Pettersson bought two litre fiascos of white wine. He waved them in the air, giving his wild yellow grin, and said: 'One for you, my friend!' Quinn took the bottle and they set off for the door.

At once the guides surrounded them again; but Quinn managed to extricate himself and found a young boy who seemed less rapacious than the others, to whom he began describing Izard and M. Beloued. The boy frowned; two tourists had started up to the crater a few minutes earlier, but he himself hadn't seen them.

At that moment there came a yell from the door; Quinn turned, to see Pettersson hemmed in by five furious guides. There was a great deal of shouting, and one of them began to weep, and another was waving a knotted stick above the Swede's head.

Quinn learnt afterwards that they had been trying to sell him lumps of lava for 100 lire each. Since the whole volcano is lava this seemed to lose its point. To Pettersson it was blasphemy. Inflamed by a particularly cloying guide he had seized a lava pebble from the ground outside the door and had offered it to his tormentor for 1,000 lire. The man, old and gnarled and ugly, had been mortally insulted.

The five of them were now threatening him with clenched fists, and the Swede rolled his eyes towards Quinn and bellowed: 'Help me, my friend!' Quinn began to elbow his way into the group, and Pettersson took advantage of the diversion to duck down and disappear through the door into the cloud; Quinn followed, with the guides howling abuse after them.

The Swede was already striding up the steep eruptive cone towards the central crater. He had begun to wheeze asthmatically. 'Thank you!' he gasped. A few moments later they heard footsteps behind them and the young guide appeared, calling that it was dangerous to go up alone. Quinn asked him how much it would cost to be taken on the same route as the two tourists who had gone up earlier.

'Four thousand lire,' the boy said smiling. The two tourists had set out on an excursion round the crater.

Quinn reluctantly counted out the money, knowing that he would not have enough to buy petrol back to Rome. But it was too late now: he would have to see the business through to the end.

He turned his face to the cone and the three of them started up the last thousand metres to the summit.

After about half an hour of strenuous climbing Pettersson got out a corkscrew and opened the wine, emptying the neck of his fiasco in one draught, while Quinn rested panting on the warm lava, puzzled that an old man like Izard could have made this climb.

They pressed on, with the guide chattering to them in Italian about his brothers and sisters, and how difficult life was in Sicily, and that one day Mussolini, the exiled King of Italy, would return to liberate them from the Mafia.

They passed more of the weird flowers and vegetable excrescences; there was one that looked like a toadstool about three feet wide; the guide kicked it and it burst in a cloud of yellow dust. Quinn imagined the floral decorations that would grace Izard's living room.

The lava was now steaming with fumes; Pettersson had fitted on his gasmask, while Quinn and the guide tied handkerchiefs over their mouths. Quinn was beginning to breathe with difficulty, and in spite of the cold was running with sweat. He was now certain that Izard could never have climbed this. Yet two people had come in the Ferrari, and they had both come up the volcano.

Somewhere above them they now caught the first sound of the crater: a deep rumbling and booming like distant artillery. Pettersson paused and pulled down his gasmask, taking a long swill at his wine; then he looked at Quinn and made a joke: 'You are tired, but you are not retired!' He beamed with delight, while Quinn nodded and took a drink from his own bottle. The sweet wine for a moment washed out the raw taste of sulphur, and he began to clamber up the last few hundred feet.

The noise of the crater had now swelled into the howl of an express train racing into a tunnel, broken by the crash of explosions. Then suddenly, only a few feet above them, they saw the jagged rim of the summit.

As they drew level with it Quinn thought at first that he was looking out across a huge misty plateau to a separate mountain range. Then the cloud parted, and he saw opening at his feet the giant firepit which many Sicilians still believe to be the back entrance to Hell.

The sides of the crater fell away in an almost vertical precipice. Quinn peered over and saw, far below, the walls of the chasm glistening a poisonous purple where the wind carried the gas and cloud up in spirals. Then for a moment it blew them away altogether, and he caught a glimpse of the lava lakes hundreds of feet below — a dull red with flickers of flame darting like quicksilver.

But nowhere could he see any sign of the two tourists.

Pettersson was hopping about like a man demented. He kept running to the edge, then jumping back and slapping his helmeted forehead. The sight of the crater, far from requiting his passions, had only excited him to further torment. The next step would be to climb in.

The guide began to lead them round the edge. The lava underfoot was warm and soft, cracked open in long black crevices, and the ground shook with the explosions. Pettersson frequently stopped to pull down his gasmask and drink from his fiasco, and was now beginning to sway and stumble.

After going a few hundred yards, they came to a small extinct crater with a hole at the bottom about four feet wide. They slithered down and Pettersson tried to look in, but the guide yelled at him to keep back: 'Motto pericoloso!' Then, picking up a lump of lava, he stepped cautiously to the edge and dropped it in. 'How deep?' cried Pettersson. 'Infinito,' said the guide simply. He added that the geological institute in Catania had tried to plumb the shaft, and had reached three kilometres without touching the bottom.

Three kilometres, Quinn thought. *Nearly two miles*. He followed the guide out of the crater, thinking: *A quiet tomb under Mount Etna*. It had poetic qualities.

They climbed over a ridge and stood looking down at a cone that burst out of the black pit of the central crater. As they watched, the mouth of the cone exploded and showers of red-hot rock and lava spat up hundreds of feet out of the swelling clouds of gas and smoke. Quinn watched the bombs — round as cannon balls, some of them as large as double-decker buses — falling and bursting in blue flashes against the side of the cone.

At that moment the guide gave a shout. Pettersson had thrown down his fiasco, which was now empty, and had begun to run down the steep slope into the crater. Twenty feet down he stumbled and fell. The guide grabbed Quinn's hand and cried: '*Pazzo!* Mad!' He seemed to think Pettersson was a German. He went on: 'The Germans are all mad! They must always conquer to be happy. They cannot conquer Etna by climbing her, so they must climb into her!'

Pettersson had picked himself up and was waving at them; then he began walking sideways along the edge of the precipice, starting to unravel the ropes from round his neck. The guide said again: 'That man will kill himself. Two Germans were killed like that only one month ago.'

It was then that Quinn caught his first sight of the two tourists. They were standing on a ridge just below him, overlooking the central crater. One was a girl in a mackintosh with a scarf tied over her mouth against the fumes; she was carrying a huge basket. The other Quinn recognised immediately as M. Beloued. But there was no sign of Izard.

Quinn forgot about Pettersson. He began to run down the narrow path, the guide shouting after him to go carefully Once he nearly lost his balance in the wind and went sliding down the slope towards Pettersson. He had come within about twenty feet of M. Beloued and the girl, when several things happened almost simultaneously.

The cone inside the central crater exploded again, this time with a deafening crack that hurled the molten lava bombs to within less than a hundred feet from where they all stood. Instinctively, M. Beloued and the girl recoiled and turned, and in doing so they both saw Quinn.

In that instant the guide caught up with him and seized his arm, pointing frantically at the exploding cone. They listened to the lava bombs thundering down against the walls of the crater. Then the clouds swirled round them, and M. Beloued and the girl disappeared.

It was only for a few seconds. When it cleared again they were both watching Quinn. M. Beloued had his hand inside his coat pocket, but there was no expression on his face whatever.

Then Quinn saw something that made him stop dead in his tracks.

CHAPTER 5

The girl had pulled down her scarf and he now saw her face.

A gust of sulphur fumes blew round him; the guide was holding his arm and saying, '*Va bene?*' — and Quinn watched her coming towards him, her basket full of the strange, evil flowers, seeing her face deadly clear against the black inferno beyond, eyes sloping up, sly and pretty, the wide mouth breaking into the flicker of a mischievous smile.

He thought of her body moving under the mackintosh — when another cloud swept round them and she vanished. At first he thought it had all been an hallucination: a trick of the wine and fumes. But then she came out of the cloud, still moving towards him, her flat little shoes crunching on the lava; and she put out her hand, and suddenly the sight and touch of her terrified him, and he shuddered away, seeing again that other image under the tarpaulin.

'What is this?' he yelled in French. 'I saw you! I saw you dead!'

She laid down the basket and said: 'I'm sorry — I can explain everything!' Her words were carried away by the wind and the roaring of the crater. M. Beloued moved up beside her, his face quite impassive, and said, close to Quinn's ear: 'So it was you, monsieur, who was following us in the little white car from Rome? Monsieur Izard and I were most puzzled.'

Quinn ignored him; he turned to Leila and yelled furiously: 'What the hell are you doing here?'

She glanced at M. Beloued, then at the basket at her side, and said: 'I came up to help pick the flowers. And also to see the eruptions. It is wonderfully dramatic up here, don't you think?'

She tried to take his hand. 'It wasn't my fault, Rupert darling! Monsieur Izard only did it to protect me. They had to pretend I was dead, or the FLN would have come after me and killed me.'

They stood looking at each other, and Quinn lifted his fiasco and drank it down till it was empty, feeling hot and dizzy and half-drunk, seeing the two faces sway and multiply, hearing Leila say, 'It must have been terrible for you, darling!'

'Who was the girl I saw dead in Casablanca?' he cried.

She frowned. 'I don't know about that. I think it was some prostitute from the Casbah.' She gave M. Beloued an anxious glance, but he remained looking coldly at Quinn. 'They found a girl about my size — with my sort of hair...'

Her laconic manner suddenly appalled him, and he broke away and ran along to where the guide was staring down the slope into the crater. At the very edge of the precipice was Pettersson, sunk on his knees, his masked head flopping against his chest. 'Your friend is ill!' shouted the guide, his eyes full of terror. 'He will burn to death!'

Somewhere behind them Quinn heard Leila calling to him. Without thinking he started to crawl down towards the stricken Swede. After a few feet he began to choke and retch with the fumes, and the wine in his belly seemed to be slopping about like seawater at the bottom of a swamped boat. The soles of his shoes grew painfully hot; his mouth filled with a bitter bile; and he cursed the Swede.

Pettersson had by now collapsed on to his stomach, his gross rubber snout resting only a few inches from the edge of the chasm. His eyes were closed behind the goggles and his tracksuit was already beginning to singe on the hot lava.

Quinn caught him under the elbows and began to haul him very slowly upwards. Twice the cone exploded and he had to pause, head down and eyes closed, while the lava bombs thudded and burst below him.

Back on the path they propped Pettersson up in a sitting position; and Leila came and helped unstrap his gasmask. The face that emerged was a grotesque spectacle: the mouth sagged open trailing saliva, and the inside of the gasmask was full of vomit. Leila cried: 'Oh, the poor man' — while the guide stood crossing himself and muttering prayers.

Presently the Swede opened his eyes: blinked at the face above him, focused on Leila, and suddenly grasped her round the knees and howled: '*Bella regazza!*' Then he wobbled to his feet, wheezing noisily, and said: 'Blardy hell, I think I have too much wine, yes?' Besides being very drunk, he appeared to be pathologically impervious to fear.

They began to lead him down the cone towards the hut, with Leila and M. Beloued following closely behind. After a moment she caught Quinn up and said urgently: 'Rupert, please listen to me…'

'I'm not interested.'

'Please, please understand!' she cried; but he walked on without answering.

Suddenly Pettersson turned his face, wet and awry-eyed, and made his second joke of the day: 'See you later, crater!' — which struck him as so funny that he had to bend double, panting with asthmatic laughter.

Leila grabbed Quinn's arm and said: 'Rupert, it wasn't my fault! When they came and took me off the train I didn't know what was happening. I was terribly frightened, because I thought that it must have been the FLN. But in the car Monsieur Izard explained everything — how they had to have you as a witness to make the FLN think that I had been killed. They wouldn't let me warn you, and put me the next day on a boat for Gibraltar, then to Palermo, and I've been staying here in a villa with some friends of Monsieur Izard's.

'It's been very boring,' she added, squeezing his arm. 'I've been swimming a lot and the sea is so beautiful — but I've missed you very much!'

He turned to her and said savagely: 'You owe me forty-thousand francs for your funeral, you little bitch!'

'Please, Rupert!'

'*Espéce de con!*' he shouted.

Her eyes opened wide. 'Do not talk to me like that!' Her mouth set hard and the soft lips curled in against her teeth.

'I don't ever want to see you again,' he said. 'You've all made enough use of me — sending me half off my head having to look at a rotting mess that was once some poor girl who never harmed any of you…' He felt himself trembling, losing control. '…Just so you can fight your little wars of independence; then, when things get too hot for you, you come and live in a big villa and play the sweet little niece to Uncle Izard and bathe in the sea every day. You little bitch!' He suddenly lashed out at her, striking the back of his hand hard across her mouth.

Her fingers flew up in defence and she pressed the knuckles against her lips; then sat down on the lava and broke into violent sobs.

M. Beloued was coming stealthily down towards them, carrying the basket of flowers; Quinn turned away and felt himself grabbed by the arm. It was Pettersson. His bony face was thrust forward, and he cried: 'You must not beat a girl!' He held both Quinn's arms and began to shake him.

'Oh get away, you stupid bastard!'

'No, no!' cried the Swede; 'you must not beat a girl.'

'Take your hands off me!' At that moment Pettersson had a spasm of coughing, and Quinn was able to break free. He scrambled on down the cone and caught up with the guide. Pettersson reached them a little later; he still looked furious, but he did not mention Leila again. She remained sitting higher up the slope, weeping next to M. Beloued.

They climbed the rest of the way down almost in silence; about the only words spoken was just as they reached the hut, when the guide turned to Quinn and asked him earnestly: 'Stewart Granger, does he still inhabit Hollywood?'

Inside the hut the guides scowled at Pettersson, as he lurched through into the lavatory; and Quinn sat down and ordered Campari.

A few moments later the door opened and Leila came in, followed by M. Beloued. She walked straight across to Quinn. 'Come down to the villa, Rupert, and talk with Monsieur Izard. He will make you understand.'

He said quietly: 'Go away, Leila. There is nothing more to understand.' He noticed that her lip was bleeding, and he looked away. She did not move, standing rigidly in front of the table, watching him red-eyed as he sipped the bitter Campari.

Pettersson came back from the lavatory; he had washed out his gasmask, which still hung round his neck, and his hair was on end. He bowed to Leila, then sat down and immediately broke into another impassioned account of how he planned to conquer the crater as soon as the explosions subsided.

Leila interrupted him: 'Rupert, you said you would marry me.'

'Go away,' he said; 'I do not want to see you again. Go away and bathe in the sea and dine at Uncle Izard's high table.'

She still would not move, even when M. Beloued tugged at her sleeve and muttered something in Arabic. Pettersson was now talking about his chances of being lowered into the central crater in an asbestos suit. The straps of his gasmask had fallen into his glass and were soaking up his drink.

Then suddenly Leila turned and ran out of the hut, with M. Beloued moving swiftly after her, still carrying the basket of wild flowers.

For some time Quinn sat listening to the chairlift clattering over the pulleys. Pettersson said gloomily: 'Is that girl your wife who is here with a lover?'

When Quinn did not reply, he said: 'If she is your wife, why does she ask you to marry her?'

'Oh shut up!' said Quinn; and ordered more Campari.

A NOTE TO THE READER

Dear Reader,
If you have enjoyed the novel enough to leave a review on **Amazon** and **Goodreads**, then we would be truly grateful.

Sapere Books is an exciting new publisher of brilliant fiction and popular history.

To find out more about our latest releases and our monthly bargain books visit our website:
saperebooks.com